"Ms. Kercheval writes with clear economy, establishing a complicated plot with apparent effortlessness, and creating a less than strictly realistic narrative . . . with sly wit and a wink at conventions that go beyond contemporary realism."

—ERIN MCGRAW, author of *Better Food for a Better World: A Novel*

"Provocative and playful, *My Life as a Silent Movie* is a lean and, yes, cinematic novel about a grief-stricken woman who escapes to Paris and soon discovers a series of secrets that both rattle and embolden her. A considerable achievement, this novel grapples with the unpredictable march of history and the way it affects the most intimate parts of our private lives."

—DEAN BAKOPOULOS, author of *My American Unhappiness*

"Jesse Lee Kercheval's precise and sharp new novel *My Life as a Silent Movie* shows us what happens in the wake of an unimaginable tragedy. Kercheval's prose is as clear as a silent film star's face, and the novel's twists and turns are wonderfully unexpected. Whether in Paris or in Indiana, readers will swoon."

—EMMA STRAUB, author of *Laura Lamont's Life in Pictures*

"Jesse Lee Kercheval brings a poet's precision to this suspenseful story of one woman's journey to find what is left of her family. *My Life as a Silent Movie* is a brilliant, heartbreaking page-turner."

—JENNIFER VANDERBES, author of *Easter Island* and *Strangers at the Feast*

"Wildly entertaining, fascinating, and deeply moving, *My Life as a Silent Movie* will make you fall in love all over again with Paris, the history of silent cinema, and the enduring, mysterious drama of being alive. I did not want it to end."

—HOLIDAY REINHORN, author of *Big Cats: Stories*

"A beautiful, evocative novel . . . Kercheval has that rare ability to bring a number of characters alive simultaneously on the page, to make us care about each one for their quirkiness, their hard-luck stories and their equally hard-won wisdom. Readers will embrace this story as it melds the magic of old movies with the redemptive power of family. An original, poignant, and truly irresistible story for our time."

—JONIS AGEE, author of *The River Wife: A Novel*

OTHER BOOKS BY JESSE LEE KERCHEVAL:

Brazil, a novel

Cinema Muto, a poetry collection

The Alice Stories, a novel in stories

Dog Angel, a poetry collection

World as Dictionary, a poetry collection

Space, a memoir

Building Fiction, a book on writing

The Museum of Happiness, a novel

The Dogeater, a short story collection

I would like to thank the Corporation of Yaddo,
David Wells and the Terry Family Foundation, and
the Graduate School and the Arts Institute of the
University of Wisconsin for their generous support.

My Life as a Silent Movie

break away books

INDIANA UNIVERSITY PRESS

Bloomington & Indianapolis

My Life as a Silent Movie

A NOVEL

JESSE LEE KERCHEVAL

This book is a publication of

Indiana University Press
Office of Scholarly Publishing
Herman B Wells Library 350
1320 East 10th Street
Bloomington, Indiana 47405 USA

iupress.indiana.edu

Telephone orders   800-842-6796
Fax orders   812-855-7931

© 2013 by Jesse Lee Kercheval

∞ The paper used in this publication meets
the minimum requirements of the American National Standard for Information
Sciences—Permanence of Paper for Printed
Library Materials, ANSI Z39.48-1992.

Manufactured in the
United States of America

Library of Congress
Cataloging-in-Publication Data

Kercheval, Jesse Lee.
  My life as a silent movie : a novel / Jesse Lee
Kercheval.
    pages cm. — (Break Away Books)
  ISBN 978-0-253-01024-7 (paperback : alk.
paper) — ISBN 978-0-253-01025-4 (e-book)
  1. Family secrets—Fiction. 2. France—
Fiction. I. Title.
  PS3561.E558M95 2013
  813'.54—dc23
                                2013006539

1 2 3 4 5   18 17 16 15 14 13

For my parents

My Life as a Silent Movie

I AM ON A PLANE LOOKING DOWN AT THE CLOUDS. It could be any country below me, any ocean. Or at least the clouds let me pretend that's true. I remember the first time I looked down from an airplane. I was a little girl, and I was crying because I was leaving France for America. I didn't want to go. I also remember flying back to Paris with my husband and daughter, although that time my daughter was the one who sat by the window and discovered the clouds. And she was laughing. The trip was a family vacation and nothing more. I am trying to pretend I am still on that flight.

It isn't working. But I am going someplace, something I thought I might not do again. I am on my way, I hope, to find family. Family I did not know I had. Living family.

But this story does not really begin on a plane. I don't want to deceive you. It started three weeks ago. With two deaths.

Three weeks ago at six o'clock, I was in the kitchen cooking dinner. It was February, which meant it was already dark. The doorbell rang and sent me running down the stairs two at a time to answer. I thought it was the UPS guy at the door trying to get me to take some electronic gadget that my neighbors—lawyers who were never home—had ordered as a treat for themselves in compensation for their busy lives.

But it was the neighbor. When I opened the door, she grabbed my arm above my elbow, like we were about to have an argument and she was afraid I might punch her in the face. "There's been an accident, Emma," she said. "I saw your car in the intersection—just now, on my way home. I talked to the police."

My car, I realized, our Subaru wagon, had my husband in it. Our daughter, eight, was in it, too, on her way home from her violin lesson.

My neighbor shook my arm.

My husband and daughter had been in the car. Now my neighbor, holding my arm tight, told me they were dead. My daughter who had played the violin. Her dad.

Just like that—I had a life, and then it was gone. I think of this part as a violent cartoon. The neighbor's words hit me like a two by four across my stomach, then *smack!* on my head. Or maybe something less Warner Brothers, more bloody, more Japanese. A sword in the gut, then *swish!* A long flying blow to the neck, and my head tumbles through the air and lands in the snow bank just beyond our front steps.

Except that would have been a blessing. To be dead. To be dead like everyone else I loved in this world. In one minute, I went from the forty-two-year-old mom of a happy—I swear to God we were happy—family to a woman who wanted nothing in this life except to be done with it.

Some time goes by here. I don't want to remember anything about what happened next. Or next after next. It was like this blankness:

But with no light like the white of this page. Also, no air.

That night—no, it was after the hospital, in the morning—I took my pillow off my side of the bed where I'd slept with my husband for ten years and got a sleeping bag out of the closet. Then, trailing them behind me, I moved downstairs into the basement apartment in our old Victorian house. We'd rented it to a long string of students, but in the months before my husband died, he'd been working on the bathroom and kitchen, trying to make them less damply peeling linoleum, trying to install tile and charm so we could move up to a better class of tenants. In the meantime, the apartment was empty. No tenant, barely any furniture. I took the pillow and sleeping bag into the dark back bedroom and laid down on the shag-carpeted floor. Except for the funeral, I stayed there.

I couldn't make myself sleep in a bed that would be so cold, so empty, all night every night. I couldn't make myself go into my daughter's room to see if she had left her beloved computer on when she'd left in a tumble for school that last morning any more than I could look at her body when the nurse at the emergency room offered me that grace. I should have. How could I not have looked at her one more time?

The nurse had not offered to let me see my husband, which meant I could guess at his injuries. The SUV that hit them ran the red light at high speed and slammed into the driver's side, into my husband. My daughter had been sitting behind him. I hoped she was flipping through her violin music. I hoped she had not been looking when the SUV came, lights bright in her face, speeding across the dark intersection. In the back seat, my daughter had been safer statistically than my husband, but that hadn't mattered. Our wagon folded in on itself like a fortune cookie, like a metal hand closing into a fist. I saw it in the intersection when my neighbor drove me to the hospital. My family was gone. The ambulance was loading the white-sheeted body of the boy—a teenager—who ran the light and killed them all. Except it wasn't a white sheet. There was too much blood for that.

At the hospital, one of the policemen told me it looked like the boy driving the SUV had been going nearly eighty and had not braked at all. Maybe he had been changing radio stations, not looking, when he ran the red light. Maybe he'd been drunk, but probably not, since it was so early, barely dark. He told me the dead boy was seventeen and had been driving his mother's brand-new Chevrolet Avalanche. He also told me the boy's name, though later I couldn't remember it for the life of me.

The cop said I would probably want to sue. So did one of the nurses and both doctors who came out to talk to me, a pediatrician to tell me my daughter had been pronounced dead on arrival, an internist who gave me the same news about my husband. So many people at the funeral mentioned lawyers and lawsuits that I forgot to keep count, as if money or vengeance would make me glad to be alive.

If I wanted revenge or money, how could I have wanted them from a mother who had also lost a son? Later, I would hear the boy was her only child, also that she was a single mother and a secretary at the college where I taught. I imagined her wanting so badly to go back in time, change her mind about lending him her new SUV, snatch away those damn keys. I wanted that, too. I knew any sympathy she was getting—useless as sympathy might be—would be blackened by the sidelong looks, people thinking, if not saying, the accident was her son's fault and so also her fault. Her son killed a man and his child. What kind of mother was she? He'd seemed an okay kid, but . . .

Though it was difficult, I thought that his death might even be harder on her than my deaths were on me. My husband was guiltless. My daughter was as innocent as on the cold winter day she was born. Being me, right then, was unspeakably bad. I couldn't imagine what it felt like being that other mother.

I meant to skip this part, what happened right after and after that. It's worth noting that I had a job, a life outside my family. I taught creative writing at a liberal arts college in this green and rolling part of Indiana where I couldn't walk across campus without half the students saying hello to me, calling out to me by name. I'd always thought I cared about that, about what I did. I found out I didn't. I didn't go to work. I had students who expected me to be there. I wasn't. I had people I worked with and friends who were so good, so worried. I didn't care.

I'll stop now, at this moment when I am lying curled in the sleeping bag in the back bedroom of the downstairs apartment. Just for a little while before I go on to what happened next.

WHEN THE FRONT DOOR BELL RANG AGAIN, I jumped as if the live wire were wrapped around the red muscles of my heart. It was March, less than three weeks later—no time at all, forever. All around the house, daffodils were poking up that my family would never see. Spring comes, no matter. The door to the basement apartment and the door to the main part of the house were side by side on the front porch. From the apartment, I'd watched neighbors and friends come by with casseroles and leave them on the porch. Sometimes I ate one or put it in the fridge for later. Sometimes I just left them for the worried neighbors to retrieve.

But the bell wasn't a neighbor. It was my Aunt Zinnia at the door, my mother's sister, the woman who my father had always called the Terrible Aunt Z.

She was standing on my front porch with her rolling suitcase. She was dressed in a sleeveless white linen dress, as if she hadn't planned on a cool Hoosier spring. She was a tiny woman with a silvery bowl of hair and a soft Southern accent. She looked helpless; she looked sweet. She was neither. She was a regular storm crow, drawn by bad luck. I'd sent her a note after the funeral, telling her what had happened. Now here she was. I watched as the airport shuttle that had dropped her off pulled away from the curb. "Let me in, Emma," she said, banging on the door. "I'm spending the night."

If my husband had been there, he would have laughed. If my daughter had been here, good girl that she was, she would have hugged her Aunt Z. My daughter had been too young to know all the family stories, to know that though Aunt Z's husband had left her plenty of money, she never stayed at hotels but only at other people's houses. If she had to, she would make it her business to meet someone on the plane, relentless in her search to find something in common. On a two-hour flight to Miami, she once discovered that she and the woman next to her had shared the same gynecologist in Kansas City thirty years earlier, a real sadist who had a twin brother who was also an ob–gyn. How do these things come up in casual conversation, my husband wanted to know. When we lived in France when I was little, Aunt Z—whose late husband was with the State Department then—came so often my father had forbidden my mother to wash her sheets each time she left. A complete waste of water, he'd said, always the frugal one. Not to mention time and soap.

Now I didn't roll my eyes or laugh. There was no audience left for Z but me. No shared jokes in my house anymore. She looked old, as if she were shrinking as well as her family. My mother, her only sister, had died three years earlier, a mere two days after my father. I hadn't seen Aunt Z since my parents' funeral. Aunt Z rattled the doorknob. I let her in. She looked around the bare basement apartment, taking in the echoing rooms. "This is ridiculous," she said. "I'm only here for one night. I am not staying down here. Take me upstairs."

So I did, taking the key out of my purse, pushing our front door open with some difficulty. Letters and condolence cards and unpaid bills had piled up just inside the mail slot. She started inside, and I followed her with her suitcase, stepping on the mail. I didn't want to read any of it.

I took a deep breath before I entered the house. Somehow, though I don't know why, I was expecting chaos. I was expecting thieves to have broken in and ransacked the place. Instead, it was neat as a pin. The carpets all vacuumed, the kitchen gleaming in the last light of the day. Even the framed silent film posters and antique movie cameras my husband collected had been meticulously straightened and dusted. My cleaning person, who came once a month, had been there.

God, I thought. I pushed open the door to my daughter's room. Her clothes— usually on the floor and desk and chair and dresser, clean mixed with dirty— were all washed and hung up or folded away. Her computer screen was dark. I sat down in the dining room and put my head on the freshly waxed table. What kind of check do you leave for a cleaning woman who acts more like a caring mom than you?

"Looks good," Aunt Z said. "Nice carpet." She was pointing under the dining room table at the red, ragged Persian that my husband had brought home last spring from a yard sale. "I have one like it." She paused and bent over to get a closer look. "But mine's much nicer." This was another Aunt Z trademark. She was always praising something—your earrings, your Thanksgiving turkey, your new refrigerator—then just when you were prepared to take the compliment, she would spring the old punch line. Whatever you had was nice, but not as nice as the ones she had, which were antique or 24 karat or brand spanking new. She really *was* terrible.

My mother, though, had talked to her on the phone every day, including the morning of the day she died. I might have been the one who took my mother and my father to their doctors' appointments and shopping and to my house for dinner on Sundays. I was certainly the one who found her body. But it was Aunt Z who was important enough for my mother to call every morning, even though it was long distance.

Aunt Z was on the move. She was looking at the family pictures on the wall in the long hall to the bathroom. "She looks like a nice girl," she said of my daughter, as if she had never seen her, though she'd met her at my parents' funeral. Aunt Z came back into the living room with a picture of my husband, daughter, and me camping on Lake Michigan. "I'd like a cup of tea," she said. "With honey, not sugar, please. But only if you have fresh bags."

I put on the kettle to boil, put some loose tea in a pot, then came back into the dining room. Nothing in my house was fresh, but it would have to do. Aunt Z was still studying the picture. "You've lost weight," she said, looking at my bathing-suited stomach in the family camping photo, then at me. I glanced at myself in the mirror over the dresser we used as a sideboard and nearly jumped, I was so spooked by what I saw. My hair was a long blonde Rastafarian tangle, and I looked nearly as thin as my daughter, as thin as I had been when I first met my husband. My pants drooped from my hips. The heavy black sweater I was wearing hung on me like the skin of some larger animal. I looked closer. I had cheekbones and hollows under them like in my high school yearbook photo, although my skin was lined in a way it never had been twenty-five years ago. I looked like something awful had happened to me, like a high fashion model on heroin. That thin. It scared me.

A friend once told me that when, during a physical, she asked her doctor's advice on losing weight, he answered, "Get cancer. That's the only way a woman your age is going to lose anything."

My friend had already had a lumpectomy and radiation. "I tried that," she said to him. "Remember?" She told me the story as an example of how stupid and sexist and horrible the doctor was. Also, of how hard it was to lose weight in our forties while feeding and caring for our families.

Now grief looked like the diet of all time. I hadn't been looking after anyone lately, certainly not me. The tea kettle whistled. I brought Aunt Zinnia her cup. She had the family albums out now, frowning over the baby pictures of my daughter. "When they're that little, babies all look alike. I can't even tell a girl from a boy," she said. "Unless they're in the bath, and I can see which has a penis." Aunt Zinnia was eighty-six, four years older than my mother, who would certainly have said "wee-wee" or used a plumbing metaphor like "fixture," but Aunt Zinnia was not one to censor herself. She flipped forward through the birthdays and holidays.

She stopped at a picture from three years ago of my parents' last Christmas. My daughter was posed with my mother under the mistletoe, pecking her grandmother's soft, proffered cheek. Looking at the picture, it was easy to think maybe the physicists who believed time did not exist were right. Surely time was an illusion. This moment was still out there. Every moment was still out there. I imagined them as single frames in a long silent movie.

I touched a finger to my daughter's lightly pink nose. "She looks a little like Mom, don't you think?" I said to Z.

"Like Livinia?" she said, calling my mother by her full name, something only Zinnia did. I suspected this was because Livinia was a fair slant rhyme for Zinnia. My father always called my mother Livvy. "Why would you think she looked like Livinia?"

"Just a little," I said. "Around the eyes." Something about the eyebrows, I thought, the way they arched. My daughter had them arched in the picture, glancing sideways at the camera, trying to keep her eyes open in spite of the flash. My mother had hers arched because she loved being in the center of the picture, loved being seen being loved.

Aunt Z shut the album and looked up at me, clearly flustered. "But they aren't related, not really." She blinked, as if she were having trouble seeing me. "I mean, you do know Livinia wasn't your real mother, don't you? I mean, surely your parents told you that you were adopted? They tried to have children for years, but Livinia could never..."

So this was how I found out that my mother was not my mother. First I felt the blood leave my face, my fingertips go first prickly, then numb, and I fainted, dropped like a dead weight onto the red carpet that Z thought looked not quite as nice as hers. I don't know why I passed out at this sudden news. I had not fainted on getting the news that my father had died of a heart attack, or on finding my mother dead, or on hearing that my husband and daughter, too, were dead, their faces cut by jagged glass and metal, bodies crushed, mere blocks from where I stood in the kitchen thawing chicken breasts for dinner.

I came around to the sight of Z, down on the carpet on her knees, chaffing my wrists, which struck me as an old-fashioned medical procedure, but apparently it was effective. I felt a warm flush in my cheeks as my blood pressure rose back to normal. Had she really thought I knew I was adopted? Or had she come all this way to blurt the news out, to get this last bit of family comeuppance off her chest? Z had three children, so it was hard not to take her news of my mother's infertility as one last Z-ism aimed at me or through me at her sister. Oh, you have a nice daughter, too bad she isn't really your child. Mine are, and that makes them so much nicer, so much more like me.

When we were off the rug and back sitting at the table, Z told me what she knew about how I had come into the world and into the family I thought was mine by birth. It wasn't much. "Your father brought you back from Paris," she said. My dad was a colonel in the army then. To the day he died, my mother always called him *the colonel* when she talked about him in his absence, as in "The colonel likes his dinner served exactly at five." We were living in Fontainebleau, where he was stationed with NATO in those days before de Gaulle kicked the Americans out of France.

My father had had a gift for languages, and since it was a rare American officer who spoke excellent French, he'd traveled to Paris at least once a week for meetings and briefings. He was often gone for days at a time. "He was always bringing

9

something back from his trips for Livinia. A dress. A hat. Some cognac, once, in a bottle shaped like a cannon. One day, it was you." Zinnia said.

"My father brought me back from Paris?" I said.

She nodded.

"Just like that?"

"Well," she shrugged.

I let the idea of me as a souvenir sink in. "Listen," I said, "if my mother wasn't my mother, was my father my dad?"

Z coughed, covering her mouth with one liver-spotted hand. "Livinia never said as much," she said, "but I always assumed he was. If you know what I mean."

She meant that my father had been doing something in Paris besides going to long meetings. I thought about it for a minute. If I couldn't be my mother's daughter, I was willing to settle for half, for being my father's daughter. "Are you sure?" I asked.

"Well, no," she said. "To be honest, I've never thought you looked the least like either of them." She put her hands on my cheeks and turned my face toward the mirror. She pulled the curly blonde tangle of my hair back from my forehead. "I mean, where did you get those eyes?" I looked in the mirror and saw my daughter's eyes—blue, big as a lemur's, deep-set, and surrounded by circles dark as bruises. *Silent movie eyes,* my husband had called them. He should have known, as silent movies were his life. He studied movies, wrote scholarly articles, whole books on them. Sometimes I thought he must have married me for my eyes.

At any rate, I could see now that they didn't look like Zinnia's, which were a jealous jade green, or my mother's, which were also green, if a bit lighter, a bit more hazel. Or like my father's, which, though he'd had blond hair, had been brown and hooded, as if there'd been a Native American ancestor or two in there with the Scotch-Irish.

I had someone else's eyes. A stranger's. I had given this stranger's eyes to my daughter, and she had taken those eyes, that mystery, to the grave. Goddamn it. Who was I? Where had I come from? Where did I belong?

After Aunt Z was safely asleep in what had been my marriage bed, I got out more photo albums. Albums not of my daughter or husband but of my mother and father and me, that first nuclear family of which I'd thought I was also the sole survivor.

There was a picture of my mother, standing on the sidewalk outside our apartment in Fontainebleau, holding me swaddled in an oversized blanket. I'd always thought it was a picture of the day she brought me home from the hospital. Had she told me that lie? Now, after having a child, I could see I was no newborn. I was at least two, maybe three months old. It also occurred to me, looking at my wrinkled face, that I did not look happy. My mother, who was forty that year, did not look happy either. She looked like someone had tossed her a roast turkey straight out of the oven without bothering to give her hot mitts.

I felt like a fool. The given of my childhood was that I'd come along to make my parents complete. Just when it seemed my mother and my father would be childless, *voilà,* the stork dropped me down the chimney. We were a family, and nothing was more important. The three of us were a little circle that, like the golden ring in the folk song, had no end. But, honestly, what in that picture was changed by what Aunt Z said? Adoption didn't make us less of a family, though I wished my parents had trusted me enough to tell me. I didn't believe my father's having slept with another woman made him someone altogether different than the man I'd known. I was too old for that. Still, I felt like a fool.

I thought about it, and then I knew. I felt like a fool because my mother had already told me the truth about our family three years earlier. At the time, it had felt like the end of the story, something I never talked about, tried not to think about. Now it seemed more like the beginning. When my daughter was in kindergarten, my father had had a heart attack while carrying a bag of groceries into their assisted living apartment a few blocks from my house. My father was eighty-five when he died, so it seems strange, silly even, to say his death came as a complete shock. He walked three miles a day. He joked often about his own father living to be one hundred and one. My mother used to joke about how many wives he would have after her death at, say, a mere ninety-nine left him an eligible widower. Though I knew no one was immortal, I thought my father was. I think he thought he was, too. All I can say is his sudden death, holding that paper sack full of cans of Progresso soup my mother had bought at the local wholesale grocery, must have surprised him even more than her or me.

Just two days later, before my father had even been cremated, before we'd finished the plans for his funeral service, my mother took two months' worth of valium and stretched out on what had been their double bed in their apartment two miles away from my house, the apartment I had picked out, had moved them into so they could be close to me. To make certain of what she had set out to do, my mother cut her wrists, elbow to palm, with one of the new Chicago Steel steak knives my father had given her for Christmas. Since she was on blood thinner, she quietly bled to death as she slept. No clotting, not even after she was dead. When I found her, she was as white as her sheets should have been. Down the sides of the bed were thin wet ribbons of crimson, and the white carpet underneath was a moist valentine pink. The room smelled like a meat counter. Standing there, I could taste the iron tang of my mother's blood.

There wasn't a note. I looked everywhere. I tore the apartment apart looking.

Then I called my husband. He rushed to their apartment to find me, wrapped his arms around me, and said, "Oh, Emma, it's the end of a love story. She just couldn't bear to live without your father." More than one friend said that my mother's suicide showed how much she loved me, loved me too much to want to be a burden. But I was there, goddamn it, just blocks away with her granddaughter. I had moved them from Florida to Indiana to be close to me. I was willing, eager to be burdened, to repay her the debt of having raised me. Instead, she left. Left her granddaughter. Left me. Left as if she had never loved anyone in this world but my father. As if I wasn't family at all. Even then, I thought, Okay, now I know where I stand.

She was dead, my father was dead, too, but I couldn't let them go. I couldn't sleep without dreaming I was waiting for them at an airport, their plane inexplicably late. Or I would dream that the phone rang and I answered, knowing my father was on the line. I would listen, hearing him breathe, and I would beg him to tell me where they were. Late one night, when I couldn't sleep and my husband was up working on his class, I finally told him how abandoned by my parents I felt. He looked at me long and hard, clearly disappointed, then said, "Let them go, Emma. Let them go. You have us."

He was right. I had my daughter, who knew only that she missed her grandparents. I had a husband, too, who needed help with his work, with his life. My students were wonderfully, endlessly needy, because that was how students always were. My teaching filled all the time my family didn't. For a long time my husband, my colleagues, my friends watched me like spotters at a gym, worried I would fly head-first off the trampoline, worried I would lose control. But I didn't. Honestly. Or maybe just a little. I lost my keys, cried easily, threw away an entire semester of student portfolios by accident. Once I slammed my fingers in the car door and was so relieved to feel real physical pain that I almost did it again. But my daughter was in the car, watching.

Gradually, I started sleeping again. Gradually, I came to think my husband was right. I could let them go. I did let my parents go. At least, I tried. Though, I'll confess, it often seemed my parents were right there, the wall in front of me no more than a membrane. They were so close I could put my palm flat to the cool gloss enamel of the paint on the wall and feel the warmth hiding there. Now, oh, God, my husband and my daughter were there, too. I closed the photo album.

Had Livvy been willing to leave me because she wasn't my mother? Or was that crazy, no more answer to the mystery of her death than anything else I had considered? Even if Livvy had loved me exactly like I loved my own daughter, that didn't answer the question of whether or not she had been my biological parent.

I got up and dug out the folder my husband kept, labeled "Important Documents," and found my birth certificate, although I knew what it said. I looked carefully at the yellowing sheet. In French, it listed my parents as my parents. Nothing had changed. It listed my birthday—or what I'd always thought was my birthday—as my date of birth. My place of birth was Fontainebleau, not Paris. Attached was a typed "official English translation." I read that, too. It was the same. A lie carefully translated into a lie.

The translation, as a matter of fact, had been written and signed by my father, by the colonel. He'd done it the night after my mother was turned away from kindergarten registration because no one at the elementary school in Florida could make heads or tails of the French. It was a family joke how no one ever questioned the authenticity of the translation. "You should have been a forger," I said to my father once.

He'd winked. "Oh, didn't you know? I used to be a spy."

Next in the folder was my naturalization paper, a stiff gray sheet folded neatly into threes like a brochure that declared me an American citizen from that date forth. Attached was a black-and-white photograph of me at four, with long fair hair held back by twin tortoiseshell barrettes. My parents had explained my naturalization as just an extra step, a precaution they'd been advised to take. If I had American parents, I was an American citizen, but since I'd been born in a French hospital, not on an American base . . .

Now I wasn't sure. My father always said I cried nonstop as we flew across the ocean to America, saying over and over I wanted to go home, back to France. The first thing I remembered was being in Washington, D.C., with its peculiar, smooth white buildings, including the one where my parents took me to be naturalized. Inside, it was hollow. The three of us crossed to the empty center on a bridge, stood looking up, looking down, floor and ceiling both impossibly distant. "What a waste," my father said, meaning what a waste of money, of space, meaning how American.

I began crying again, kept crying even when the man we'd come to see took my picture and asked me why I wanted to be American. "I don't," I said. "I'm a little French girl."

He laughed and stamped my papers. "Not anymore, you're not," he said.

He was right. Now, looking at the picture he'd taken, I recognized the dotted swiss dress Livvy had made for me, but I swear the girl was a total stranger. Her lips, pursed, disdainful, were definitely French.

When I was a junior in college, I'd gone back to France for the first time and made a side trip from the excitement of Paris to staid Fontainebleau. With no address, no picture, I'd found the block of flats where we used to live, sat on the same stone bench where I used to play while Livvy watched over me. The block had been built by the U.S. Army and was full of NATO families when we lived there. By the time of my junior year visit, it was as French as could be. There was no one we knew there. Now, four decades after we'd lived there, no one in all of France would remember my family and the years we spent as expatriates. Except for Aunt Z and her children, neither of my parents had any family. Who could I possibly ask where I had come from, who my parents really were? Who would know?

Then I remembered Apolline. She'd been our maid in France, and after we came back, my parents had sponsored her into this country. She'd lived with us for a year, studying hairdressing, and then she'd moved to New York. She'd gone straight to work for a famous salon, her French accent her meal ticket. She did the hair of rich old ladies, and her clients gave her seats to the opera and ballet. She traveled with them, too. Often, it seemed, their hairdresser was their only friend.

When I was little, Apolline always came down to Florida from New York for Christmas with us. In the photo album were shots year after year of her picking oranges or tangerines in our backyard. Photo by photo, she had distinctly different hair colors: red, black, one year a color she called champagne. "The hairdresser's curse," my father said. "They always practice on each other."

She was always after my hair, even then a long, unfashionably curly tangle that was my mother's bane. Apolline wanted to cut it short. Like Twiggy, she said when I was very little, then like an ever-changing list of crop-haired fashion models. Whenever I saw her with a pair of scissors, I ran.

When I was in high school, I visited Apolline in New York, and she took me to see Balanchine's *Swan Lake* and then to the Rainbow Room for dinner, a dream night out for a sixteen-year-old. Then Apolline drifted into her own life and stopped visiting us, even when she came to Florida with a client or friends. But I know my father had occasionally exchanged cards with her. With a sudden flush of guilt, I realized I hadn't let Apolline know about my parents' death. I opened the last photo album again. In the very back I found a Christmas card from Apolline, dated four years ago, still tucked in its holiday green envelope with the return address neatly inked in one corner. *Astoria, Queens.* Surely that was the same apartment I'd visited on my first trip to New York.

Had Apolline been standing just outside the photograph in Fontainebleau the day I came into my parents' lives? When I came, not from the hospital as I had always believed, but from somewhere unknown. *From Paris,* said Z. From Paris with my father on the train.

Why did it matter? I asked myself, testing this new sense of urgency I felt. What did it matter who my parents were? I shook my head. It did matter. Maybe I had a mother still alive somewhere, a mother who had always missed me, who would welcome me back. Or, at least, be glad I was alive. If I really was the last one of my whole family, if I had no parents, no husband, no children, I wasn't sure I had any reason to keep living.

I had to find out what was true. I would go to New York to see Apolline.

3 ✍

THE FALL BEFORE THEY DIED, my husband and daughter had been in a short film my husband made with his silent film class called *The Magic Tree*. Besides studying and writing about old films, my husband used the antique movie cameras he collected to have his classes at the college try their hand at a short silent film or two. In *The Magic Tree*, the first title card explains:

> After his family is killed in a railroad accident,
> a man wanders without hope.

In the opening shot, he is walking through a deep forest with his few precious family mementoes in a sack. The man is my husband, made up with his eyes so wildly corked in, so dark, he looks like he had spent his grief in a coal mine. The film is dark, grainy black and white. I remembered my husband complaining about the difficulties he had shooting it. The late fall sun in Indiana had barely been up to the task of lighting the old-fashioned, insensitive film stock he used for reasons of authenticity. The class time had made for a late shooting schedule. My daughter had complained about how cold it had been in the woods in her thin cotton costume.

Still, the film had turned out to be beautiful, so striking I was surprised when I saw it projected at the school, the pianist playing some Erik Satie to set the mood. Each leaf on the ground, each bare branch seemed etched on the screen. We watched, me, my daughter, my husband, his class, holding our breath.

After the announced wandering, the man, passing by a massive oak, stumbles over a rock with an inscription:

What you have loved
What you have lost
This tree returns

He offers the tree all his money, pressing oversized bills onto the rough bark with both hands, his every gesture telegraphing *desperate.* Then he opens his sack and takes out the last reminders of his family, a small white stuffed bear and a picture of the daughter—our daughter—with his wife. The wife is one of his students, dressed for the period in a trailing white dress, her hair piled on her head. In the framed photograph, she sits with my daughter smiling in her lap. The man tosses first the stuffed bear, then the photograph, and they disappear mysteriously into the tree.

Then out of the tree—*magic!*—step his wife and his daughter. My daughter looks younger than eight in a white sailor suit. The father hugs his wife. His daughter. They hug and hug—*such joy.* Then he tries to lead them away, but the wife pulls back, shaking her head. She kneels and brushes some leaves away from the rock and shows her husband the rest of the inscription:

Whatever you have loved
Whatever you have lost
This tree returns
But at great cost

In life and in magic, always there is the fine print, the sub-clause, we would all be wise to read. At this point, students in the audience gasped. No matter that the film was sentimental, no matter that it was hand-cranked and slow. Loss is loss, even to an audience of twenty-year-olds.

The husband and wife exchange a long look. Then, hand in hand, the student-as-wife, then the daughter, and then the husband disappear into the tree. My daughter and my husband *there,* then gone. Together in this alternate reality, smiling, as they disappear, one after the other, through the magic of the camera into that thick, unyielding oak.

The night before I left for New York, I watched the film on video again and again, and all I could think was, "Why can't I go with them?" Though I knew the rock was carved and painted Styrofoam, and the tree was an oak in the city park behind our house, it was all I could do to keep from running into the night to find it.

Near dawn, I put the tape away and got ready to leave. Most of my bills were paid automatically, deducted from our checking account. My husband had been keen on that. The others—bills I picked out from the mail scattered on the floor inside the front door—were mostly things an empty house could live without, like cable TV and magazine subscriptions. I wrote notes on the bills, canceling them. I left a last check for my cleaning person with a note telling her I wouldn't need her anymore and wrote the insufficient words *Thanks for Everything!* in ink on the bottom. My husband had been raised to be careful with money and had always kept six months of our salaries in savings. I moved all that money from savings to checking.

After the accident, I'd taken sick leave for the rest of the spring semester, so I was still getting paid every month even though someone else was teaching my classes. I wasn't scheduled to teach again until the fall. I wanted to go now before I changed my mind, before my friends I taught with at the college got over their shyness at my grief and started crowding around with suggestions for ways to fill my newly empty life.

First I would see Apolline, then I would see what I would see. I didn't pack a suitcase. I just tucked a spare pair of socks, two changes of underwear, and my toothbrush next to my credit cards in my purse. I didn't want to think about how long I might be gone or what to take or not take. I could buy what I needed. In case nothing came of this, I also took the three-year-old bottle of Valium the doctor had prescribed for me after my mother took all of hers and her own life. I couldn't bring a steak knife on the plane, but the world was filled with objects that were just as dangerously sharp.

In the morning, I gave Aunt Z more tea. I had done nothing about getting another car, so I called the airport shuttle and arranged for it to pick us up. Then we rode, side by side, to the airport in Indianapolis. "Are you going to be all right?" Aunt Zinnia asked, as I checked her in for her flight. "Because if you aren't, I won't go."

This didn't sound like her at all. She had never been one to linger. She was a frequent visitor, but always in, then out. She took my hand and looked into my face. Whatever she saw did not reassure her. She looked as if she might cry. "I'll stay if you ask me," she said. "Livinia would have wanted me to stay." Her family was an iceberg, melting under her feet. Soon we would all have to swim for it.

I shook my head. "No need," I said.

As she was about to go through security, she turned one last time. "You were always a good daughter," she said. I waited for the Z punch line, but she just waved. "The best," she said, and was gone, a tiny old lady being kind, genuinely selfless, maybe for the first time in her life. I watched her disappear, on her way to her son's house in Portland, then I went to the counter and asked for a one-way ticket to New York.

The ticket agent looked a little puzzled. Not many people bought tickets at the counter. "This is for today?" she asked.

"For the next flight." She took my credit card and noticed my complete lack of luggage. "There's been a death in the family," I explained.

"Oh," she said and looked relieved. "Of course." She looked at the black turtleneck sweater I was wearing, as if realizing that black was the color of mourning. Actually, since I was a writer, or had been one, as well as a professor, almost every sweater I owned was black, the house color of intellectuals and artists. Almost all the clothes I owned, except the blue jeans I had on, were black as well. "If you call this 800 number, they'll tell you where to send a copy of the obituary." The agent circled the number on the ticket jacket. "Then you could qualify for the family bereavement fare. If it was a close relative?" She looked up at me.

"Yes," I said. "Very."

"Well, good then. I'm sure you'll qualify," she said, handing me my ticket. "Sorry about your loss."

So that is how I ended up on a plane, looking down at the clouds, on my way to find my mother. Or at least to find out who she was.

As soon as I landed at Kennedy, I called the salon on the Upper West Side where Apolline worked. I asked for her, and someone with a Liverpool accent put me on hold. Apolline's home number was unlisted. I'd checked that the night before, so either I reached her at the salon or I would take my chances on a surprise appearance at the address in Queens.

An older man came on the phone with a French accent that sounded half Maurice Chevalier and half Pepé Le Pew. It was the famous stylist himself, the one who ran the salon. I knew from Apolline he had started life in Dothan,

Alabama. I asked for Apolline, and there was a pause. "She has retired," he said. "The last year. But I think she is staying still in New York, unless she returned to our beautiful France."

I said I needed to contact her. My parents, dear friends of hers, had died suddenly. He put me on hold and then came back. "This was her number," he said. I wrote it down. "If you talk to her, tell her I said *allo.*"

I called the number he'd given me. Apolline picked up on the first ring. "Hello?"

I told her it was me. I said I was in New York. I wrote down her instructions, from Kennedy to the subway to her block, and then I followed them. I'd thought about telling her all the bad news on the phone, so she would have time to get used to the overwhelming amount of it, but she hung up before I had a chance.

I reached Queens with no difficulty. Not surprising, really, that Apolline knew her way in from the airport to her own house; she'd done it often enough. As I walked from the subway station, I was amazed at how well I remembered the neighborhood when I had only been there once, so long ago, when I was sixteen. I could have found the apartment without her instructions, without the address even. My first trip to New York must have made a lasting impression on me. Except now either the neighborhood had changed for the better or I had seen more—and worse—cities. I remembered how Apolline had made me clutch my purse under my arm as we walked up the hill to her door. Now people passing me gave me odd looks and a wide berth. Me, the mad widow with the wild eyes who looked like she'd slept in her clothes. Except I hadn't—slept, that is.

I passed the Swiss butcher shop on the corner. I remembered stopping with Apolline, who bought us two boned chicken thighs for dinner. We had that, wine, some salad. When all the fuss had come out in the American press about how the French ate everything—butter, cheese, pastries—and never had heart attacks or high cholesterol or got fat because—oh, French miracle—they were protected by their habit of drinking red wine, I thought the people writing those articles had never really spent time with anyone French. Maybe they had been to France to visit, but that was the France of restaurants, and that was different. Apolline never ate sweets, never had more than fruit for dessert, and had told me, the time I visited her, that a woman should stand on the scale every day, and if she had gained so much as an sixteenth of a kilo, she shouldn't eat that day. I had been skinny as a cat then, and I had laughed at what she said. Now I was that skinny again, but not laughing.

I rang the bell, and Apolline buzzed me in. She held me at arm's length, looking at me. Her hair was the color of Thanksgiving cranberries. Otherwise, she looked remarkably the same in her sixties as she had in her forties, leathery, thin, her eyebrows carefully penciled in above her dark eyes. She kissed me on both cheeks; she still smelled overpoweringly of Chanel No. 5.

My little girl, she said in French, then switched to accented English to ask me how my parents were.

I told her they were dead.

She asked me how my family was.

Dead, too.

Oh, merde, she said, and led me into her kitchen. I told her what had happened, minus the violent details, the blood, but I could tell she knew what I was leaving out. She had grown up in Nazi-occupied Paris. She knew blood. Whatever family she had started with was gone by the liberation. When she'd come to work for us, she was an orphan with only distant cousins to call family.

"Your poor little daughter," she said. She got a bottle of brandy out of a cupboard and poured us each a juice glass full. We drained them. "I should have kept in better touch with your parents," she said, pouring us another brandy.

I shrugged. I had been in touch. Every day. It hadn't saved either of them.

After the third glass of brandy, I told her what Aunt Z had told me. Did my mother bring me home from the hospital, or did my father bring me home from Paris? I had brought the snapshot of my mother holding me outside our apartment, and I showed it to her.

Apolline touched the blanket. "First he brought me from Paris to Fontainebleau," she said. "Then he brought you."

Suddenly I understood everything. My father had once told me, apropos of nothing, that in France if your maid got pregnant, the law assumed you were the father and charged you for the child's support until the child turned eighteen. He'd said it lightly, as if it were a humorous but slightly illuminating difference—brie versus Kraft singles—between the American idea of family and the French. But Apolline *had* been our maid. I thought of her on all those Christmas mornings, sitting on the floor with me, watching me open my boxes of Barbies and Barbie clothes. Once even, I remembered, a miniature Barbie convertible. She had watched me grow up thoroughly, irredeemably American. "You're my mother," I said.

Apolline shook her head. She touched the picture again, this time putting a red fingernail on a shadow I had not noticed before, one that stretched across the ground at my mother's feet. The shadow of the photographer, my father, that U.S. Army colonel. "I should have been," she said. I was confused.

"But were you?"

"No," she said. Then she patted my arm, got up from the table, and brought back an old copy of *National Geographic*. She flipped open the cover. I saw a small cache of $100 bills inside and a handful of snapshots—Apolline's combined safety deposit box and savings bank. She pushed a small black-and-white square across the table to me. "This is your mother," she said. "We were roommates in Paris. We worked at the same bar."

I peered down at the photograph, at a young woman with dark brown curls— a perm? She had on a tight white blouse and full skirt, and she was laughing, her head thrown back a little. I couldn't really see her eyes, which were half-closed. I looked harder, expected some click of recognition. Some physical manifestation of *ah hah*. But I felt nothing. "What's her name?" I asked Apolline.

"Sophie," she said. "Anne-Sophie Desnos. Or so she always told me."

"Desnos," I said. "Like the poet?"

"What poet?" Apolline said.

I told her what I could remember, that Robert Desnos had been a Paris-born surrealist poet famous for automatic writing. How during the war he'd worked with the French Resistance, had been deported, and had died of typhus just after the camp he was in was liberated. What I remembered best was a story about him moving among the prisoners, reading their palms, trying to confound the guards, who told them daily they were all going to die, by predicting for each a long life. I had named a character in my only novel *Desnos*. Now I had hopes of a connection to both a hero of France and another writer.

"I can't imagine they were family," Apolline said, doubtful. "Sophie said she had grown up in Alsace. She came to Paris right after the war. Lots of girls did." She paused to look at the picture. "I did think maybe she was a Jew. I couldn't ask her that, though, so who knows? Was Robert Desnos a Jew?"

"No," I said. "I don't think so."

"Still," Apolline shrugged one shoulder. If my mother was Jewish, then I was, too.

"What else can you tell me about her?" I asked.

Now Apolline gave a truly Gallic shrug, one that implied the general mystery of the universe—or at least of the facts in question. What Apolline did know is that they had worked in the same bar and lived in the same small attic room for nearly two years starting in 1957. It was at the bar that they met my father, the colonel, who came in sometimes with French officers they knew.

"So my father went out with Sophie?"

"Went out?" Apolline raised her plucked and penciled eyebrows. "Were they lovers? Maybe, but I don't think so. I don't think I ever saw them do more than talk over a drink. She certainly didn't bring him back to our room, but then she wouldn't have." Apolline frowned, and I wondered if Sophie had not brought the American colonel back to their room because of some mutual agreement about not bringing men into what sounded like the tiniest of garrets. Or was it because she knew or guessed how Apolline felt about the colonel? *I should have been your mother.*

"Sophie was clever," Apolline said. "She could keep a secret. I'll say that for her. She didn't tell me everything. That's for certain." She pulled the other photos out from their hiding place in the magazine and pushed them across the table. Apolline and Sophie smoking beside what looked like a narrow industrial canal. Sophie on a ramshackle carousel, riding a one-legged horse. Again, there was a shadow on the ground. Was it the ride operator? The photographer? My real father, whoever that was? I looked at the shadow, trying to compare it to the one the colonel cast in the photo of Livvy with me. It was impossible to tell.

The last picture in the pile wasn't a snapshot but an old-fashioned postcard addressed to Apolline, or so I guessed. The looping fountain-penned handwriting was illegible to me. "Do you know who my father was?" I asked, turning the postcard over to look at the front.

Apolline leaned forward and tapped one finger on the front of the postcard. It was a hand-tinted photograph of a man in a dark suit, wearing an immaculately knotted silk tie. His hair was combed straight back, and his bright blue eyes were looking directly at the camera, past the camera, with an expression so intense I felt it. He looked like a movie star. A caption was printed at the bottom of the card. *Film Albatross.*

"My God," I said. "This is Ivan Mosjoukine."

"You know who he is?" Apolline said. "How do you know that? No one knows who he is anymore."

"My husband," I started, then stopped. It seemed too complicated to explain to Apolline what my husband had done for a living, that he watched and wrote about old films no one else had any desire to see, that his passion had pulled us all into his world, our daughter growing up watching Fatty Arbuckle and Buster Keaton, our family vacations spent near film archives where he was doing research or attending silent film festivals. "He liked old movies," I said, and let it go at that. I knew who Mosjoukine was because my husband had thought about writing an article on Albatross, a film company formed in Paris by White Russians who'd fled the revolution. Mosjoukine, who'd already been a success in Russia, had been their biggest star.

We'd watched the only Mosjoukine movie my husband was able to get his hands on, *Kean: Disorder and Genius,* a bio pic about the great English Shakespearean actor Edmund Kean. The film was famous among film scholars, if little watched, for a furious fast cutting scene where Mosjoukine as Kean dances, Cossack style, in a pub. He dances and drinks and dances again, fueled by his impossible love for the wife of an ambassador from somewhere—Norway? Venice? A woman who was also the mistress of the Prince of Wales.

In the end, Kean, the most popular actor in England, defies the Prince of Wales and is booed from the stage. He dies, abandoned by his public, nearly alone and in poverty in a famous deathbed scene. A very long deathbed scene. One where he quotes *Hamlet.*

My husband had found *Kean* slow and sentimental. I had been stunned. Mosjoukine, I thought, was amazing. I'd felt every stab, every turn of love or jealousy. Even in the fuzzy bootleg print we saw, he burned on the screen. I made my husband run the film again. Maybe my enthusiasm was one reason he dropped the project. "Next time we're in Paris," he'd said, putting off the project in the name of all the research it would take at the Cinémathèque Française, where they had the rest of Mosjoukine's French films.

"He's my father? Ivan Mosjoukine, the silent film star, is my father?" This seemed absurd.

Apolline nodded. "He was crazy about Sophie. He said she reminded him of some Russian actress, Vera Holo-something. He called Sophie his little Vera."

"Vera Holodnaya," I said, naming the Russian silent film actress who had died young of Spanish influenza, right after the revolution. When she died, thousands upon thousands had turned out in Odessa for her funeral. The scene rivaled the riot in New York after Rudolph Valentino died. Now she was even more obscure than Mosjoukine, her films nearly all lost, but she had a small devoted following as a doomed film diva, as someone whose fate had been as tragic in life as in film. I looked back at the picture of Sophie by the canal. Dark hair, darker eyes. *Vera Holodnaya.*

Then I remembered that Mosjoukine, too, had died young. Hadn't he? Although he'd survived to leave Russia after the revolution and, in doing so, clearly outlived Vera Holodnaya. I thought I remembered a sad death after sound came to film, when he was already broke, already forgotten. That was the great cliché about silent film actors, that sound killed them all in the end. It was a legend that lived on in Gloria Swanson's role as Norma Desmond in *Sunset Boulevard,* fading away in her grand mansion, waiting for one last great role, calling out as the police take her away for murdering William Holden, "I'm ready for my close-up, Mr. De Mille." But just because it was a cliché didn't mean it wasn't true. Or was I just remembering the crushingly sad end of *Kean?*

"You think I am making this up," Apolline said.

"Well," I said, "it is hard to believe."

For the second time in as many days, someone took my face in their hands and made me look in the mirror. *Know thyself.* Apolline held the picture of Mosjoukine up beside mine. Blue eyes. His sharper than mine, more focused. Then she held up the snapshot of Sophie, the skin around her dark eyes black as kohl. Silent movie eyes times two.

4 ⟡

I WENT INTO APOLLINE'S BEDROOM and called the chair of my husband's department, another film scholar who was an old friend. In my husband's office at home in Indiana were a half-dozen books I could have checked for information on even such a forgotten film figure as Ivan Mosjoukine, but that was there and I was here.

"John," I said, when he picked up the phone.

"Good Lord," he said. "Emma."

I could hear people talking in the background, the sound of forks on china and glasses clinking. "Oh, you have guests."

"To hell with them. Where are you? Tricia said she went by the house this afternoon looking for you. There was mail piled everywhere and no one answered the bell. She was about to call 911 when a neighbor came by walking her dog and told her she'd seen you leave in the airport shuttle this morning."

Tricia was John's most recent wife, a poet who taught in my department. A good one. Would she really have called 911? Yes, Tricia wrote whole books of poems about dying. She had a sestina about jumping off the Golden Gate Bridge that made suicide sound like the best high dive ever. She knew enough about the magnetic pull of death to be worried about me. "I was taking my aunt to the airport," I said.

"So you're home now?"

"No, I'm in New York, but that doesn't matter. Listen, I need you to look up some information for me. I need a bio for Ivan Mosjoukine."

"Who?" John's specialty was Japanese film.

"He's a silent film actor from the '20s." I could hear John cover the phone with one hand and whisper something to someone. Tricia probably. I didn't want this turning into an intervention.

"Pick up the other phone," I could hear him mouthing to her. "Mojo...who? How do you spell that?"

I spelled Mosjoukine. "He was Russian," I added. "So probably there is more than one way of transliterating it. I think I've seen it with a Z."

"Give me a number," John said. "I'll call you right back."

I heard Tricia pick up. "I'll call you," I said and hung up. Whatever Tricia wanted to tell me about John, her writing, their newborn son, her faith in the power of really good meds, whatever it was that kept her going day to day, I didn't want to hear it. She still had her family.

I gave John a half hour, then I called back. This time, wherever he was, in his office in their attic probably, there was no extra noise. Also no Tricia.

"Can't I fax or email this to you?" he asked.

I looked around Apolline's apartment. As far as I could tell she didn't have so much as an answering machine. Even her phone was a pink princess, the old-fashioned square push buttons yellow from use. I fished a pencil out of a coffee cup on the phone stand, got a pad of paper. "No," I said. "Just go slow."

"Well, get ready to write it down. Ivan Ilyich Mosjoukine, born Penza, Russia, 1889, the son of a prosperous landowner," John read. "Sent to Moscow to study law, he skipped from the train at the first station and joined a traveling theater troupe. Went to Moscow and was a success on the stage." John was summarizing now. "Started making movies in Russia in 1911. Played roles from Tolstoy, Pushkin. 'Developed a style of psychological realism,' says one place. 'Was famous for burning, mesmeric eyes,' says another." John paused. "He became the biggest Russian star. Then came the revolution. He and his director, producer, other actors—do you want their names?"

"Not now," I said.

"They fled to the Crimea, then on to Constantinople, and finally made their way to France. Formed a film company..."

"Albatross," I said.

"Ill-omened name," John said. "Yes, and Mosjoukine—by the way, that's the French spelling. Do you have any idea how many ways you can spell it?

Mosjukin, Mozzhukhin, Mozhukin, even *Moskine.* Then there is *Ivan* and *Iwan* and *Jwan.* Anyway, he was a nearly instant success in France as well. More praise. Jean Renoir said he decided to become a film maker after seeing *Le Brasier Ardent,* an experimental film Mosjoukine wrote, starred in, *and* directed. In 1924, Jean Tédesco wrote that while people used to say, 'You should have seen Sarah Bernhardt die,' after *Kean,* they say, 'You have to see Mosjoukine die.' Whew," John said. "How come I never heard of this guy? He was in comedies. Someone here compares him to Chaplin. Also epics and period films, the Jules Verne historical drama *Michel Strogoff.* I read that as a kid. A version of *Casanova* that has some great stills here from Venice, and a film about the actor Edmund Kean. Want a complete filmography?"

I didn't. What I wanted was to find out what happened in the end. When the end came. "No, what happens after sound?" I asked.

"Well, first there was other stuff. A contract in Hollywood. One movie made from an old Broadway chestnut about a shetel girl and a Cossack falling in love. He was Ivan Moskine over here. Disastrous reviews. Seems he just left. Went to Berlin. Made a series of movies there for European release. Those were successes, too, though maybe they don't get quite as many glowing adjectives. At least in the bios I found. Then . . ."

"Sound," I said.

"Sound," he said. "To quote the British film historian David Robinson, Mosjoukine 'approached sound films bravely, but the roles for an actor with a heavy and ineradicable—and it is sometimes said, unintelligible—Russian accent were clearly limited.' Sounds like he'd been generous with his money when he had it. By the '30s he was broke. He drank. Says he died of tuberculosis alone in a hospital in Neuilly-sur-Seine in January 1939 at age forty-nine. He was buried in a pauper's grave."

It *was* the death scene from *Kean,* but minus the faithful friend at his side, the last-minute appearance of the woman he loved. In a movie, it was heartbreaking. In real life, both sordid and sad. "Jesus," John said. "It just plain sucks. I mean, how can you be so famous and then be so completely forgotten?"

"Alexander died, Alexander was buried, Alexander returneth into dust," I said.

"What?"

"It's the line from *Hamlet* Mosjoukine recites when he's dying at the end of *Kean.*"

"Guess he got that right," John said.

Why was it, I wondered, Mosjoukine seemed to have known what was coming, or was that just an illusion I had looking backward, comparing *Kean* with the end of Mosjoukine's own life?

"Emma," John broke into my thoughts, his voice wrinkled with worry. "What is this all about? Isn't there something else I can do? Something real?"

"No, no, John, but thanks. Give Tricia my love." I hung up before he had a chance to ask me anything else.

Mosjoukine had died in 1939. I was born in 1958. Hard to father a child when you have been dead nineteen years.

I pointed this out to Apolline once I was back in the kitchen.

"He wasn't dead," she said. "Not when I knew him, anyway. Who are you going to believe? Me or some book?"

I shook my head. I was a professor. I tended to trust books. But I found myself thinking of the colleague in my department who was convinced that Christopher Marlowe, author of *Dr. Faustus,* had not died at twenty-nine in a tavern brawl from a knife through his right eye, but had been whisked away, hidden from his enemies, and gone on to write all the sonnets and plays we mistakenly thought had been written by William Shakespeare, a mere theater owner who acted as Marlowe's front. Then again, my colleague was quite old and quite mad.

To quote John, he had died "alone." In one of the sad, always unfashionable suburbs outside Paris. What if Mosjoukine had faked his death to escape debts, his failed career, to start over?

If he had lived—just if—how old would he have been when I was born? I did the math in my head. He would have been sixty-nine. Not young, but not dead. That part, at least, was plausible. John, for example, was sixty-five, and he and Tricia had a three-month-old son.

"Okay," I said. "Maybe he was alive. Maybe. Barely."

Apolline snorted. "He was handsome," she said. "Not some old man."

"But Sophie must have been forty years younger than Mosjoukine," I said.

Apolline rolled her eyes. "Sure, he had white hair, but when he was looking at you with those blue eyes of his, you forgot all that. And he had such lovely

29

manners. Only men born before the first war had manners like that. Plus he was working for the Americans and had money like no French boy did. He even had a car. Sophie had nothing. No family. Less than me, and I had less than nothing. You don't know, you can't, what it was like growing up an orphan during the war, trying to live after. We never had a chance at school. Then grown, what were we supposed to do? It wasn't just Sophie or me. In those days, none of the girls who worked at the bar had more than the clothes they went to work in, maybe an extra pair of stockings. Paris was dust. France down and out. No matter how hard de Gaulle beat the drums to make it sound as if we were a strong nation again."

"So it was all about money?"

"No." Apolline shrugged. "That's making it too simple. Mosjoukine and Sophie, what can I say? When they were together, it was like watching a love scene in a movie. They just burned up the place. Even then it seemed crazy." Looking back, she raised her shoulder, let it drop.

We had left the brandy behind and were working on a bottle of single malt Scotch that had a yellowing gift card from a client attached. Judging by the age of the card and the face Apolline made every time she took a sip, Scotch was not her favorite drink, but we both felt a strong need of it. Apolline sighed. "Mosjoukine had such beautiful clothes. Honestly, anyone would have gone to bed with him. Though he only had eyes for Sophie. Only your father"—she stopped herself—"only the colonel, in his American uniform, came anywhere close."

I imagined the frantic bar scene from *Kean*, my father and Mosjoukine tossing back drinks, then arms linked with the men of the neighborhood, the French officers, dancing the sailor's hornpipe until dawn. I laughed. The room spun, tipped, righted itself. I'd had a lot to drink on a stomach so empty I couldn't remember the last time I'd eaten.

"What?" Apolline said. "You are laughing at me?"

"No," I said, putting my head down, half on the table, half on her arm. "I was just thinking of how long it's been since I went dancing." Apolline clucked her tongue and rested her free hand on my head.

The only trace of Sophie Desnos that Apolline had was an old address, 44 Rue Ste-Odile, which she said was not far from where they'd lived together off the Canal St-Martin. The address was written on the back of the first photograph of Sophie. After the colonel had taken her to Fontainebleau to help care for me, Apolline said, she'd tried to keep in touch, but she hadn't written or heard from Sophie since she'd come to America in 1962, so the address was nearly forty years old.

"Forty years!" I said. I was sitting up again, though slanting badly in my chair. It seemed hopeless. "A forty-year-old address?"

"Who knows?" Apolline said. "In France people don't move around like here. She could still be there. I've been in this apartment for nearly that long."

Apolline had not seen Ivan Mosjoukine since he'd gone away—south, maybe to Nice, she thought—before Sophie even knew she was pregnant. As far as she knew, if Mosjoukine was my father, he had no idea he was. "Men slept with a lot of women then," she said, "and women got pregnant. Not all the time, but not never like now."

After we finished the Scotch, Apolline helped me from the table to her bed, and then she stretched out, fully clothed, on the other side. I had the spins and hung onto the blanket she'd put over me with both hands.

"Did you ever sleep with my father?" I asked her. Apolline laughed.

"Which one? Mosjoukine? No. He was too pretty for me."

"No, no, the colonel," I said. She sighed.

"I wanted to. God knows, I wanted to. But he loved Livinia more than life," she said. "God knows why. She tortured him. She was so jealous. Jealous of his job, of the people he worked with, of me. Of you."

"Of me?"

"You never knew that?"

I shook my head, though that was a mistake. For a minute, I thought I might be sick.

"*Ma pauvre enfant,*" Apolline said, patting the blanket over me. "Sweet little fool." Then she let out a deep breath, and before she could take another, she was snoring.

I lay awake in the dark of Queens, car alarms going off outside, thinking that Apolline was right. She should have been my mother. It would have been simpler.

I dreamed I was watching the one film I had seen with Vera Holodnaya, the Russian diva my mother was said to have resembled. I heard my husband's voice lecturing me, *See how close the director keeps the camera? Look, look at the light coming through that window.* Only in the film, I also *was* Vera, playing a rich Russian girl filled with ennui, with a vague sense that life is more than her mother's drawing room. I was Vera stabbing a man, killing him, and then fleeing back to the smothering safety of her mother's house.

I was Vera, washing and washing my hands in a white porcelain sink. I felt a sharp stab of irritation at my husband, lecturing me on a rare early tracking shot. Why was he talking, talking, talking all through this silent film? I couldn't even hear the music. What music was the pianist playing? So softly, too softly. Shut up, I snapped at my dead husband, the husband I loved.

Then I was awake, shaking so hard my teeth chattered. I made it the bathroom, hugging myself, still shivering, though I wasn't cold. I inched the door shut, trying not to wake Apolline, snoring on the bed. I turned on the light, wincing at the sudden brightness and looked at myself in the mirror. My eyes were bloodshot. I was still good and drunk. I had no idea what time it was, except that it was dark. I washed my face.

What was it about silent movies? I'd asked my husband when I first met him. I was thinking of the Keystone Cops. I thought *silent movies* and found the whole idea about as interesting as the Three Stooges or Jerry Lewis, inheritors of that early manic comic style. Not my taste at all. I hadn't yet seen a silent spectacle like *Napoléon* or the stunning sexuality of Louise Brooks in *Lulu* or even one comedy with Buster Keaton, his deadpan style so self-deprecatingly ironic, so modern.

"It was a universal language," my husband said to me then. "When you made a film—in New Jersey or California or Berlin or Rome—the world was your audience." To my husband, when sound came in, it was the Tower of Babel all over again. The world broken into warring nation-states, divided by the unnecessary static of the spoken word.

Paradise, in the form of silent film, had been sadly short-lived. I remembered a quote from a textbook my husband always printed in big bold letters at the top of his silent movie course syllabus: "In an astonishingly short time—1895 to 1927, little more than thirty years—the silent cinema evolved into a unique, integral, and highly sophisticated expressive form and then, overnight, became extinct."

Extinct. The word had a new reverberation for me. I stopped shaking. My heart stopped pounding behind my sore ribs. I washed my hands in Apolline's sink and was comforted to see there was no blood, that it had all been a dream. Then, as the sun came up over Astoria, I crept back to bed and under the covers. Before it was full daylight, I was fast asleep.

I should have felt ghastly when I woke up later, but I didn't. I hardly ever drank, and usually even a glass of wine made me first giggly, then sleepy. My husband had teased me—*cheap date.* As I stood again at the bathroom sink, this time brushing my teeth, Apolline came up behind me and gathered the waist of my jeans in her fist. "You are too thin," she said. "I never thought I would say that about an American, but you are." She dug through her drawers and lent me a thin black leather belt to keep my jeans from falling down as I crossed the street, though that would have made a good silent movie moment.

"You are going to eat breakfast," she announced, threatening me with croissants and cream, real cream, for the coffee. Then she went out to the bakery.

While she was out, I called John again, this time at his office on campus. "I need another favor," I said.

"I'll send someone to get you," he said. "Tricia could come."

I stopped myself from saying, *God, no,* and instead said, "I need you to fax a request on letterhead to the Cinémathèque Française. Tell them I am coming to do some research in the collections. Tell them"—I paused, trying to think up something plausible—"that I am working on my husband's last book." The Cinémathèque was notoriously picky about letting researchers see their films or work in their collections, but they'd known my husband. In the small world of silent film, everyone had.

"You can't," John said. "You can't go to the Cinémathèque."

"Why not?" I felt a sudden flush of anger so hot that my cheeks burned. "Why the hell not?"

"Because the archives are closed. They are supposed to be moving to this high-tech wonder palace in Bercy, but the place never seems to get done. I think they are predicting two years now before the opening."

I opened my mouth and then shut it. I had not expected this. "But I'm going to Paris," I said. "I'll be there tomorrow, with any luck."

John made a sound like a tire deflating, caught short of words for once. "Listen, I know the director, some of the archivists. It's Mosjoukine material you want, right?"

"Yes," I said. "Mosjoukine."

"I'll make some calls. It'll take a few days, though, and I don't know what will be possible. Can you stay in New York until I find out? Or, better still, come back here?"

I thought about the address I had for Sophie. Forty years and counting. "No," I said. "I have other research to do."

"Research?" he said. "What's this all about?" John knew full well my husband had not been working on a book on Mosjoukine. "Are you writing?" In theory, I was a fiction writer. I'd published one novel. I got paid to teach students how to write. I just didn't do it myself anymore. I hadn't written a word in years. I could feel how much John needed to believe I was up to something as sane and worthwhile as researching a novel, but, honestly, I wasn't.

"No," I said. "It's not that. Listen, I'll call you from Paris, okay?"

"Okay. You'd better. But give me until Wednesday to see what I can set up."

I thought about that. I had completely lost track of time. "And this is what day of the week?"

"Jesus, Emma, it's Thursday—in Indiana and New York. Won't you please let somebody come get you? I could come. Today, even. You know I'd do that for you."

I shook my head. I knew he couldn't see me, but my silence was enough.

He was silent, too. Then he coughed. "I found some more Mosjoukine bio stuff. Not much, but more than you're gonna want me to read on the phone. Are you sure there isn't a way for me to send it to you?" Behind me I could hear Apolline coming in from the bakery. I covered the phone with one hand and asked Apolline if there was somewhere in the neighborhood I could get a fax. She pointed at a number on a slip of paper taped to the wall, a copy shop near the subway station.

I gave John the fax number. "I'll stop on the way to the airport. Send whatever you can find."

"Okay, I can do that. Listen, if I see Gwen," he asked, "what should I tell her?" Gwen was the chair of the English department at my college, a woman with violently red curly hair who wrote short stories that managed to say more about the world than any novel. We'd been colleagues for fifteen years, and neither of us had ever missed a meeting or class or refused the most boring committee assignment. Together we'd built a program we were proud of. Gwen was as passionate in her defense of it as she was about her own writing. But I hadn't seen her since the funeral, though I knew when I heard the phone ringing upstairs at least half the time it had been her wanting to talk about what we always had—classes, students, former students, their lives, jobs, and books. I'd let the phone ring. I didn't want to hurt her, to break her heart, but I just didn't care anymore, not about what happened to my classes or the writing program or the whole damn college.

"If you see Gwen," I said, "tell her I'm okay. Tell her I say hello." It was worse than nothing. It was the best I could do. Apolline was pouring me coffee, putting the croissants out on a plate. "I have to go, John," I said, and hung up on him for the third time.

Apolline watched me eat, intent on making sure not a crumb stayed on my plate. For her sake, I chewed, I swallowed, but the buttery croissant could have been stale Wonderbread for all I could tell. I seemed to have lost my sense of taste along with my appetite. "Why do you want to go to Paris?" she said. "There's nothing for you there. I know. I left. If you can't bear to live your old life, you should start a new one in America, in some new city. There are so many here. You could start a new life every year and never run out."

"You may be right," I said, though I couldn't quite imagine choosing a strange town at random, then moving there to stay. "But first I have to go to Paris. I need to find out if Sophie is still alive. You can understand that, can't you?"

Apolline frowned. "I shouldn't have told you so much," she said. "It was the Scotch. And the shock of your news." She watched as I finished the last bite of croissant, then she cleared the table.

"Do you have pictures of your family with you?" she asked.

I thought about that for a moment. How could I have taken the picture of me as a baby and left behind every one of my own daughter, newborn and growing? Then I remembered my wallet. Like most moms, I had my kid's latest school picture tucked in next to my credit cards, my driver's license. Also one of my husband holding a trout. That was it. I took them out.

The school picture was, as usual, not particularly good. My daughter's eyes were downcast so you couldn't see how blue they were, and she had an unnatural grin as if the photographer, with the cold soul of a dentist, had told her

35

to show every one of her new permanent teeth. "She looks like you," Apolline said, using the present tense, though whether that was out of kindness or a slip I couldn't tell. In the snapshot my husband, no fisherman, was holding up his prize and grinning. We had been on one of our family camping trips, and my daughter, six at the time, had actually snapped the picture. He looked young. He had more hair than I remembered and different glasses. Behind them, his eyes, like my father's, were serious and brown.

I had the oddest feeling my husband was living through time backwards, getting younger every year instead of older, the way Merlin in Arthurian legend was said to have done. Every second, my husband was slipping further and further away from me. We'd made love the night before he was killed, after he'd come to bed late from previewing yet another silent movie for the class he was teaching. It had been the wordless, comfortable sex of two people who know each other well, maybe too well, to need speech. I remembered what must have been our last kiss as I slipped back into sleep, then—nothing. Why? I could remember the last *Have a good day!* I'd called after my daughter the next morning with Technicolor vividness. But what was the last thing I'd said to my husband? Remember you're taking your daughter to violin? Or, maybe, Don't you have a department meeting today? Nothing personal. No more than a secretary might say to her boss as she handed him his mail. I closed my eyes and tried to remember the last time we'd made time to talk, to say more than dueling sentences—*Did you? Don't forget to?* That week? That month? And now, it would be never.

Here I was in New York wondering who had or had not had sex in Paris more than forty years before, when I was a widow who would never make love to her husband again. Might never have sex again, period. Suddenly my head felt too heavy to hold up. I put my face, cheek down, on the table again. It was getting to be a habit. Maybe the Scotch was finally wearing off. The back of my skull was throbbing, and my eyes ached.

"Do you want more coffee?" Apolline asked, resting her hand on the back of my neck. My hair hurt.

"Do you still have your scissors?" In the old days, Apolline never came to Florida without a kit of freshly sharpened shears and fine toothed combs. Just the sight of them made me hide.

36

"Yes," she said. "They're mine. Good stylists always own theirs, never the salon."

"Cut my hair," I said, sitting up. "Short." I gathered a great handful of it and lifted it off my neck. It felt like it was strangling me.

"I don't do hair anymore," She held up her hands, and for the first time I noticed how swollen her knuckles were, how her hands trembled.

"Please," I said. "Just cut it all off. You can do it."

She did. First, she just took off a couple of inches, but I begged her to cut more, so she kept going inch by inch toward my scalp as I pressed her. My hair fell around her feet like blond leaves, drifting in funereal curls. As she cut, I thought of the wreaths and flower arrangements the Victorians made from the hair of their dead, how they often put both the arrangements and their dead under glass. As she cut, I thought of the scene in Carl Dreyer's great silent movie *The Passion of Joan of Arc*, where the jailers cut St. Joan's hair down to her scalp as they prepare to burn her at the stake. In Dreyer's tight close-ups, Joan is crying.

As Apolline got closer to my skin, I could feel her hands shaking. The scissors caught my scalp and the sudden pain made my eyes water. I missed my daughter. I missed my husband so badly. I wanted Apolline to cut and cut and keep going until the pain, the real blood, was a noise in my head so loud I couldn't feel this other, unbearable hurt. Then I was crying, sobbing so hard Apolline had to stop for a while.

When I was done crying and she was done cutting, Apolline held up a mirror for me to see. I didn't look like myself. My hair was a bare inch, too short to show curl and very blond, as if I had been in the sun. I looked like the baby in Livvy's arms, or like my baby, the day I brought her home from the hospital. So little hair, such startled, shocked eyes. "After the war, they did this to the women who were collaborators, who'd slept with German soldiers, you know," Apolline said. "Punishment for sleeping with the enemy."

"I know," I said. What was I punishing myself for? Losing my family, I thought. *Losing*, as if I'd been unforgivably careless. *For being alive.*

"Well," Apolline said, brushing the blonde hair off my black sweater. "At least on you, it looks good."

Before I left, Apolline packed me an extra croissant and an orange, then kissed me on both of my cheeks. She unlocked her apartment door. The early spring air of Queens felt cold on my nearly bare head. "Is there anything else you can tell me about my mother before I go?" I asked. "Anything?"

Apolline paused, as if she were considering a list of possibilities. "She was a communist," she said. "A fierce one. She had fights with both of your fathers about that! Neither of them liked it one bit. One a White Russian, the other a colonel in the almighty American Army." Apolline laughed. "Imagine."

5

I BOUGHT A ONE-WAY TICKET TO PARIS. Every time we'd flown to Europe, my husband, who'd been six feet three, had complained bitterly about how close together the seats were in economy. In his honor, I bought a seat in first class. He'd paid for all that frugality, and now I had three credit cards with nothing on them and limits that added up to more than my yearly salary. This time, at Kennedy, the ticket agent wasn't even curious. People bought tickets there at the last minute to every place on the planet you could possibly fly.

As soon as I got to my seat, the flight attendant, a man about my age, asked me if he could bring me a beverage. He had the most beautifully buffed nails I'd ever seen. I had him bring me a double Scotch. Then I fastened my seat belt. Now there was no going back.

First class was nearly empty, and once the curtain was drawn it was like being on a separate plane, steerage a faint din behind us. The flight attendant had his hands full with a pair of Japanese businessmen who kept ringing before he'd fulfilled their last urgent desire. There was only one other woman, sitting a few seats ahead of me. I couldn't help noticing her. She was beautiful. She was maybe ten years younger than me, in her thirties, or maybe she was my age but with great makeup, maybe even great cosmetic surgery. I knew I was naive about such things. Her skin was as smooth as my daughter's had been. How was that possible? To move through the world and show no signs of age or wear. She had short, sleek dark hair like a seal and teeth as subtly, as expensively white as natural pearls.

She was with a man at least ten years younger than she was, and he watched her lips, his lips parted, apparently holding his breath, as he waited for her to speak. Was she a movie star? Some hotel heiress? She looked familiar. Everything about her—clothes, hair, makeup, purse, shoes—was perfect. Like the clothes Mosjoukine wore in the postcard. Just looking at them made you want to touch them, touch her. Her skin and the baby alpaca of her sweater would be equally soft.

Could you change your life, your luck, if you had better clothes? I guessed Sophie Desnos, ardent communist, probably would not have thought so. A month earlier, I would have agreed with her. You were who you were on the inside, and I measured people either by what they knew—I *was* a professor—or by what they had given to life. That part of me was pure mom. Who did you love? Who loved you back?

Now, I wondered, if you looked invulnerable, would the devil, the grim reaper, God himself or herself, stand back and let you stroll by, untouched? All I knew was I had the profound feeling I wanted the seal woman's life. I wanted it like sex, like religion, like heroin, maybe. I could taste it in my mouth. Instead, I ordered another double. In first class, all the liquor you needed or wanted was free.

Dinner found me too far into my Scotch to be hungry. Even in first class, the feature film was a Sylvester Stallone movie I didn't think had been released in the States. Impossible to watch even in the name of needed distraction. I got out the envelope with the fax John had sent.

One bio said Mosjoukine had gotten his start as a double for Valdemar Psilander, the great Danish actor, in new endings filmed for the Russian market. It was one of those odd movie facts I had heard before, how, in the silent days, distributors would film sadder endings to suit the lachrymose tastes of Slavic audiences. If, in an American or French or German film, a drowning couple was rescued, in the Russian ending they died. My supposed father had been one of the lovers going under. Not exactly an auspicious beginning for a happy film life.

Another talked about how much Abel Gance had wanted Mosjoukine to play the title role in his epic six-hour *Napoléon*. There had been much correspondence, apparently. Would that be at the Cinémathèque Française? My husband would have known. In the end, Mosjoukine declined. Maybe, one source suggested, because of the time involved or the money, but Mosjoukine had written Gance to say he had decided no one but a Frenchman should play

Bonaparte, the greatest Frenchman of all. Gallant, that refusal, smooth. Like his picture.

Another short paragraph mentioned Mosjoukine's many women, including, briefly, Kiki de Montparnasse, that spirit of Paris in the '20s. Mosjoukine was almost as famous a lover in real life, this writer implied, as on the screen. All in all, it sounded like one hell of a romp, one that ended, the authors of these various brief biographies were all unanimous in saying, in the hospital in Neuilly-sur-Seine. One author said Mosjoukine had been buried in a grave marked only by a rude wooden cross. All of them had him dead in 1939.

I put the fax in my purse. The flight attendant was standing in the aisle by the seal woman's seat, laughing at something she was saying. She was an alto, her voice musically low and a little rough. I closed my eyes.

If the colonel and Livvy believed in making safe choices, Mosjoukine clearly had not. Mosjoukine had left a secure life as a landowner's son and future lawyer to become an actor. His early success in Russia made the chance he had taken seem like a bet on the roulette wheel that paid off handsomely. He'd been rich. He'd been famous. At least until the revolution. Again, he'd chosen risk, fleeing to France, and there his good fortune returned. He spent his days writing and acting and directing, doing the very things he'd jumped off the train to Moscow to do.

Then sound swept his world away. But how could he have seen that coming? Even if he could, there was no stopping it, any more than he could have stopped the Bolshevik revolution. Where was there a life that pain could not touch? Look where the careful woman who raised me had ended up, in a bed soaked with her own blood.

I opened the paper bag of food Apolline had packed for me. I took a bite of the leftover croissant, but my mouth felt so dry I couldn't chew. She'd tucked the photographs of Sophie Desnos, including the one with the address on the back, and the Mosjoukine card next to the croissant. I laid out my alleged parents like a game of solitaire on my little meal tray and looked at them in the bright hot spot of the reading light. Mosjoukine had a high forehead, a strong, straight nose. But it was his blue eyes, so large in his face, that defined him. Sophie's dark eyes were even more overwhelming. She had a button nose, a trembling bow of a mouth, but her eyes swallowed the light, pulled me in. Could we really be related? They were both so handsome, so much more handsome than I was. Mosjoukine looked out at me, one eyebrow slightly raised, as if he, too, questioned the entire idea.

After a while, I put these people I did not know in my purse with the pictures of my other family and ate the orange, reminder of my childhood, small Florida sun, that Apolline had packed for me. For good luck. *Bonne chance,* I thought, trying to warm up the woefully rusty French side of my brain. When I was little, when we were newly arrived in the States, my father and I had spoken French to each other every day, usually when my mother wasn't around. On the way to a Disney movie. In the pool at the officers' club. My mother, increasingly, had disapproved, sensing there was something between us she couldn't share. By the time I was in sixth grade, without ever talking about it, my father and I stopped.

After that came years of no French, then four years of bad high school French teachers. When I was in college and returned to Paris for the first time, I could get by, even have moderately deep conversations, but no one accused me of being French. It was clear as soon as I opened my mouth that I was yet another American.

I closed my eyes and tried to sleep. But in my head I kept seeing lights flashing, hearing brakes squeal. The sound of metal on metal. In the real world, inside the pressurized tube of the plane, I heard someone new joking softly with the seal woman. I opened one eye. The pilot was perched on the armrest of her seat. She had her hand on the blue sleeve of his uniform jacket. Didn't she ever sleep? Or frown? He was looking down at her with an expression on his face like the ones the Wise Men wore when they beheld the baby Jesus, the child they found by following a star. The pilot basked in her glow.

I felt the opposite of luminous, like a chunk of bituminous coal in my itchy, heavy black sweater prickly with cut hair. I felt tired and sticky. Had I ever glowed, a candle in somebody's night? Had I been the light of the world for my husband? I thought so. Maybe. For my own daughter. God, I hoped so. I closed my eyes again and made myself keep them shut until finally I did go to sleep, though I was so much less comfortable in my first class reclining leather seat than I had ever been tangled, leg to leg, in economy class with my husband, I couldn't bear to think about it.

Morning in first class came with coffee and steaming hot towels. Then after a steep descent that made my bones feel leaden with gravity, we landed with a bump and a squeal at Charles de Gaulle.

We all stumbled down the jetway. Paris, we were finally in Paris. Right away, there was an ATM machine. I put one of my credit cards in, got a cash advance in euros. Just like that, I was living in a different economy. I stood at the baggage carousel watching the suitcases go around for a good five minutes before I remembered that I had nothing to claim. The seal woman was chatting with her companion, pausing every now and then to point out another piece of matched black leather luggage as it went spinning by. He would hop to get it and add it to the growing stack. I saw another, a small rolling suitcase, slip down the chute and head onto the conveyor belt. I could see it. They could not, the pile of already retrieved luggage momentarily blocking their view. Before they could, I reached out and grabbed the handle. Then I headed for customs, the stolen suitcase rolling smoothly behind me.

I slid through customs, declaring nothing. My heart pounded. The French official looked barely awake. What could an American, a blonde American in baggy, unfashionable jeans and sweater, possibly be smuggling *into* France? Any second, I expected to hear the seal woman's voice behind me, low, melodious, "Excuse me, I think you have my suitcase."

Or something sharper, her companion shouting, "Stop, thief!"

I shot across the lobby and out the automatic doors. I heard them suck shut behind me and stood blinking in the cool sunlight of a March morning in Paris. "Taxi, Madame?" a voice asked me. When I had been in Paris before, by myself or with my husband, I had always carefully taken the RER, the train, into the Gare du Nord. Never a cab all the way into the city. Too extravagant, too foolishly expensive. I heard the doors open behind me, heard the sound of many tiny squeaky wheels on a host of suitcases. I didn't turn around to see if they matched the bag I was pulling.

"Yes, taxi," I answered in French, then I hopped in the open door, pulling my suitcase in beside me. "Go," I said to the driver, scrunching down in the seat. "Please." He went. The driver was young, maybe Tunisian or Moroccan. Once we were free of the airport, we flew past the concrete suburbs where the new immigrants who worked at the airport lived. After a while, I saw the sign up ahead for the Périphérique, the ring road around Paris built where the old city walls once stood.

The driver looked at me in the mirror, one eyebrow raised. *Where now?*

"Gare du Nord," I said. I would get off there and take the Metro. And head where? I dug in my purse for the photograph of Sophie. "No, wait, I have an address. It's near the Canal St-Martin." Leaning over the seat, I showed him the address Apolline had given me. He looked at it for a full ten seconds, then put his eyes back on the road. He shook his head.

"No," he said.

"No, what?" I asked. "No, you won't go there. Or no, you don't know where it is?" We shot through the Porte de Clignancourte, still headed for the Gare du Nord.

"It isn't a real address," he said.

"It is," I said. "Or, at least, it was."

He didn't answer, but sighed loudly, as if I had deliberately set out to ruin his day. We went spinning past the great doors of the Gare du Nord, and then he pulled up in the queue at the taxi rank, braked to a hard stop, and got out of the cab. He waved over an older driver. They both looked at the address. The older man shook his head, too.

I should have bought a Paris map at the airport, I thought. I shouldn't have been spooked into the cab. Okay, I shouldn't have stolen the suitcase. My driver got back in the cab. He pointed to the older driver. "He says the street isn't there anymore. That it used to be, in the sixties. But no more. The government tore down the old houses to build apartment blocks, and the old alleys like this got wiped away."

The older driver was looking through the window at me, as if he were waiting for me to insist. I thought, He knows where it is. Or rather, was. Then someone came running out of the station and got in his cab, and he was off.

Okay, okay, I thought. Stupid to go there first, anyway—an Aunt Z sort of thing to do. Show up at the address and say, "A woman who might have been my mother used to live here. Can I spend the night?"

My cabbie tapped the steering wheel with the ring on his right hand, clearly restless. He seemed to have suddenly noticed how odd I looked, with my razor cut, my wrinkled clothes, and expensive bag. "A hotel, perhaps, for Madame?"

he suggested, as if I, in my current deranged state, might not have considered that possibility.

I hadn't. "Yes," I said, "a hotel then. Hôtel Batignolles," I added. "On the Rue des Batignolles, near the end, almost to the square." As soon as I said it, I regretted it. We pulled back into traffic. The Hôtel Batignolles was where my college put up faculty and students on their way to its far-flung foreign studies programs. My husband and I had stayed there. Someone might well be there who knew my whole sorrow-soaked story. I caught a glimpse of myself in the taxi's bead-festooned rear mirror. This time I kept myself from jumping at the sight, but I thought, No one is going to recognize me. I wouldn't have recognized myself, not even in the *International Herald Tribune* under a banner headline with my name.

"Okay, Hôtel Batignolles," he said and took me straight there, cutting down Clichy to the Boulevard des Batignolles to the much smaller Rue des Batignolles without a second's hesitation, proving he did know Paris, if not the street where a woman named Sophie Desnos once lived.

Batignolles was a neighborhood that had once been a separate village, as was true of so many stray parts of Paris, and it still looked like it, with small shops and a worn grassy park behind a church at the end of the street. It was cut off from the rest of the city by the steep rise of Montmartre to the east, by the Gare St-Lazare to the south and its endless tracks to the west. It was still mostly a working-class part of town, and it was not near anything, in the touristic sense of that word, not even a convenient Metro stop, though a bus ran down the street to the Gare St-Lazare, and then further, to the Opera.

The taxi driver dropped me in front of the hotel, which was neat white stucco with a courtyard, as if it had wandered from the south of France and come to rest here in Paris. It was small and very clean and someone, sometime, had gained the loyalty of our dean of students and the deans of a half-dozen other midwestern liberal arts colleges, so there were usually little knots of blonde co-eds waiting for the bus in front of the bakery next door, with maps and guidebooks clutched in one hand, on their long way to the Louvre or Notre Dame or whatever it was they had been told by their teachers they must go and see.

When I got out of the cab, though, the street was empty except for an old man in a fedora walking an equally elderly dachshund.

45

"Good morning, Madame," he said, tipping his hat.

"Good morning, Monsieur," I replied, as if we were in a small town, as if we had known each other, at least by sight, all our lives. For a moment, I wanted to pretend I had stepped back in time and might run into Sophie, Apolline, Mosjoukine, and the colonel on the sidewalk in the Paris of the 1950s. Instead, I went into the dark lobby of the hotel.

I managed to check in without anyone seeing me except the desk clerk. A large sign announced in English, German, and Japanese that the check-in time was 3:00. It was barely 11, but the clerk, taking in my advanced state of dishevelment, handed me the room key.

In my room, I locked my door. The room was small, clean, and absolutely ordinary with a single bed and a small black-and-white TV. I put the suitcase on the bed and unzipped it. Inside was a single matched outfit, packed separately, as if for a quick overnight trip. I shook out a pair of black rough wool pants, a soft grey shell, a long merino and silk sweater with subtle gold and green flecks. Also, a cosmetics bag with more makeup than I owned, not a hard feat. In it was a large vial of Percoset, more than anyone who wasn't dying or in chronic, crippling pain should have. No wonder the seal woman had kept smiling. I pulled off my black sweater and jeans, old dead clothes, and stripped to the skin. Then I threw myself down on the bed beside the suitcase and closed my eyes.

When I opened them, it was late afternoon. The sun slanted through the window. I went into the bath and took a long hot shower, using all the hotel's small largess of soap and shampoo. It felt strange to wash what was left of my hair. I ran my hands over and over the smooth shape of my head. I washed out my underwear, hung it in the shower to dry. I got a clean pair out of my purse and put it on. Then I slipped on the black pants, the loosely knit shell and sweater. They fit like no clothes I had ever owned, like a soft second skin.

I took the makeup kit into the bathroom. Early in my husband's silent movie making, he had press-ganged me into helping with the makeup. He'd gotten old manuals on film makeup out of the depths of the college library. He'd raided Walgreen's for some dark and primitive colors. Really, I'd shown no talent for it. I only owned one tube of lipstick, which I wore on occasions like New Year's and to friends' weddings. Each semester, he had at least one female student who knew lifetimes more about makeup than I did. But now I wanted

46

this stolen makeup to complete my transformation. I wanted nothing about me—not hair, clothes, or skin—to be the same. I wanted magic. I wanted to be wearing a mask. I stared and stared at myself in the mirror, unsure what to apply where.

Finally, I gave up and tucked the makeup kit in my purse. I would think about it later. Now I wanted to find a good map, and for that, I needed a bookstore.

In the lobby, two co-eds were sitting at one of the small tables where they served breakfast, drinking with straws from cans of Coca-Cola. I glanced at them. They looked familiar, in a generic sort of way. Were they my former students? My husband's? One of them, with long purple hair, was wearing the perfect makeup. Eyes shaded in, brows dark. In my husband's class, she would have been the makeup artist.

"Um, hi," I said, stopping in front of them at the little round table. I held out the makeup kit. "Could you guys help me with this makeup? I'm a little out of practice."

The girls stared at me for a moment, then at each other. I thought they might burst out laughing. Then the one with the purple hair nodded. "Oh, sure," she said, with a nice round midwestern O. "I could get into that."

We crowded into the small WC off the lobby, the makeup girl, me, and her friend, who was chunkier and boyish but who wanted to act as consultant. "I like your hair cut," said the girl with the purple hair. "So what kind of look do you want?"

"Like yours," I said.

"Really?" her plainer friend asked, doubtful. She went back to the lobby for her pack and brought back a couple of wrinkled American magazines, a *Vanity Fair* and a *Cosmo*. This was a full consultation now. We flipped through the pictures, and I picked one.

"Kind of like that," I said, pointing at a hyper-thin girl in a fashion spread. Her eyes were raccooned with dark shadow and her lips blue-black.

"Are you sure?" the purple girl said. "I mean, I can see going there. But I think she looks like her boyfriend beat her."

I dug in my purse and pulled out the picture of Sophie. I wished I'd had a picture of Vera Holodnaya in full film makeup to show her. "Like this," I said.

"Oh, okay. Diva, right?"

47

"Diva," I repeated, a bit of the silent film world slipping into this crowded, twenty-first-century space. Amazing how styles outlived artists like Vera Holodnaya.

The makeup artist carefully circled my eyes, then shaded the hollows above them. Her friend chipped in a pair of tweezers from her Swiss army knife and watched as the makeup artist shaped my eyebrows, each pluck making me wince. "Not too thin," the friend said, pointing to the picture of Sophie. "Hers are pretty full."

The makeup artist nodded. She penciled my blonde eyebrows a soft sable. Then she dug in the bag for some lipstick and came up with a dark garnet. She painted my lips into careful bows, trying to make them look as full as Sophie's. She made me smack my lips on a Kleenex to blot off the excess. She frowned at the result. "It should be brighter," she said. "More kissy. You should maybe buy some."

She stepped back, and I looked at myself in the mirror. The eyes were definitely Vera. Or at least Sophie. My hair, though, short as a man's and still slicked back from my shower, looked like Ivan Mosjoukine's.

"Thanks," I said to the two girls. "I really appreciate it."

"No biggie. It was fun," said the makeup artist.

"Can I ask you a question?" said the friend.

I nodded, afraid what it might be.

"Is there something wrong with your feet?" she asked, pointing down at the clogs I was wearing. "Because, I mean, if there isn't, you definitely should not be wearing those shoes."

I looked down at my feet, the feet of a woman who had stolen better clothes, but not better shoes. "What should I wear?" I asked.

"Boots," said both girls at the same moment. "Definitely."

"Okay, boots," I said. "I'll get boots."

I waved over my shoulder as I opened the door of the WC and slid into the lobby. Behind me I heard the friend say, "Do you think she just got out of prison or something?"

"I think she was a nun in a convent," the makeup artist said. "And now she's on the run."

I caught the bus outside the hotel. The sun was setting over the train tracks as we neared the Gare St-Lazare. The street lights came on. It had rained while

I napped or showered or got my face painted, and the pavement gleamed with the headlights of the cars.

The last time I had been in Paris was nearly six years ago. My daughter had been two and a half, and though she'd outgrown it at home, she spent most of the trip in her old stroller. My husband, with us in tow, had headed straight to look for discounted film books at a large store a friend had recommended near St-Michel. Probably it was still there and would have maps and guidebooks. I would go there. At least from the window of the bus, a bit fogged by the rain, Paris looked as if it hadn't changed, as if six years were nothing. I felt like I was the one who had aged a century.

From Gare St-Lazare, I took the Metro to St-Michel. The bookstore was there, not looking any different, though there was a Chinese restaurant next door to it, something I didn't think had been there six years ago. Vietnamese maybe, but not Chinese. Inside, beyond the guidebooks and the full color coffee table books of Matisse, Renoir, and the Masterpieces of the Louvre, I found a copy of *Plan de Paris par Arrondissement.* If I were going to find a trace of the Rue Ste-Odile, it would be here, where, page by page, every square inch of Paris was covered even if the names of the streets were nearly small enough to need a magnifying glass to read.

After I paid, I went back outside. The street was busy, people rushing to do a little shopping before dinner, teenagers and backpacking tourists hanging out by the fountain with its gilt statue of St-Michel, sword raised. A girl walked by and stared pointedly, or so I thought, at my feet. I stepped into the Chinese cafe next to the bookstore. In the glass case, displayed the way the potato salad or coleslaw would be in an American deli, were platters of stir-fried chicken, egg rolls, and a great round casserole of white rice. Rice had been my daughter's favorite food. My husband always joked that she had been Chinese in her previous life. Would she be in her next one? I wondered. If there was a next one.

I ordered some rice and stir-fried vegetables and sat at the one small plastic table by the pay phone while the girl behind the counter heated the food in a small microwave. The counter girl brought the plastic plate to my table and watched as I took the first bite or two. When had I last eaten a hot meal? Suddenly, it tasted better than anything I could remember eating. I ate the rest with my head bent low over the plastic plate, shoveling the rice into my mouth with the equally plastic fork. When I was done, the girl brought me a paper cup of tea. She nodded at my empty plate. "Good?" she asked.

"Very," I said. The girl smiled.

"My grandmother makes it." We smiled at each other again. Grandmother, a granddaughter, maybe a mother in between. I felt warm from the rice, the tea, this bit of order in life.

"Listen," I asked, "is there a good place nearby to buy boots?"

She looked me over, taking in my clothes and my clogs. "Are you looking for a bargain or something classy?"

I thought about the first class ticket and the money the clothes I was wearing must have cost. "Classy," I said. I was about to add, "Just not too expensive," but I stopped myself.

She leaned forward. "Well, if someone were paying for me," she looked at me as if waiting for me to confirm that this guess of hers were right, "I'd go to Jean Gabot. It's down the street, then right. There a pair of boots is going to cost you 300 or 500 euros." She watched me to see if I would blanch. I passed her test. Then she cleared my table, throwing my dishes in the trash, and said, more to herself than me, "Most girls I know would do most anything for a pair of boots from Gabot."

So I went to Jean Gabot, trying not to think about how I was going to talk a French shoe clerk into believing I would buy a pair of boots that cost more than a hundred pairs of clogs. It turned out it was not hard at all. Like going off the high diving board, the hardest moment was pushing off, opening the glass and brass door of the shop. After that it was like falling through clear blue air to the water below.

It didn't matter that I didn't know my European shoe size, or what color or design of boot I wanted, or that I had no idea what type of leather. I was the only customer in the shop, and the two clerks—one in charge, the other her assistant—threw themselves into finding me boots. Better I should have no preconceptions. They, the professionals, would find me the perfect pair. Boxes appeared, disappeared. Boots were held up to my foot and considered, eliminated. Black, red, with stiletto heels or flat. Ones that laced, zipped, buttoned. Some even made it onto my right foot, only to be pulled off, rejected, by vote of either the head clerk or her assistant.

I closed my eyes, feeling like a dog in the hands of a skilled groomer, listening to the murmured, *Maybe,* followed by an emphatic *no, no.* Finally a soft black pair appeared, with low heels and buttery leather that reached to just below my knee and ended in a soft fold. Cavalier boots, the assistant called them. They looked like the boots that Puss wore to London to visit the queen.

"Good," the head clerk said. "Very good."

"Perfect!" said her assistant. "Yes, Madame, you agree?"

I stood up, the leather cradling the back of my calves like the hands of a lover. I took a step, a seven league first step. My stride was longer, the heel clicked as if my feet knew where they were going. "Yes," I said. "Definitely."

I charged the boots, then walked out in them, letting the assistant clerk dispose of my clogs, something she was eager to do.

Then I let my boots walk for me, down the quay, across the Seine on the Pont Neuf, move me through the crowds out on this Friday night as they swept from neighborhood to neighborhood. As I walked in my five hundred euro boots, it was Paris that seemed changed, not me. There was more graffiti, though I knew that was a plague that came and went in all big cities. The buildings seemed more worn. The euphoria for the future I remembered from previous visits seemed gone. Nothing looked really new. The shopping mall at Les Halles, that monument to the hubris of the '70s, looked run-down, was filled with teenagers on skateboards.

Near Les Halles, I went underground, meaning to catch the Metro back to Batignolles, but somehow, almost sleepwalking now, I went in the wrong direction, and by the time I realized my mistake, it was too late. I got off at the Trocadéro, came out opposite the Palais de Chaillot, where the Cinémathèque Française had been before it went into limbo. I stood on the steps before the Trocadéro, looking down at the river and puzzled over the Metro map in the back of *Plan de Paris par Arrondissement,* trying to plot the easiest way back to the hotel. The print really was infinitesimal. The trick with the Metro was to choose the line that let you get where you were going with the least number of changes. Otherwise, you arrived feeling as if, between the long white-tiled tunnels and the multiple flights of stairs, you had walked most of the way. I decided it would be best to cross the river and catch the RER east.

I started down the stairs to the river. On either side were carousels, whirling, illuminated. I smelled the sticky sweetness of waffles, saw the vendors ready to offer me one dusted with powdered sugar or burdened with Nutella. When we brought my daughter here, her father had bought her one. I remembered it as if it had happened that morning. I remembered him carrying her in her stroller down the long flight of steps, me trailing behind them. I felt sick. I'd left my home, flown all the way to Paris, and still my dead family was all around me.

With my daughter, we had to do three carousels before we could cross the river, letting her ride a dragon, a unicorn, and a swan before we could interest her in moving forward through Paris. On my left, I saw an old woman in a baggy polyester sweater guarding the first carousel. If she was not the same woman who had been there six years before, she was remarkably similar. Are they all sisters? my husband had asked when we finally got to the third carousel and paid another old woman in a sweater for that one as well.

This old woman stood bathed in the red light of the canopy as taped music, a distorted version of a calliope, came squealing out of the speakers. The luminous green dragon my daughter had ridden was still there. I'd found this first carousel seedy, but my daughter loved it.

I hurried down the steps, trying to look ahead, to look only at the bridge. But there was my daughter's unicorn, one among a herd of unicorns on a much fancier two-tiered carousel trimmed in gilt and silvered with mirrors. Another old woman stood in its shadow taking tickets. Then the swan, more of a boat than a bird. I'd sat with my daughter in the swan on that third carousel, helping her hold her waffle. *Oh, God.*

That time we hadn't been headed anywhere, then suddenly we were across the river, fleeing from animals that spun for small girls only if their parents bought and paid for ticket after ticket. And there was the Eiffel Tower. In all my visits to Paris, I'd never been up it. Never wanted to pay for the ticket for the great elevator to the top. My daughter insisted.

I retraced our steps, crossing the bridge, half blocked, as it had been then, by young Africans selling bracelets, carved statues of couples having sex, umbrellas, and little models of the Eiffel Tower. My daughter had wanted one of those, too, but we hurried by. At the foot of the tower, more African vendors flew small mechanical birds, birds that somehow flapped and soared in great arcs to land at your feet. If you stooped to pick one up, the vendor was there in an instant. My daughter had wanted the bird, too, of course. She cried as we handed the windup pet back to its keeper.

So, to stop her from crying, we'd gone up the tower. Had we really been such chaotic and clueless parents? Giving in to our daughter's every whim? Yes. No. What difference did it make now? I only wished we'd bought her the miniature Eiffel Tower, the mechanical bird. A whole flock of them.

Now I walked across the concrete base of the tower, past the vendors, their birds soaring all around me. There was no line for the elevators. Maybe it was the rain. Maybe March was too early for the big crowds of tourists. No one was around at all. The sun was setting, the haze of twilight spreading under the tower. I paid for a ticket to the top. When I was in the elevator, just as the doors were closing, two more Americans ran up and jumped in. They were young guys, one black and one white. As the elevator doors closed, the white one said to me, "Can you believe it? We're Air Force pilots, and he's afraid of heights." He nodded at his friend, who had his eyes half-closed, clearly uncomfortable, as the open cagework of the elevator lurched, then rose slowly up the great iron leg of the tower. The black pilot's arms bulged inside the short sleeves of his Polo shirt, and yet his muscles were no help at all.

We made the switch to the smaller elevator for the ascent to the last stage. The lights of the city were coming on, block by block, below us. The black pilot was shaking now, his eyes closed tight. "Hey, man," his friend said. He had his hand on his buddy's arm, leading him. "We're almost there."

Why had they wanted to do this? What did a pilot in the Air Force have to prove? No one had to pilot the Eiffel Tower through takeoffs, landings, bombing runs. None of us were in charge, though, and for the black pilot, maybe that was the problem. He could fly thousands of feet above the earth if he were the one making the decisions. Now he wasn't.

We got off at the top, not even 300 meters from the ground, and still he was shaking. I wanted to tell him my new point of view—that we were never safe—but I had enough sense to keep my mouth shut. The white pilot headed for the men's WC. My husband had done the same thing. As if, for men, there were some mysterious attraction to urinating so far up in a tower that was, like all towers, in some ways a penis.

Six years ago, as my daughter and I had stepped away from the elevator, it started raining, justifying the eternal optimism of the umbrella salesmen on the bridge. We'd stood in the rain anyway, looking over the rail, down at Paris stretched like a toy city below us. "Look," I said to my daughter. "There's Notre Dame." We'd been to the church earlier that day. She and I had cruised the aisles of the nave while her dad climbed the tower and took photographs of the gargoyles and the pigeons. He wanted to compare them to the silent film set in Lon Chaney's *The Hunchback of Notre Dame.*

Poor kid, her sorry parents hadn't taught her anything about God or religion. We hadn't known what we believed, hadn't known what to say, and so we said nothing. In the house of God, she was full of questions. "Who is this Jesus?" she asked. We examined a nativity, still up from Christmas. The stations of the cross. Hard to explain such suffering, but she listened with great patience.

When he finished in the WC at the Eiffel Tower, my husband joined us at the railing, and my daughter mimicked my earlier gesture for the benefit of her father, pointed toward the cathedral. "Look," she said, "that's the house where God lived when he was a baby." He smiled at her. "You know," she'd added, "before we went wrong and killed him anyway."

Now I leaned my forehead against one of the iron bars that held the mesh designed to keep jumpers from throwing themselves off the tower, though they still did. One had jumped just a few months earlier. Some American tourists on their honeymoon caught it on video. The news channels had run the footage over and over. A man falling just past the left shoulder of the smiling bride. The iron bar felt cold. My daughter, I thought, she would never get married. Would never visit Paris again with me. My baby. Where was she? I banged my forehead against the iron softly, then harder. Thud, thud. It felt so good, I kept going. Thud, *bam*, thud. It felt so good, I couldn't stop.

The black pilot reached me first. What compassion moves a man so afraid of heights to come to the rescue of a woman standing at the very edge of the world? "Please," he said, "ma'am, step back." He put his hand on my arm. His fingers burned, they felt so hot, but the iron was cool. *Bam.* And hard.

A minute later, the guards were there. They were less polite. They grabbed me above each elbow, one on either side, and pulled me away from the railing, the heels of my new boots scraping over the iron grid of the platform under me.

They dragged me backward all the way to the elevator and kept a good grip on me as we waited for it to arrive. I looked for the black pilot. His friend was standing beside him. "I swear she was going to jump, man," the white pilot said. The black pilot kept his eyes on me, his face unutterably sad, as if I *had* jumped, as if he'd known me a long time, and now I was gone. The elevator doors opened, and the guards pulled me inside.

"Jesus loves you, sister," the black pilot called after me. Then the doors closed, and he was gone. The guards did not let go until I had both feet on the earth. It was night now. The tower loomed, illuminated, over our heads. Then one, who seemed more senior, took my passport and wrote my name in his notebook. He picked up a phone outside the ticket booth, waited until someone answered, and then he reported what had happened. He nodded. He said yes. He said no. Arrest was mentioned. Also the word *ambulance.* I tried to look calm, rational. I tried to look like I had nothing dangerous in mind.

Finally, the senior guard handed back my passport. "Clearly," he said, "it would be unwise to return to the tower."

"Clearly," I said.

"Go home," he said, letting me go.

"What a good idea," I said, thinking, *And where would that be?*

I left, feeling their eyes follow me as I recrossed the pavement under the tower. A bird landed with a small metallic clink in the dark at my feet, and a young man ran over, eager as always. I reached into my purse and pulled out a fistful of coins, handed them to him without looking. Then I picked up the bird.

"Thank you, Madame. Many thanks," said the young man, smiling broadly, his teeth gleaming. "Many, many thanks."

When I reached the river, I lofted the bird as high as I could into the air. It soared up and over the river. I stood long enough to see the yellow of its wings catch the spotlight headed for the tower and burn a brilliant, luminous gold. Then I turned away before the bird could start to lose altitude, before I could see its inevitable fall into the cold muddy water of the Seine. Or maybe it never fell. Maybe it flew and flew. Maybe it is flying still. That they flew at all—metal birds!—was a miracle to me. That birds fly at all, wings beating. That we live, hearts beating, if only for such a painfully brief time.

6 ✑

AFTER THAT, I TOOK THE TRAIN AS I'D MEANT TO, though I could feel
a bruise rising between my eyes. I changed from the RER to the Metro, headed
safely and sanely in the right direction. But when it was time to change lines at
the Gare St-Lazare, I made another mistake and got on the wrong one. As soon
as the doors hissed closed, I realized what I'd done. "Screw this," I said, loud
enough to turn the heads of the two teenage girls sitting in the jump seats just
inside the car, and I got off at Pigalle, meaning to cut over to Montmartre and
come, that way, down into the flat lands of Batignolles.

I walked up Pigalle, past the strip clubs, sex clubs, and adult bookstores inter-
spersed with the odd, brightly lit gyro stands. Women and men in singles and
pairs passed me, some offering me things no French class covered. I kept walking. "Nice boots," a tall transsexual in front of one of the clubs called out to me.

"Thanks," I said. He was wearing black lace-ups with wicked heels and tight
red fishnet stockings that followed his legs up into a scant circle of skirt.

"But, my dear," he stepped back to consider my complete outfit, "you really
should show more skin."

Skin, I thought, moving on by. I felt my skin hanging on my body like a coat
of chain mail, that heavy, that alien and unfeeling. What difference did it make
if I showed my body? Maybe my next step would be a leather miniskirt. What
would be wrong with that? Or taking off my stolen clothes for the short busi-
nessman who came up behind me on the crowded sidewalk and slipped his hand
over the tired muscles between my legs as he passed. Then, in the rush, he was
gone. I should have been afraid. I should have at least held my purse under one

arm, as Apolline had taught me to do. But I didn't give a damn. They could have my money. They could have my credit cards, empty promises of something for nothing. They could have any part of me that would do someone the least bit of good. My head hurt like hell. I wished it hurt more.

I turned off Pigalle and began the steep climb up the Rue Lepic. I knew this neighborhood because, when I was a student, I'd stayed at a hotel here, one labeled by the government as not only having no stars but as one "incompatible with tourism." Most of the tenants worked in the clubs off Pigalle and paid their rent in cash every Monday. One of them had showed me how to get more of my clothes into the tiny washer at the laundromat near the hotel by packing my jeans down with a broom handle she kept for the purpose. During the day, Lepic had been a cascade of food shops, skinned lambs hanging in the shop windows, tables with rows of perfectly aligned endive, each in its own little paper sleeve.

Now, at night, it was damp and silent. The pavement was still wet from either the earlier rain or the shopkeepers' last cleaning. I could smell cheese through the glass window of the closed shop on my right. I could smell the blood and hair of the horse butcher's. I turned west off Lepic, and then I knew where I had been headed all along: the bridge over the Cemetière de Montmartre. The longest I had ever spent in Paris, the one time I'd considered it conceivable, maybe even possible, that I might stay there was when I'd been researching my novel. This was before I met my husband, right before I got my job teaching. I'd walked the streets of Paris and thought about nothing but my characters, two lovers, in Paris in 1929.

I'd set part of the novel in the cemetery, which I found romantic. I was so stupid and young, I think I'd even found the idea of death romantic. Now I stood on the bridge, looking down at the white roofs of the tombs of that miniature city of the dead, and it seemed no time had passed. I could hear the cats below, the dozens who lived in the cemetery. They lived in rag nests their admirers built for them in the houses of the dead. The same people came to feed them every day. The toms howled, the females in heat answered. I heard the soft mews of the spring's early kittens. I had written the novel, published it, and never written another. Never mind that I taught students to write. I had stopped. Why? Because I had married, had a child? Not really a good excuse in these latter days.

I leaned over and smelled the rank ammonia scent of the cats, so alive below me. I stopped writing because I was afraid. I had always been afraid. If, as in *Kean*, genius came hand in hand with disorder, I would pass. I wanted a happy life. A good life. A safe life. I remembered hearing a story about Faulkner, about how when his daughter asked him why he had missed her birthday party, he told her no one even remembered if Shakespeare *had* a daughter.

So cruel. Is that what art took? Where had Mosjoukine been when Anne-Sophie Desnos found out she was pregnant? Where was Mosjoukine when she gave me away to an American colonel to be raised on the other side of the cold Atlantic? I had given up writing in a bargain with God to protect my life, my family, my happiness and theirs. Then it turned out God was as unforgiving, as unfair, as the goddamn IRS. Better to be a girl on Pigalle. Better to be a cat rutting in a tomb. What are we but eating and fucking and pissing animals? I loved my daughter. I loved my husband. The cats below me were raucous with love. What difference did it make in the end? As I stood there, looking down, I realized I could feel warm pools in my boots by my toes. I had walked until my feet bled. I hadn't even felt it.

I made it back to the hotel. I kept patting the book of maps in my purse, thinking, Here is what I have to do. Here is my work for the night. In my room, under the flat light of the florescent tube, I opened the map and poured over the streets on either side of the Canal St-Martin, all of the way from the Seine to the old slaughterhouses at La Villette. I stared until my eyes stung, until I had rubbed the dark paint around my eyes into a blur that stretched from cheek to cheek, that matched the purple bruise rising between my eyes. The young taxi driver had been right; there was no Rue Ste-Odile.

I took out the stolen bottle from the stolen suitcase, opened it, shook out two Percoset, and swallowed them dry. Then I thought about it and took one more. I fell asleep on the bed in my stolen clothes, my new boots still on my bloody feet.

7

I DREAMED I WAS DYING. I dreamed I was Vera Holodnaya. I had the Spanish influenza, and I was drowning inside my own body. Someone had propped me up on white pillows, but still I couldn't breathe. A curtain moved in a soft breeze, in and out of the window, but the air was not there for me. I wanted to cry out, but when I opened my mouth, my scream was the scream in a silent movie, full of emotion, quiet as the grave. I awoke covered with sweat, shaking, ran to the bathroom and threw up, the white rice I'd eaten the night before floating like little islands in the water of the toilet.

The sun was just coming up outside as I showered and brushed my teeth twice. I washed out my underwear and my bloody socks. The broken blisters on my feet were dry and hard, as if my thin skin were in a hurry to be calloused. In the mirror, my face looked whiter than rice, except for the bruise between my eyes, which was shading toward a yellowish green. I put some foundation on it, rubbing it gently over the tender skin, then did the rest of my face, trying to remember what the makeup artist had done, but also trying to go slightly less *diva* than the night before, not wanting to look so much like the girls on Pigalle. Putting my face on calmed me. War paint, my father had always called my mother's heavy foundation, rouge, tubes of red lipstick.

I took two of the three credit cards out of my wallet and tucked them inside the suitcase. Last night I hadn't cared if I was robbed on Pigalle, but in the morning light, it seemed foolish to carry all of them with me and risk having to cut short my search if they were stolen. I tossed in my bottle of Valium to keep the Percoset company and away from me for now. I put the suitcase in the closet and went outside. The bar across from the hotel was already serving coffee. I ordered. I felt chilled, though the sun was up, the day heading for lovely. I shivered, my hands shook, and I had to lean low over the cup, holding it between both palms.

It was Saturday. The bakery was open. The other shops would be raising their metal shutters soon. Since the Rue Ste-Odile wasn't on the map I bought last night, I would just have to find an older map to see where it had been. Or find an even older taxi driver. Someone in Paris had to know. I thought of the book stalls along the Seine. They seemed a likely place to start. Failing that, I would just start walking through the neighborhoods on either side of the canal. Someone would know, I kept thinking as I drank my coffee. Someone had to know. This was Paris, not Brigadoon. Streets did not just disappear without some record. People were another story.

I ordered another coffee. Standing at the bar, I could see the Hôtel Batignolles across the street and somehow, because of the plate glass window or the lighting, it seemed far away, like a slide in a magic lantern show. Who knew what I might find once I started looking for Sophie Desnos? Would I be back at the hotel that afternoon, that night? The idea that I didn't know sent a small wave of panic up the back of my legs, but I resolutely ignored it. I paid for the coffees, then crossed the street and went into the lobby. The night clerk was just closing out, getting ready to head home.

"Madame?" he said.

"I have some business," I said. "I may not be back every night. I might even be gone for a few days at a time. Will you charge the room to my card until I check out?"

He woke his sleeping computer with one flick of his mouse, checking to make sure they had my credit card number. "Certainly, Madame. Do you have any idea how long you—" he paused, since what we were really talking about was an empty bed, left luggage, and not me—"will be staying with us?"

I shook my head. "I may know tonight. Or so I hope."

He took his turn nodding. The day clerk came out from the office behind the counter, a cup of coffee in his hand. The night clerk finished entering my open reservation with a final tap of the computer keys. "It's done, Madame," he said. "Good luck with your business."

By the time I got to the Seine, the little book stalls along the quay were beginning to open. I strolled along, checking out the yellowing novels in French, the thumbed art books. I stopped at a stall on the parapet. A man with a long beard like Santa Claus, slightly yellowed around the cigarette he was smoking in place of St. Nicolas's pipe, was just unlocking. The sign he had set up on the pavement read, *Maps. Etchings.*

I asked him if he had any old copies of the *Plan de Paris par Arrondissement.* He flung back the cover on his stall, revealing an entire row. "How old?" he asked, pointing to the ragged and broken spines, "1914, 1929, 1946, 1960 . . ."

I pointed at the 1960 edition. "That should do," I said. Then just for old time's sake I had him give me the 1929 edition as well. When I'd been researching my novel, I'd checked out a 1929 Paris *Baedeker* from the library of the university where I was a graduate student and brought it to France with me, accumulating enough overdue fines to have bought it many times over, but good girl that I was, I'd returned it. Now I wanted those happy days researching my novel back.

I paid Santa for the books and took them to the nearest bench. First, I flipped open the 1929 book. Just looking at the style of the print made me realize why Paris seemed so changed. Paris for me was the setting of my novel. How often had I walked the streets, even after the book was long done, and seen only things that would have been there in 1929? The old shops with the glass and gilt fronts, the posts that had once held gas lamps. Paris in 1929 was, in some odd but real way, my Paris. And I realized it had been Ivan Mosjoukine's. My novel's lovers could have seen his fine car sweep by on the street, might have gone to see his popular film serial *House of Mystery* in weekly installments. Some film of his, at any rate. But they hadn't. It made me sad, as if I had missed my one chance to connect with my father, even if that connection was fictional. Hell, all of it still seemed fictional to me.

I looked in the index, and there it was, plain as print, Rue Ste-Odile. I found the page. It was not right beside the canal, but rather four or five blocks east. It made a crooked dog leg between the Haussmann-style Boulevard de la Villette and the compound of the Hôpital St-Louis, which sprawled over several city blocks, nearly down to the canal. Off the Rue Ste-Odile ran a little dead end, the Place Ste-Odile. I took Sophie's photograph out of my purse to look at the address again. The ink was smeared. I had thought it read *Rue,* but perhaps it was *Pl,* the abbreviation for *Place.* Maybe the address was 44 Place Ste-Odile.

I opened the 1960 edition of the same map. The Rue Ste-Odile was gone, displaced by a large new building at the hospital and replaced by a straighter, wider road that ran from the boulevard to the canal. But part of the Place Ste-Odile was still there, a little bump on the straight road of progress.

I opened the book of maps I'd bought last night. I found the hospital, but no Place Ste-Odile. Or was there? The road past the hospital still seemed to have a strange wart on one side, a bump that could have been a printer's error, a spot of ink on the rough paper. It was not labeled. Did that mean the Place Ste-Odile was still there? I flipped to the Metro map in the back. The nearest stop was Goncourt.

I put all three maps in my purse—as well equipped now as any time traveler—and walked to the station at the Hôtel de Ville. Hôtel de Ville to Goncourt was a short run, with no changes of line, and as I went underground, I found myself wishing the trip could be more difficult. If I did penance by descending the stairs to the platform on my knees, would God or the universe reward me with my mother or at least some sign of my mother at the other end of the journey?

I came up into the sunlight at Goncourt and strolled down the wide Avenue Parmentier, which I vaguely thought was probably named after the same distinguished Frenchman as the potato dish. I tried to remember what, exactly, were Potatoes Parmentier? Did they have cream, or was that Potatoes Dauphin? My daughter would eat only plain mashed potatoes, but she was eight. She would grow into more adventurous tastes. I stopped. Except, of course, she wouldn't. I took a deep breath.

At the end of the avenue stood the enormous compound of the Hôpital St-Louis. Nurses and doctors moved down the sidewalk ahead of me, and I followed them, let them carry me along, past a hodge-podge of modern outer buildings through an archway into the central courtyard. I stopped, taken by surprise. It was a secret garden. There were large trees, dotted with buds, and thin spring patches of fenced grass. In the very center, a bed of tulips was beginning to open, a blood red heart. I turned in a complete circle, admiring the surrounding old buildings, the elegant brick and stone of their façades, their tall mullioned windows. Then I sat on a stone bench, got the 1960 map out of my purse, and oriented myself. *This way,* I said to no one but me. I pointed. *It's this way.* A man in an expensive but wrinkled gray suit passed me as I sat there pointing east like a weather vane. He looked at me like he knew a crazy woman when he saw one. I looked at him and thought, He slept in his clothes. Was he a doctor? The relative of someone dangerously ill? He left the courtyard by one entrance. I left by another.

I followed the map, but still I almost missed the Place Ste-Odile. The entrance was a narrow passage that ran under a brick arch between two large postwar apartment blocks. No wonder the taxi driver had no idea where to find it. It was barely wide enough for a motorcycle, let alone a car. It looked like the entrance to a yard behind the blocks of flats, someplace where the neighbors kept their garbage cans. I eyed the passageway. It was probably just the chemical illusion our brains create that even Americans have learned to call déjà vu, but I had the strong feeling I had been there before. As I stood on the street, the man I had seen in the hospital courtyard brushed by me. "Pardon me," he said. Then he was gone as quick as a rabbit down a hole.

I followed him through the arch. In the Place Ste-Odile, time had stood still. There was only a single narrow house on either side, each three stories high with attic windows in gables poking through cracked slate roofs. The abbreviated block ended in the blank back wall of a tall apartment block. The two surviving houses of Place Ste-Odile leaned toward each other, as if to hide whatever business went on in the narrow, paved court between. Neither was in good repair, the plaster on the masonry walls cracked, the eaves sagging. Neither had been painted recently enough to show any color other than smog gray. Were they condemned? Abandoned?

I heard voices. The man from the hospital was talking quietly to a large, middle-aged woman wearing a faded housedress in front of the house on the right. She was sitting on an old wooden kitchen chair, scrubbing what looked like flowered curtains in a pan of soapy water balanced on a low stool. Her forearms were strong, muscled enough to remind me of Popeye. When she saw me, she glared. The man leaned forward and whispered in her ear. The house number, faded and barely legible, over her door read 43. Surely that meant the one opposite was 44 Place Ste-Odile, but it had no number that I could see.

The man finished his business with the woman washing curtains and passed by me on his way out. "Pardon," he said, for a second time. This time I could see he had a stethoscope in his suit pocket. What was a doctor from the hospital doing here? Did physicians in France still make house calls? He hadn't stayed long with his patient. I glanced at the woman. She was still staring at me, her eyes steady and black. While I watched, she wrung her curtains like the neck of a chicken.

I turned my back on her and examined what I hoped was Number 44. Next to the peeling front door of the house were three doorbells. Two of the tarnished name plates above them were blank, but the third had a barely legible name engraved on it: A. Meis. I laughed. It was hard not to take it as a joke, as in "Nobody here but us mice." I dug the picture of Sophie out of my purse. *44 Pl. Ste-Odile.* But there was no flat or floor number as part of the address.

I rang all three bells and waited. Behind me, the woman stopped strangling her wash. I could feel her eyes on me. No one answered. I rang again. Was this building abandoned? The ground floor windows were shuttered, but I stood back, staring at the upper floors. One pane in the attic was broken. But heavy, red velvet curtains hung in the second floor windows. Faded, but velvet nonetheless.

I heard a swish behind me as the woman put her curtains back in the tub. I turned. She didn't look down or pretend she hadn't been watching my every move. I crossed the narrow courtyard. "Good morning," I said.

She waited a moment before she answered, "Good morning." She had an accent. Polish? Romanian? But it was buried under what sounded like a half century of Paris. I bent down to show her the address on the back of Sophie's picture. She smelled strongly of onions and sweat.

"Is that the building?" I asked.

She studied the photograph, then the building in front of us. She shrugged, admitting it was the address. I turned the photograph over, pointed at my mother.

"I'm looking for this woman. She'd be in her sixties now. Her name is Anne-Sophie Desnos."

The woman took the photograph, looked at it even more carefully than she had the address, her every movement slow, deliberate, colored with a certain hostility, as if I were just another boss in a long line of bosses asking her to work harder for less pay. Then she shrugged so slowly—her broad shoulders first rising, then falling—it was as if we were standing neck deep in thick winter mud instead of the clear sunlight of a spring morning. If she moved slowly enough, her gestures seemed to say, I would give up and go away, leave her alone. I was sure it was a tactic she used every day.

I didn't go away. I took back the photograph, then repeated the name, Anne-Sophie Desnos. I spelled it D-E-S-N-O-S, speaking almost as slowly as she would have.

She made a clucking sound. "Desnos?" she asked.

I nodded. Now we were getting somewhere.

"I don't know her," she pointed at the picture of Sophie in my hand. "But there's a guy who lives in that building." She bent, picked her flowered curtains out of the washtub with one hand. "His last name is something like that. A Jew."

I looked up at the front apartment with the faded red curtains. "Is he there now?"

She started another glacially slow shrug, then seemed to give up on lethargy as the best way to be rid of me. She slapped her curtains into the tub so hard that the water flew, splashing us both. She'd had enough. I won.

"He's working," she said. "He's a guide on one of the tour boats they run up the canal to the old slaughterhouses in La Villette they've turned into some park." She made a puffing sound with her lips, as if dismissing the very idea of paying money to ride on a canal boat like so much meat.

"Where can I find . . ." I started.

She waved her hand in the direction of the Seine, dismissing me at the same time. "They start at the Port de l'Arsenal. But don't expect them to let you on for free." She then rose, tub in hand, went inside, and shut the door behind her with an audible click of the lock.

I stood on her wet doorstep and consulted the map. She must have meant the long basin labeled as the *Port de Plaisance de Paris Arsenal,* which I took to be the first part of the Canal St-Martin as it left the Seine, though it was hard for me to be sure because the water disappeared at the Place de la Bastille. Then there was no sign of the canal again until nearly the hospital.

This time the trip was ridiculously difficult, transportation as stasis. Three separate Metro lines, changes at two of the biggest Metro stations, Republic and Bastille, long walks underground to transfer from line to line. I should have gone on foot, aboveground. I found myself running through the complicated tunnels at Bastille. I wasn't sure why. I had no idea when the tour boats sailed or how I would find a man with a last name that sounded something like Sophie's, one man among many on what might be one of many boats. Or what I would say to him when I did. But I was an American, just a harmless tourist. I could buy a ticket, get on a boat, then figure out some way to ask. I ran as if my flight were leaving in ten minutes, as if I had heard the last boarding call.

As it turned out, there was only one boat docked by the side of the Seine, a narrow wooden barge with a small pilot house. It was dark green with the name *La Sirène* painted in red and gold on one side. It had a short ramp running up to it. A banner hung from poles on the quay: "Guided Tours! The Canal St-Martin, *13 Euros!*"

A queue of elderly women waited to board. From the back, they looked like the woman in the courtyard. Even from a distance they smelled nearly as strongly, as if they, too, did heavy housework day after day. They were uniformly short and heavy, dressed mostly in flowered dresses covered by knit sweaters, a concession to the morning chill, as were the scarves on their heads. As I came up behind them I caught the soft swoosh of Slavic vowels. Great, I thought, I was trying to slip inconspicuously into a tour group composed entirely of Polish grandmothers. The woman directly in front of me, who wore a thick string of amber beads around her throat, turned to stare. Then they all did, a long rank of round grandmotherly faces. The line stopped moving.

A man's voice from somewhere beyond the head of the queue called cheerfully in French, "Hurry, my dear ladies, and please have your tickets ready. We're running late, and we have thirteen locks to go through today." The grandmothers murmured in Polish and stared at me. The line stayed perfectly still. The man started down the line. I could see the top of his head over the shorter, scarf-clad heads of the grandmothers. Then I could see him.

It was me. He was me, though he still had my blond curls, his hair worn in a long ponytail down his back. He stopped, his face as surprised as mine.

I had a twin.

"Vera!" he said. I thought for a moment he was calling me by Mosjoukine's pet name for Sophie. Then for a crazy moment I thought he thought I was Vera Holodnaya. Then I realized my mother had named me Vera. Apolline had neglected to mention that or the matter of my brother.

Now my brother grabbed me by the shoulders, kissed me first on my left cheek, then on my right so hard I was sure I'd have bruises like bookends to set off the one between my eyes. "Here," he handed me a torn ticket stub. "Get on the boat." Then he headed back up the line, snatching tickets from each outstretched, arthritic Polish hand.

8

MY BROTHER WAS TALLER THAN I WAS. And he spoke much better French.

I noticed both these things once I was on the boat and settled between two buxom grandmothers. Otherwise the resemblance was unmistakable. That was why the whole line of Poles had been staring at me on the quay. Now I heard the grandmothers whispering, heard *siostra,* which I took for the Polish word for sister, maybe modified by the Polish word for twin.

La Sirène had a crew of two. The captain, an older Frenchman, started the engine. My brother unlooped the heavy lines from the quay and tossed them on board before jumping on himself. He was taller than I was by a good six inches. Close to five eleven, I guessed. He looked tall and thin in worn blue jeans and a long blue sweater the color of his eyes and mine. I also noticed he, unlike me, moved like Mosjoukine. Spontaneous—jumping up and over the bow without seeming to notice he was moving—and effortlessly graceful. His boat shoes made white blurs as they arched through the air.

Then he switched on the microphone and started the tour. "Hello, good morning, my lovely fellow sailors," he began in French. Then he paused and said his greetings again in Polish, or maybe it was Russian mixed with a little Polish, smiling at the grandmothers so warmly I could see them all around me preen a little, blush, coo. "I am your guide for this trip through time and across Paris, up the historic Canal St-Martin. My name is Ilya Desnos and . . ."

Ilya. Ilya and Vera.

"We will be together three hours this morning, making our way the length of the canal, through all thirteen locks, until we reach the basin at La Villette,

where you will have time to stroll and visit the gardens at the Parc de la Villette, then all of you—well, nearly all," he glanced at me as he added this, "have
tickets for the Cité des Sciences et de l'Industrie this afternoon, and your trip to
the museum will be followed by a performance at the Cité de la Musique." Ilya
waved a hand toward the bow as the captain maneuvered *La Sirène* through the
narrow opening of the canal. "Now we step back in time. We are a barge making
our way from the Seine to La Villette when it was the busiest port in France and
the slaughterhouse for all of Paris." Again, he repeated himself in what seemed
to be a working melange of Slavic languages, to judge by the whispered questions that went through the grandmothers when he finished with his translation
and the delayed laughs his jokes often got. They hung on every word.

Ilya's mouth had the tight corners I noticed around my mouth in the picture
taken at my naturalization, although his, through years of French, had firmed
into thin, deep lines that set off his frequent smiles for the grandmothers like
parentheses.

We moved toward the iron mouth of the canal, that meeting of nature—*the
Seine*—and artifice—*the canal's first lock*. The Canal St-Martin was ready for us,
opening even for such a slight cargo as one mixed-up American, two French-
men, and twenty Poles. We entered the first lock and sat at the bottom of what
seemed like an empty concrete swimming pool as the metal gates swung shut
behind us. The water began to rise, taking us with it. We inched very slowly up
the concrete walls. When we reached the top, another man jumped in the boat,
a young African with a shaved head and large gold earrings. "My regrets," he
said to Ilya, apologizing for being late. "I was helping my cousin."

When the lock was full, the gates ahead opened. The African helped Ilya untie
the lines that had held the boat steady, kept it from bouncing against the sides
of the lock. The wind at our back off the river suddenly felt chill. It had taken
a good fifteen minutes to rise from one level of the canal to the next. Thirteen
locks, my brother had said.

It was so odd watching him, half like looking at myself, half like staring at a
total stranger. Some of the gestures were so familiar. *There*, he stood listening to
a question with one hand open as if to catch a ball, as if to let the words gather
in his palm like rain from heaven. My daughter had teased me about that one.
"Crazy Momma," she said to me, "you think you can hear with your hand."

Others reminded me painfully more of her. The way my brother tilted his head first to one side, then to the other, if one of the grandmothers asked a question he didn't quite understand. The puzzled dog look, my husband had called that one, when our daughter listened to our instructions—clean your room, take a bath—with her blonde head tilted as if what we were saying was unintelligible.

My strongest feeling was that here was someone besides my daughter who looked like me. The two people who raised me had not. Aunt Z had been right about that. The mystery was why I'd never seen it, never even guessed. Apolline had been trying to prove that point when she held Mosjoukine and Sophie's pictures up to my face and made me look in the mirror. But Ilya *was* the mirror.

He was talking again, giving the universal Slavic rendition of what we were seeing. The grandmother sitting beside me patted my knee and offered me a cough drop. I shook my head. "He's good," she said. Her French was better than mine. She felt no need to listen to the translation of what we'd just heard. I nodded, proud of my brother. "We've had a lot of guides. They take us here. They take us there. Yesterday to Notre Dame and then to the Mémorial de la Déportation. Have you been there?"

"Yes," I said. My husband, daughter, and I had visited that splinter of the past buried in the tender tip of the Île de la Cité. I remembered my daughter staring at the illuminated crystals—numerous beyond even a grown-up's ability to count them—that represented those deported from France to the camps, all the Parisians who never returned.

The Polish grandmother shook her head. "Interesting, I suppose," she said, "but nothing to do with me."

I looked at her. Nothing to do with her? I wanted to whisper the word *Auschwitz* in her ear, but then I remembered how tired and impatient I had been at the memorial after having already waited so long with my daughter in Notre Dame for my husband to finish climbing the bell tower. Standing right in the dark heart of the memorial, I'd asked my daughter if she would like to get some ice cream. Would I feel differently now that I knew my mother was French, possibly a French Jew? I hoped so. Then my own sorrow would have taught me something. Then again, I hoped not. What did it say if I only cared about the deported, the dead, if they were related to me?

We moved through a wide open stretch of the canal. Up ahead, I saw the stone arch of a tunnel where I had seen the canal disappear from the map at the Place de la Bastille. "That great planner and architect Haussmann," Ilya was saying, "that perfect expression of his emperor's will, covered the canal, stinking as it was with commerce, smelling too clearly of what made Paris all her money, to build yet another grand boulevard." We all watched as the mouth of the tunnel approached and swallowed us whole. Then we were inside where it was so dark all of us blinked, and several women let out small startled cries of alarm.

Ilya's voice echoed through the dim, chill air. "Haussmann put the work of the city—and its working class—out of sight beneath the sidewalks of the bourgeoisie. But Haussmann, Kind Dictator of the New Paris, also built skylights, barred portholes, to let air and light into the tunnel and hid them in the parks of his new aboveground world." Ilya waved an arm above his head just as we passed under the first skylight. Green vines trailed down through the opening to meet us. We moved forward through the circles of wavering sunlight that Haussmann had granted us. The reflected lights bounced off the walls, shivering as if they, too, were cold. *"Ghosts,"* Ilya said in a stage whisper, pointing at the apparitions cast up on the walls. "Poor dead," he said, "they didn't want to leave their Paris."

In the gloom, I saw a rat run along the tunnel's narrow tow path, his eyes as bright as bits of sky in what began, as we moved slowly along, to seem like a daylong darkness. I imagined being born as this dark and this uncertain. Not to mention sickness, the soft sibilance of death. I imagined my daughter on the barge, along for this ride.

Just then, from the front of the barge came the eerie swoop of a violin. The *Gavotte in G Minor* by Bach. My daughter had played that piece in her second year of violin lessons. I leaned forward, trying to see where the music was coming from. It wasn't her ghost. It was Ilya, standing on the bow, one foot resting on the tall coil of ropes he and the African used to tie off the boat each time we entered a lock. My brother drew the bow across the strings with a flourish. To be honest, my daughter would have found his technique both flamboyant and spotty.

The grandmother next to me poked me with her thick, sweater-clad elbow. "I told you he was good," she said, nodding her head. Then she rubbed her thumb and forefinger together, predicting the tips the violin solo would win him and nodded again. "A real pro." An actor, I thought, from a line of actors. But not me. Even in my classroom, I was more a good listener, a quiet and careful lecturer, than the kind of performer that had students lining up for the chance to take one of my classes. Ilya would pack them in.

The melody ended just as we emerged into the light, leaving the tunnel behind us and passing beneath what my brother announced was the Swing Bridge of the Barn of the Beautiful, which stood above the lock of the same amazing name. In the sun, we blinked at the horse chestnuts and at the pedestrians who lined the bridge above us—one per step—as if posing for a group photograph, as if they were a choir assembling to welcome us to life or, at least, to their forgotten piece of Paris. In the sudden sun, my brother looked older, nearly as tired and thin as I was. He stopped his Slavic translation for a moment, coughing, then began again, explaining to the grandmothers about the swing bridge.

"Do you have children?" the grandmother asked.

"Yes," I said, then, "no."

She didn't seem to be listening. "Because there is a children's museum, La Cité des Enfants, at La Villette, too. It's supposed to be wonderful." She handed me a brochure she had for La Villette, for all the attractions at this abattoir turned pleasure park. "I wish I had one of my grandchildren with me so I could go." She sighed. "I think I would like this more than the science museum," and she pointed to the picture of small children wearing construction helmets, building a wall with oversized blocks of foam. She sighed more heavily. "Or the concert of experimental music." I glanced at the brochure. Beside La Cité des Enfants there was a huge metal slide shaped like a dragon. I closed the brochure. I had no children. None. I had to remember that, and I wasn't a child.

We passed the Hôtel du Nord which, Ilya informed us, had been made famous by the Marcel Carné film of the same name starring Arletty, who, when accused of having sex with a German officer, replied, "My heart is French, but my ass is international." The grandmothers chuckled. I recognized the quay in front of the hotel from the photograph of Apolline and Sophie together by the canal.

We passed the Hôpital St-Louis, me for the second time that day. "The hospital was built to care for the plague victims of Paris," my brother told us, then added that it had a famous medical museum of skin diseases started by a Dr.

Alfred Baker in 1865. The doctor had commissioned an artist to make wax moldings of various diseases, thinking them more useful to the students than the usual drawings. The collection had been used for teaching until the 1960s and was still open to the public. Among other things, Ilya told us, the museum featured over *six hundred* casts of sexual organs deformed by syphilis and gonorrhea. The grandmothers loved this one. They blushed as red as if they were sitting on radiators instead of cold wooden benches.

Then the locks began to blur, the slow swooshing rise of water, the sound of time flowing by. The Polish grandmothers began to nod, chin on cushioned chin, until we reached the Lock of the Dead, which brought us all, even the oldest, briskly back to life. Ilya explained this was the site of the Gibbet of Montfaucon, *mont* for mount, a site so high all Paris could see who was executed here, hanged from sixteen ropes on two levels so the hangman could drop thirty-two into the next world at one time.

"Even in death," he said, "the aristocrats were up on top and so had the better view of Paris. Imagine," he whispered, "the ravens pecking out the eyes first. Corpses left to hang for weeks. In the foreground, perhaps a pile of freshly quartered pieces from the guilty executed in the city center."

Then he waved a hand. "Thinking of having lunch?" he asked, with a wicked smile. "Let me recommend a restaurant."

Finally, we rose inside the thirteenth lock and sailed at last out of the Canal St-Martin into the basin at La Villette. If this trip had been birth, then we were born. If death, then wherever the dead go, we had arrived.

In the distance, I spotted the slide shaped like a dragon. The Polish grandmothers crowded around Ilya, most pressing tips into his hand, many kissing him on one or both cheeks. Then they disembarked, headed toward the promise of a garden.

My brother helped the last grandmother down the ramp, then jumped back on board to grab his violin case and a rucksack. "Come on," he said. "Let's get some lunch. Then we can talk." He put out his hand, and I took it. It was the same shape as mine, fair, freckled, though his was warm and mine felt, even to me, like cold meat.

He led me down the concrete path into the park. It was an odd place, with long raised walkways covered by metal roofs like waves. What I assumed was the Cité des Sciences was an enormous blue glass fortress built on the stone foundation of one of the old slaughterhouses. Red stumpy pylons of varying heights—art? lights?—were spaced with monotonous regularity across the flat, open grass. Like the shopping mall that had taken the place of the old open air market at Les Halles, this abattoir turned space-age park seemed like a vision of a future that had never come true. Now it had a run-down, deserted air. More traditional amusements had moved in, an attempt to make the vast scale more human. We passed an ice cream stand, another with sandwiches and fries, cold drinks.

There was a carousel, this one apparently made of animals rescued from a century of carnivals. As we passed, a faded wooden rooster winked his one glass eye at a donkey who nodded his broken head but failed to catch a speed boat that rose and fell, always just ahead. Only two children were riding. A girl a little older than my daughter, maybe eleven, too big for her poor earless pig, and a boy, maybe four, a tiny Patton in his green tank. He aimed the tank's gun at a tin horse that had already lost a leg. What was one limb in a place like La Villette, butcher for all of Paris, La Villette, the Verdun of animals. The grass glowed a bright cemetery green.

"I have some fruit," my brother was saying. "Everything in the park is ridiculously expensive. Usually I get some bread at the bakery by the Metro." Suddenly I fell, went down on my knees on the sidewalk. I could hear what my new brother was saying, but I couldn't see him. Everything had gone dark. I was so cold I couldn't stop shaking. I pulled my hand away from his and wrapped my arms around me. "My God," I heard Ilya say, then I felt his arm, warm around my shoulders. "Here, let's get you on this bench."

I felt the curve of cool concrete under me, then I put my head between my knees. Ilya pulled off his blue sweater and wrapped it around me like a shawl. I could see a little now, but everything was swimming with dots, as if the air were alive with the kind of black flies that must have once found a home in the slaughterhouses. Ilya put his hand under my chin, lifted my head, and looked me over. "Did you take anything?" he said. "Are you on something?"

I shook my head. "I haven't eaten," I said. "I forgot."

"Forgot for how long?"

I closed my eyes, everything was fading again. I shrugged.

He left me on the bench, and I shook so hard that I bit my tongue and tasted the sweet salt of my own blood. "Here," he said. "Take a sip of this." He slipped a straw between my numb lips. I sucked the straw, not knowing any more than a newborn what to expect. It was Coke, warm, sweet Coca-Cola. The sugar went straight into my blood, rushed to my brain, and the TV picture that was the world clicked on. First in black and white, then in color. Two more sips and even the black static of the flies was nearly gone.

"Now this," he said. He was holding a chunk of banana. He must have gotten one from his rucksack and peeled it. He slipped it into my mouth as if I were a baby chimp, being careful of my teeth and his fingers. "You need the potassium." He kept feeding me bite by bite, until I took the rest of the peeled banana from him and began to feed myself. I could feel him looking at me—smeared makeup, brutal haircut, bruise like a third eye in the middle of my forehead. "You're a mess," he said. He brushed his palm over my head, ruffling my inch of hair.

"At least I'm here," I said, meaning at least I made it this far, at least I'm alive.

Ilya only shook his head again. He gave no sign he'd heard me. "And your French is awful."

"Fuck you," I said.

He laughed. "Oh, my little sister, that would be so wrong."

After a while, we got up and walked slowly out of the park, Ilya holding me by the elbow in case my legs failed me again, his sweater draped over my shoulders as if I were an elderly invalid aunt. In season, Ilya explained, *La Sirène* ran tours in both directions. This early, there weren't always enough bookings to make the less popular La Villette to the Seine route worthwhile. Jacques, the captain, and Nolo, who'd helped with the ropes, would take the boat back down to the river. We would take the Metro into the city and be there in a fraction of the time.

"Where are we going?" I asked, when we were at last seated in a car half-filled with suburban youths headed into Paris for Saturday afternoon, Saturday night.

"Well, to my apartment, I guess. You have questions, right?" he looked at me.

"Right," I said, though at that moment, floating along on a small sugar high from the Coke, I couldn't think what, exactly, those questions might be.

"You still look like shit. You're not going to throw up, are you?'

I shook my head, then half-closed my eyes. I hoped not. "Good," Ilya said, and got a book out of his rucksack and started to read. It was a French translation of the life of Harry Houdini.

By the time we got off at Belleville, I was feeling better. The late afternoon sun was warm on my head as we walked down busy Boulevard de la Villette. I gave Ilya back his sweater and he pulled it on, though neither of us really needed it now. The leaves were just coming out, pale green against the blue sky. Spring was too new, too fresh to be sullied by the exhaust of the cars that rushed by. As we walked, Ilya whistled the *Gavotte,* going over the tune he'd played on the boat. I noticed he made the same mistakes. A missed sharp here. Half notes for whole. Not careful enough, I thought, not serious. I begin to suspect this as a flaw, as a sign of larger deficiencies in his character. My brother, God bless him, I imagined myself explaining to some mythical someone, is not serious. I, on the other hand, *was* serious. I had always been serious.

Look what that got you, the other side of my brain answered. We turned off the boulevard, went down the hole that was the entrance to the Place Ste-Odile. The neighbor was outside her house, perched in the same rickety chair. This time she was scouring a pair of muddy rubber boots with a stiff brush.

"Madame," Ilya nodded, coolly, I thought. The woman dipped her chin, barely acknowledging him. Not friendly neighbors. He unlocked the front door with a large brass key, the kind they sold in antique malls in America. He held the door open for me. "The first floor," he said. I waited for him to open the door just off the entryway so we could go into his apartment. "Not that one." He pointed to the narrow, wooden stairs. I'd forgotten that in France the first floor is what would be the second in America. On the landing was another door that had to be unlocked by another brass key as long as Ilya's index finger. He turned it, then pushed open the door with the toe of his shoe, and I stepped into the room I'd seen from the street, the one with the faded velvet curtains. The room was velvet dim. I put out a hand, afraid I might stumble.

Behind me, Ilya flipped the light switch, and a chandelier flickered to life. I stood, blinking, just inside the door. This is what I saw: a movie set from *Kean.* No, a room from a museum labeled *Paris, 1929.* No, that wasn't right either. I saw a living room with a red plush carpet patterned with roses as big as babies. The plaster walls matched the somber green of the flowers' thorny stems. The room was small, an apartment-sized space, but it was as stuffed as an antique store with heavy, dark mahogany furniture. To the right of the door sat a red velvet sofa with carved lion heads on its arms and claw feet. Facing it in a semicircle were four equally clawed matching chairs. At each end of the sofa, round marble-topped tables stood covered with black-and-white photographs in ornate frames, autographed photos of Mosjoukine and a dozen other carefully made-up faces that must have belonged to silent film actors and actresses, though I couldn't put names to them.

"Welcome to the past," Ilya whispered in my ear.

9

I MUST HAVE SWAYED A LITTLE, BOBBLED. Ilya, afraid I might faint again, took me by the elbow and plopped me into one of the claw-footed velvet chairs. A cloud of dust rose up to meet me. I sneezed, sneezed again, then when my eyes stopped watering, I saw a framed picture of Vera Holodnaya on the marble table beside me. Stuck in the bottom of the ornate silver frame was a snapshot of Sophie Desnos, holding two newborn babies, one in each arm. Ilya and Vera. My brother. Me.

Ilya went through a doorway into the kitchen and made coffee, put lots of sugar in it for me. He handed the cup to me with a slight, polite bow, then he sat cross-legged on the floor and watched me drink.

"So?" he said. "What do you know? What do you want to know?"

"This," I said looking around me, "this was Ivan Mosjoukine's apartment?"

"Yes," Ilya said.

Ilya had pulled open the curtains, and I could see the living room more clearly. Time had not stood still. The curtains were not the only thing that had faded. The sofa looked more rust than red plush. Squares of an even deeper green checkered the walls, marking spots where paintings had once hung before being taken down, perhaps sold. On some of the tables were stacks of photographs, as if some of the frames, maybe valuable sterling ones like the one that held Vera Holodnaya, had been sold as well. There was still a stunning amount of furniture. Now I could see a baby grand piano pushed up against the wall at the end of the room. From where I sat, I could read the oversized gilt letters of the maker's name over the keyboard, *C. Bechstein, Sr. Major der Kaisers und Königs*, a piano fit for a king. Next to it, a large armoire and two dressers with beveled mirrors that really belonged in a bedroom huddled together, as if they had come into the living room for company, for safety in numbers. The style wasn't 1929. The furniture would have been terribly out of date by the twenties. It was the sort of dark, nineteenth-century furniture that would have filled a flat in Moscow before the revolution or even the house in Penza where Mosjoukine had been born.

A good half of the forest of photographs were of Mosjoukine. I got up, wandered around the room looking. Photographs in frames were arranged on the piano as well. I touched two fingers to the piano keys. One key made no sound, the other made three strings sound at once. All the framed photographs were studio shots, the kind stars used for publicity pictures. I counted four shots of Mosjoukine from *Kean*, all signed *Ivan Mosjoukine* with the large looping hand that I recognized from the back of Apolline's postcard. In another, a young Ivan posed on a couch with a lustrous black poodle, his signature at the bottom indecipherable in Cyrillic.

Also, Mosjoukine in costume from a dozen other movies I didn't recognize. In one, he wore the robes of an Orthodox priest. A heavy beard and makeup aged him into the old man he had apparently survived to be. There were also plenty of head shots of him dressed in expensive street clothes, like in Apolline's postcard. Wearing shirts with French cuffs and heavy gold cuff links. In one, a snappy fedora. He started young in them, then started to age, shot by shot. The focus got softer, but there was no hiding the soft flesh under the eyes, the lines on either side of his mouth that Ilya inherited. I guessed from the clothes Mosjoukine wore that the latest picture was probably from the early thirties. Taken at the dead end of his career, then—*nothing*. Even in the later ones, he had the most magnetic eyes. They looked out of the photographs like the eyes of the living, saying, *Look at me.*

I held up the photograph of Mosjoukine as priest for Ilya to see. "And Ivan Mosjoukine, the silent film actor, was my—our—father?"

"Yes."

"Jesus," I said. Somehow, until that moment, it hadn't seemed real. I sat in the overstuffed armchair, sending up a second cloud of dust. "And this," I pointed at the picture of Sophie holding her twins, "is our mother?"

Ilya tilted his head to look at the photograph. "Yes, that's Sophie, our mother."

"Anne-Sophie Desnos?"

He sighed. "So she said." His answer was as vague as Apolline's.

"Does she live here?"

"No," Ilya said. "She doesn't. She's been dead for years."

Oh, no, not her, too, I thought, looking at the photograph of our mother. I picked up the heavy silver frame. I'd come all the way to Paris to find her, and now this was as close to her as I would ever get. "But you knew her?" I asked my new brother, looking for something, anything more. "She raised you?"

"She was my mother," he said with a slight shrug, as if that explained everything.

"She was my mother, too," I said, setting down the frame so hard, I saw my brother jump. "So why the hell didn't she raise me?"

"Come on," he said, helping me up from the smothering depths of the armchair. "You need to eat."

He talked while I sat at the kitchen table and watched him fix dinner. The kitchen was spare, an old two-burner gas stove, a zinc sink, a refrigerator about the size my students had in their dorm rooms. The black metal telephone mounted on the wall looked like it belonged in a museum. On top, a handset rested in a cradle while another round earpiece hung from a hook on one side as if the phone were designed for early conference calls or eavesdropping. The only furniture was a folding table with two folding chairs. Either Mosjoukine had not felt the need to furnish a room as mundane as the kitchen or what had been there originally had gone the way of the silver picture frames.

"I am making you an omelet," Ilya announced, cracking four eggs into a bowl, as if he thought an American might not know what an omelet was. It struck me that he was more comfortable talking to me standing up, as if I were still on *La Sirène* and his presentation of our history were part of the tour. "Listen, for what it's worth, Sophie always said she tried to get the American colonel to take both of us." He looked at me, then turned to whipping the eggs. "She said she hadn't meant to separate us like that, but the colonel said he was too old to raise a son, that he wasn't going to be playing catch in the yard with a boy when he was sixty."

I could imagine the colonel saying those very words. I once heard him snap at a local Scout leader who offered him sympathy for not having a son to take camping, "I slept in enough damn tents in the Army, thank you." With me, he'd played Scrabble, not ball. I might understand the colonel, but Sophie, a mother who'd wanted to give away both her children, was a mystery to me.

Ilya turned on the gas, lit a match, and the burner caught with a whoosh of blue flame.

"How did Sophie know the colonel?" I asked, though I thought I knew the answer to this one from Apolline. He'd been a customer at the bar where Apolline and Sophie worked.

"Mosjoukine introduced them," he said. He melted butter in a sauté pan. "Mosjoukine worked for the colonel." He turned to face me, lifting the pan off the stove for a minute so the butter wouldn't brown. "You did know that, didn't you? Your father's work . . ."

I interrupted. "Mosjoukine's?"

He shook his head. "No, Mosjoukine is *our* father. *Your* father, the colonel. You know what the colonel did for his American army, don't you? He was in intelligence. Mosjoukine was one of his contacts, his sources. The colonel was Mosjoukine's boss." He added the beaten eggs to the hot butter and swirled them deftly so they rose slightly up the sides of the pan.

"Both my fathers were spies?"

Ilya shook his head. "Don't be so dramatic. You sound like Mosjoukine, making life into a movie. It was the cold war, and the Americans didn't know anything about Russia or Russians, really. Mosjoukine had some answers, that's all. He knew people, knew what they did, what jobs they held. Things like that."

"Why Mosjoukine? Just because he spoke Russian? Paris must have been full of musty, aging White Russians."

"He'd been back. Mosjoukine said his father kept writing him letters about how he was starving, how hard everything was back home in Penza. When Mosjoukine couldn't get work in films, couldn't send any more money, he went back to help."

"After he faked his own death," I said.

"After he left the hospital," Ilya agreed. He flipped the omelet with a well-timed flick of his wrist and held it out for me to see the perfect tan crust on the eggs. He was showing off, but it smelled delicious. "Mosjoukine was in the Soviet Union during the war. He was on the radio there under his American screen name, Ivan Moskine. The authorities knew who he was, but during the war even Stalin had the sense to take what patriotic help Mother Russia could get.

"After the war, in 1949, somehow Mosjoukine got out. Lucky guy. Before your father, he was working for this crazy American general who was launching balloons stocked with propaganda leaflets in Austria so they would drift over Czechoslovakia. The balloons said 'Svoboda' on them—*Freedom* in Czech—and their drops were triggered by melting dry ice so the pamphlets would fall on Prague and not some potato field. Mosjoukine loved to tell stories about that one.

"Then in 1953, he made it to Paris and went to work broadcasting in Russian for Radio Liberty. Practically the first story he read on the air was an announcement of Stalin's death. He enjoyed that. He hated Stalin. The Americans at Radio Liberty fixed him up with a new French passport. He picked the name Adrien Meis for that one."

"The name on the bell plate," I said.

"In his film *The Late Mathias Pascal*, Adrien Meis is the name that Mosjoukine's character takes after everyone thinks he's dead."

"Apt," I said. Ilya nodded.

"It appealed to him, though he didn't use it except when he had to. With people he knew, he preferred being Ivan Mosjoukine. By that time, nearly twenty years after his last picture, fifteen years after his 'death,' it wasn't like anyone was looking for him anymore."

"And somewhere in here, he meets our mother?"

"So she always said. And, *ta-da*," he divided the omelet in half with a fork, then slid a portion onto each plate with a flourish, "then there were four." He chopped some onion, a potato, and added them to the now empty pan.

"Where was Mosjoukine when we were born?" Watching Ilya was making me dizzy, like following a juggler or a magician.

"Well, he was there for the beginning, obviously," my brother said. "Then off on some business for the colonel. You know, just like his movie, *Michel Strogoff*, where he is the secret courier for the czar? Have you seen that one?" I shook my head. "You probably should. It's one of his best. It's very dramatic. He gets blinded by a red hot saber." Ilya held up his paring knife in front of his eye for a second. Behind him, the potatoes sizzled.

"According to Sophie, Mosjoukine didn't know about us until the adoption was over and all he had left was a son, me. He was furious. Apparently he got in such a shouting match with the colonel that the bar owner where Sophie worked called the police on them. Only Mosjoukine was charged, of course." Ilya patted his shoulder where my father's oak leaf cluster insignia would have been. "They didn't put American officers in jail for a little thing like making a scene in a bar."

"Did he really do that, Mosjoukine? Get into a fight over me?"

"Well, he's the one who told me. So—*maybe*. Maybe. It was always hard to be sure with him. He liked a good story. It would have made a great scene in a movie, though if he were younger there would have been punches thrown. There's a fist fight at the end of *Strogoff* that goes on and on until Mosjoukine is a bloody mess and practically naked. But you shouldn't forget, it wasn't just Mosjoukine. If the story is true, both your fathers were fighting over you. Over their little girl." He took the potatoes off the stove, divided them between the plates. "Your father never told you about any of this?"

I shook my head. "Not a word. I didn't even know I was adopted." I watched as my brother added a little salad to our two plates, set them on the table. Then he got out forks, two mismatched glasses, and two bottles of red wine. He opened one bottle, poured some into the glasses, handed one to me. I hesitated, still feeling shaky.

"Builds the blood," he said. "Take it." I took a sip. He took a long pull on his, then looked at me over his glass, his blue eyes so clearly Mosjoukine's eyes. "Growing up in America," he asked, "did you miss having a brother?"

Had I? I'd been aware of being an only child, of my friends at school having to share rooms, having brothers and sisters to fight or play with. Had there been some indefinable sense of loss? When I was sad, when I cried at my naturalization or, later, hiding in the orange grove behind our house in Florida, what was it I felt was missing? Who was I missing? My real mother, real father, twin brother? *God?*

"Eat," Ilya said, waving his fork at my plate. "That wine won't do you any good on an empty stomach." I put a bite of omelet in my mouth, chewed, tried to swallow. It tasted as good as it smelled, but I seemed to have lost the knack of eating. "You don't remember, do you?" Ilya asked. "How you came back here?"

"Here?"

"Your mother brought you back."

"Livinia?" I dropped my fork on my plate.

Ilya nodded. "*Livinia,* if you say that was her name," Ilya said. "She brought you back when you were almost three and left you downstairs with a neighbor. We found you when we came home from the market. You lived here with us for nearly the whole summer." He waved his fork at the apartment. "Nothing looks familiar?"

I thought about the passage into the courtyard, my sense of déjà vu. I looked at Ilya and tried to imagine him smaller. I remembered playing with a boy who my father had always told me was our neighbor in Fontainebleau. Rocks, I remembered playing with rocks. We collected buckets of pebbles to cook rock pies, to made muddy pots of rock stew.

"Stone soup," I said.

Ilya smiled, the wrinkles on either side of his mouth cutting deep into his cheeks. "Ah," he said, "even then I was the good cook. You," he made a face, "were a bad one. Too much dirt in your bisque." I took another bite of the omelet. I wasn't eating much, but Ilya ate even less.

"What happened after the summer?"

"The colonel came and got you. He found out where you were. Maybe he'd been away on Army business. At any rate, I don't think he had any idea how your mother discovered where we lived."

Apolline told her, I thought. It had to have been. She knew where Sophie was. Had she told Livvy for my sake, to reunite me with Sophie and Ilya? Or had she done it to hurt Livvy or the colonel? Had she done it to hurt Sophie? I'd been raised to think people's motivations were direct and simple. Now it was hard to guess where this knot started or where it would end.

Ilya refilled our glasses. "The colonel came looking for you, and when you saw him, you ran across the courtyard." Ilya opened his arms wide. "Like this."

Then I remembered the sensation of running, the freshly dry-cleaned smell of my father's uniform as he picked me up, spun me around. I thought I remembered leaving in his arms, not even looking back. Damn, both my mothers had given me away, Sophie twice. What kind of charmless child had I been? I would never have given up my daughter. Not for anything or anyone. From the moment I had first seen her in the delivery room, my heart burned with love. This is what the mother lion feels, I remembered thinking woozily. I would have killed to keep her safe, would have died. In the end, my love hadn't been any protection. I put my hand to my stomach, remembering how it felt when she was still safe inside my body.

Then I noticed Ilya. He was pushing the salad around on his plate. I put my hand on his blue sleeve. I had never seen a man look sadder, his eyes downcast. His face was pale. I had come to Paris to find family, to find someone who cared if I lived or died. Now, here was someone who had loved me and missed me. All these years and I had never even known.

"You thought I should have stayed," I said. "You thought I should have chosen you."

Ilya shrugged. "We were children. We didn't make the decisions." He got up and began to clear the table, piling the dishes in the sink. "Let's go in the living room," he said, grabbing the glasses and the bottles of wine.

This time we sat on the floor in front of the baby grand, the glasses balanced on the thick rose-patterned carpet. He kicked off his boat shoes, but I kept on my boots. It wasn't my apartment.

"You grew up here, then, with Mosjoukine and Sophie?"

He shook his head. "She wouldn't let him back in his own apartment after the fight in the bar. He would come by, bring a little money, toys or candy for me. Once he brought me a red bicycle. But she wouldn't let him any further than the stairs. Then, when I was three—the autumn after you went back to your other family—we left."

"Left for where?"

"For Prague. Sophie believed Czechoslovakia had the best chance to become a true workers' paradise. She thought Russia never would. It was too agrarian, too backward to be the perfect communist state. She wanted to live what she believed. It sounds crazy now, I know, but then . . ." He poured us more wine. "Okay, then it sounded crazy, too. She talked the Czech embassy into visas for us, packed our clothes, and off we went on the train. She didn't tell anyone she was going. Mosjoukine would have killed her. He hated the communists, always went on about how Lenin had ruined the lives of his friends in the Russian film industry, how Stalin had killed his father, his whole family, along with millions of Russians before, during, and after the war. Your father would have tried to stop her, too, if he'd known, though maybe he was on his way back to America by then.

"So I grew up a good communist. We lived in an apartment block with other foreigners, mostly from America, some from rich families who owned skyscrapers in New York. Such believers! They sacrificed everything to move there, so they had to see what they wanted to see. Our Czech neighbors used to throw things at us sometimes. Called us Jews."

"Was our mother Jewish?" I asked. I was lying on my back on the carpet, my head spinning. "Are we?"

"Was she? Who knows. For Sophie, God didn't exist. She had no religion but communism, and she wanted that ideology pure as snow." Now Ilya was flat on the carpet, too, both of us gazing at the cracked plaster ceiling as if at the stars. "Let me tell you a story," he said. "When I was six, every day she took me to this store that sold pots and pans and dishes in our neighborhood in Prague. Every day, as we walked home from school, she would go in and ask if they had plates. My mother and I were sharing one plate and one bowl then, though we each had a fork. Every day, the clerks behind the counter would say, *No, Comrade Desnos, no plates have come from the ceramics factory. Try again tomorrow.* The shelves of the store were bare, no plates, no anything, except some enamel pots that were so badly made they blew apart like hand grenades when they got hot.

"All along, of course, there were plates, but like everything worth having in Czechoslovakia, they were out of sight in the back room. To get them, you had to trade something: some meat from the butcher shop where you worked, a dental exam for one of the clerk's children that didn't overlook cavities the way the compulsory ones in the schools did. Everybody knew that. I was six, and even I knew it. Everyone knew except Sophie.

"Finally, she wrote to the director of the factory. She demanded—in her very poor Czech—to know why his factory was not producing its quota of dishes for the workers of Prague. When would there be plates? The manager wrote back, thinking she was just crazy enough to report him and get him in trouble for not doing his job. He wrote her and said, *Dear Comrade Desnos, the Proshuka Ceramic Works delivered twenty boxes of plates to Store Number 4 on the first of this month. This should have been more than enough dishes for the workers of your district. Yours, etc.*

86

"Sophie snatched me up by the hand and dragged me down the street to the store. I didn't want to go. I knew there was going to be a scene, but she had me like death. She banged open the door and when the clerks started in with their usual *Nothing today, Comrade,* she waved the letter in their faces. They got scared. They opened the door to the storeroom and showed her the cartons of dishes. 'Take as many as you want, Comrade Desnos,' they said to her. They were afraid of her now, wanted to buy her off. But Sophie made the clerks carry all twenty boxes out and pile them on the counter.

"She made me climb up and sit on top of them, just to make sure all twenty stayed there. Then she marched to the front door of the shop, threw it open, and shouted, 'Women of Prague, we have plates!' She stood there until the clerks had sold every plate and bowl at the marked price." He laughed, then started coughing, hard, nearly choking. He sat up. I sat up, too, ready to pound on his back, but he poured himself more wine, took a sip, and was better. "Only then did we go home with our one new plate. To have more," he sighed, "would have been bourgeois. Though I remember wishing we could at least have gotten a second bowl."

"When did you come back to Paris?" I asked.

"In 1968, the Prague Spring, yes?" Yes, I nodded. I remembered watching the footage on the evening news with my parents. It had been a break from the endless coverage of the war in Vietnam, which my father, retired Army colonel or not, had bitterly opposed. He didn't believe in fighting wars we couldn't win, he'd told me. "One day I came home from school," Ilya went on, "and there was a big car, a foreign car, like a diplomat might drive, and there, standing next to it, was Mosjoukine. He'd come to get us. He had all the paperwork and wanted us to leave that night. 'The Soviets will come,' he said to Sophie. 'They won't let this experiment go on. I know.'

"'Good,' Mother said. She thought Dubcek's reforms were heresy. She hated him. She was a Stalinist to the core. 'When the Red Army comes, I'll be in the street cheering them.' He said she was blind. She said he was a class enemy. Things like that. Worse. He was cursing her in Russian. She was cursing him in French and Czech."

Ilya said he'd fallen asleep listening to them fight, then woke up when Mosjoukine picked him up off the floor. "Shhh," Mosjoukine had said, carrying

87

him to the car. They crossed the border just before midnight. By the end of the next day, Ilya was back in France. Two days later, the Soviet tanks rolled into Prague. No more spring. Ilya said he had seen our mother on French TV waving the hammer and sickle.

Mosjoukine brought him back to the apartment at 44 Place Ste-Odile, and they'd stayed there together for three years, until Ilya was nearly thirteen. Then Ilya had gotten very sick. Spinal meningitis. The doctors thought maybe he would die, or go blind, or be left brain damaged. They thought anything might happen. He kept crying out "Mother!" and one of the doctors asked Mosjoukine if there wasn't anything he could do to bring her to the hospital to see her son.

Mosjoukine wasn't working by then, as far as Ilya could tell. Things had been disappearing one by one from the apartment. Sold for money or traded for the things they needed. But Mosjoukine told Ilya's doctors he would get his son's mother. He told Ilya he was going to bring Sophie from Prague if he had to drug her and put her in a suitcase. Then he left that night. "I got better," Ilya said, his voice dropping so low I had to lean close to hear him. "But he never came back. I waited and waited."

The police searched for him, first as Adrien Meis and then, at Ilya's insistence, as Ivan Mosjoukine, but they couldn't find any sign. The French embassy in Prague made inquiries. Nothing. When Ilya was finally well enough to leave the hospital, he was sent to a boys' home. After a year, he ran away and came back to live in Mosjoukine's apartment. No one had been there while he was away. No one ever came to collect rent. As far as Ilya knew, Mosjoukine had owned the flat since he arrived in Paris in the '20s. When he was rich, he'd used it as a retreat. When he was broke, a place to hide from bill collectors. As far as Ilya knew, Mosjoukine's name was still on the deed. Ilya had never bothered to find out. All he knew was he'd taken the extra keys hidden in the drain spout and moved in, starting life on his own at fourteen.

"I thought he would turn up," my brother said. "I was going to beat the shit out of him, old man or no, for letting the colonel take you, for taking me away from our mother. For running, just when I needed him. I was sure he hadn't gone after Sophie when I was sick, had never so much as set foot on Czech soil. But he never returned. So I got over it. Then one day, I counted up the years and realized: The son of a bitch. He must be dead."

88

"I think I need coffee," I said. We'd finished the last of the wine. Ilya made a pot, stronger this time. No sugar.

Over the years after he left Prague with Mosjoukine, Ilya said, he'd written and written to our mother, but she'd never answered. Of course the mail in those days was so uncertain. In Czechoslovakia, even the censors had censors. Then in 1989, in those last months before the wall came tumbling down, when all the Skodas started pouring out of Czechoslovakia by way of Budapest and Vienna, when it became clear no one was stopping them anymore, not the border guards or the secret police or the army, he'd borrowed a friend's Fiat and driven to Prague to find Sophie. "I was the only car headed east," he said.

He'd found only his old neighbors, still Reds, still sure the Soviets would come to their rescue one more time. They told him Sophie had died the previous year. She'd fallen down the steep concrete stairs of their apartment block. They told him they were sure that the dissident who had been forced to work as the janitor—*class traitor*—had loosened the bulb to make the stairwell dangerously dark. They were sure that he, or someone else in the building, someone who was not loyal like them, had tripped her or pushed her, just to see a good woman fall.

Thinking of Sophie, thinking of her in the dish shop, in a thousand scenes in the building where she reported someone for the smallest infraction of the rules, Ilya was sure that was probably what had happened. Some neighbor had finally had enough and given her just the smallest of shoves. I thought of Sophie in the instant she realized she was falling. *What had she been thinking?* I wondered. It was probably too much to believe it was of her lost children.

Ilya got up, opened a window, letting cool night air flow into the room, then he came back to our spot on the carpet.

"Your turn," he said.

So I told Ilya a little about growing up in America with my parents. As he listened I could tell he was thinking, *What would it have been like to be an American? Would I have been happy?* I told him about being happy, about having a husband and a daughter I loved.

Then we were silent for a while, sitting surrounded by all those pictures of men and women who had made silence their profession.

Then I told Ilya about finding my father dying and finding my mother dead and about the car accident. I got out the pictures of my husband and daughter.

"How can they be dead?" he asked, touching their faces.

"They're dead," I said. Then, for the first time since the accident, I let myself say their names. My husband *Ben*. My daughter *Julia*. "She was only eight," I said, staring at her last school picture. "Is that fair? Is dying that young ever fair?"

Ilya put his hand on my wrist. "Eight years is eight years," he said. "It's not nothing. At least she had that."

As we sat on the floor in the living room, it seemed we were surrounded by death and the wreckage of lives. The furniture had held up better than the people who had owned it. The couch alone was probably a hundred years old. Sitting on the dusty carpet—crying, I was crying again—I was sure I would never make it that far.

"Are you tired?" Ilya asked, after we had been quiet for a while. "You should sleep."

I shook my head. "Bad dreams," I said.

My brother stood up, brushing off the front of his jeans. He offered me his hand. "Then let's go out. Enough of all this talking. Let's find someplace with music loud enough to keep us from thinking. Let's go someplace and dance."

10

WE WENT BACK TO BELLEVILLE, climbing the steep streets toward the shadowy heights of the Buttes Chaumont. But we didn't get that far. We turned into a neighborhood of apartment blocks, more bad postwar urban planning. We stopped at the end of one dark street, in front of an especially faceless six-story block. Ilya looked at the bells, picked one, rang it two, three, then four times. A crackle came from the speaker. "Who?" a male voice said. I could hear music behind him, pounding away.

"It's me," Ilya said. "Let us in." The buzzer on the front door sounded, and we went in, crowded into an elevator barely big enough for the two of us.

Ilya pressed the button for the basement, and the elevator sank with a sickening jerk. As soon as the elevator stopped and Ilya stepped out with me behind him, a man bounded up and grabbed Ilya around the neck with one arm. I jumped back, hitting my head on the open elevator door. "You came," the man said. It was Nolo, the African from *La Sirène*. "Good, good," Nolo was saying, "And you brought a girl. Better and better."

We followed Nolo into a vast basement with plywood storage bins down one side, the numbers of the apartment units stenciled on them with spray paint. Lights, hot spots, were strung from the ceiling, and a DJ was set up at one end playing music. The noise hit me like a wall, like a kick in the chest. Under the lights a solid mass of people were dancing, their arms waving over their heads like a field of wheat in a strong wind.

"Nolo is from Mali," Ilya shouted. "The DJ is his cousin. Come on," he said, and tried to lead me into the crowd.

I pulled my hand away. I couldn't imagine joining such a crush of people. "In a minute, " I shouted. I thought I saw a table covered with bottles in the far corner of the basement. "I need a drink." Ilya shrugged, pushed forward into the dancers. In a minute, his arms were waving among all the others—black and white, all bare but Ilya's. I kept seeing the blue arms of his sweater even though, between the lights and the bodies, it was as hot as if we were diamond miners inside the earth, much further below ground than a single story.

I went to pour myself a glass of wine, but there was a fish bowl on the table filled with bills, with one and two euro coins, and that stopped me. I'd left my purse in Ilya's apartment. I didn't have any money. "Here," a voice said in my ear. A hand dropped a coin in the bowl. I turned. The voice belonged to a tall woman in an African robe though she was white, paler than me. She handed me a plastic glass, picked up one of the bottles and filled my cup. She poured herself a glass, too. "Chin-chin," she said and clicked her plastic cup against mine.

It was quieter at this end of the basement. A tangle of pipes and duct work blocked the speakers, though the music still bounced off the far wall and came back a little delayed, an echo, as out of sync as I felt.

The woman leaned forward. "You came with Ilya," she said into my ear.

I nodded.

She touched a square leather pouch she wore around her neck. "My name is Mei-mei. I read cards," she said. "Want me to tell your fortune?"

I opened my mouth, sure I was going to say no. Then I thought of Robert Desnos, passing down the ranks of the condemned in Auschwitz, whispering Long Life, Long Life as a blessing. "What do I do?"

She took the pouch from around her neck, hung it around mine, then put my left hand on it. The leather felt warm from her breasts. "Think about what you want the cards to tell you. Ask them a question," she said. Then she refilled my glass. "I'll be right back." I could feel my heart beating through the cards in perfect time to the drums in the music Nolo's cousin was playing at the other end of the basement.

Where is my daughter? Where is Julia? I asked the square edges of the cards pressed between my breasts.

Then Mei-mei was back. She gestured for me to follow her. She lifted the padlock off one of the plywood storage lockers. Inside was a vinyl couch, a badly bent metal garden chair, and a low coffee table held up at one end by a concrete block. A single bulb hung from a cord over the table. On it, a candle was burning. Otherwise, the compartment was plywood walls and a concrete floor. It had all the ambience of a cattle car. She saw my expression. "It's only my office for tonight," she said. "One of the boys broke the lock for me. Sit down." She waved at the couch.

I sat, put my wine on the table. She had me give her back the cards, and I watched as she shuffled, dealt them out in a cross shape on the table. I'd been expecting Tarot cards, with their elaborate drawings. When I was in high school, no sleepover or slumber party had been complete without a Tarot deck which someone was always using to read fortunes aided by a paperback with a title like *Tarot Made Simple*. This was a regular French deck, perfectly ordinary to American eyes, with its four suits the same as ours.

Mei-mei studied the cards. She frowned. She pulled on her lower lip. She sighed. Outside, Nolo's cousin put on something slow, though it still had a strong drum track. A sad female vocal burbled over it. I had no idea what language the woman was singing, but I could feel the tears, hot, hotter, flowing like lava. I had asked the cards a question beyond their power to answer. Her song seemed to tell me, *Gone is gone, and there is no going after.*

Mei-mei looked at me. "Do you want to tell me your question? You don't have to."

I shook my head. "No," I said.

"Well, then I'll tell you what I see." She pointed to the queen of diamonds. "That's you. All around you are other diamonds," she pointed. "Do you come from a close family? They are standing so near you."

I took a deep breath, but said nothing. She stared at the cards again. Then she clucked her tongue and looked up at me. "They're dead, aren't they? These are your dead. They are all around you, watching everything you do."

Suddenly, strongly, I wanted to be somewhere else. I must have started to stand, because I felt Mei-mei's hand on my knee, forcing me back down. "They're worried," she said. "They are worried about you."

I looked down at the cards and saw a wet drop fall on the two of diamonds. Then another. I wanted the water to be sweat, to be my body trying to make sense of itself, to cool down. But they were tears. Saltwater rolled out of my eyes and down my nose as if I had nothing to do with it at all. I put my hands on my face. Even with my eyes covered, I felt a shadow fall across the cards. I looked up. Ilya was standing in the doorway, leaning on the plywood frame.

"Do you want to ask another question?" I heard Mei-mei ask me.

"She wants to know when she'll be happy," Ilya said. "Isn't that what everyone asks, pet?"

Mei-mei shrugged by way of acknowledging the truth of that. She looked at the cards again, then at me. "Something is holding you back," she said.

I pointed at the cards around the queen, "The people I . . ." I couldn't bring myself to say "lost." I hated to think of them as lost.

She shook her head. "This is something you're doing. Or did. I see it as fear, as a thick rope holding you back. Otherwise, I see talent. I see great achievement." I tried to imagine a rope tied around my leg. Or maybe my neck. A rope keeping me from moving forward as real as the lines Ilya and Nolo used to tie off the canal boat.

Ilya laughed. "Ah, everyone Mei-mei sees is so talented."

Mei-mei laughed. "Not you, you bastard," she said. "I have heard you play violin. You are the black hole of no talent."

Ilya threw up his hands. "Come dance, both of you," he said, losing patience. Then he turned, shouted something to someone across the room.

"Sure," Mei-mei said. She swept the cards together, put them back in her pouch. "You okay?" she put her hand on my knee again. "Want to dance?"

I shook my head. I rapped on the top of the broken coffee table. "I feel like dead wood."

She took a small box out of a pocket in the side of her robe, opened it, and handed me a yellow pill. It had a happy face on it, but one with its eyes closed—a happy dreamer. "Here," she said, "one problem solved."

"What is it?" I asked.

"Do you care?"

Honestly, I didn't. I washed it down with my wine, and then I followed Mei-mei and Ilya to the dance floor.

I danced. One minute I was standing there, not dancing, and then I was. I was one person moving in a mass of moving. The music passed through the crowd like a current, like fast running water, and we were swimming like trout in a clear steam, swimming all out just to stay in the same spot. I thought, *I don't exist.* Then, *No one exists.* By that I meant as single bodies, as lone sets of legs walking on an uncaring planet. A botanist I'd once met at a party told me that in Michigan there was a single fungus that was the world's largest living creature and that it covered hundreds of acres. They'd always thought it was many separate funguses, but now they knew they were wrong. Trees in a forest were not separate organisms either, he said. Their roots knit them together. Infect one, and the disease would spread to all. Feed or water one, and all the trees would be greener, taller. I'd thought he was stoned. I'd thought he was full of shit. Now I was higher than high, and what he'd said made all kinds of sense. I was dancing with more legs than I had, waving more arms than I could count.

Sometimes Ilya was there, sometimes Mei-mei or Nolo. Most often I danced with people I didn't know but who looked so familiar. They looked like people I'd grown up with or taught or the young teachers who had taught Julia. Why worry about who was family, I found myself thinking over and over, each realization the same revelation, when all humans looked so much alike, when you couldn't tell them apart once they started dancing. At some point, I flung off my stolen sweater. Who knows where it went. The heat was so thick I felt it like a second skin. I think we danced for hours. Maybe we danced for days. No one stopped. The crowd changed sometimes, more white, then darker, more men, then more women. It never got smaller.

Finally Nolo tapped me on the shoulder. He gestured for me to follow him. I smiled at him, grabbed his hands. I wanted him dancing. He shook his head, led me by both hands out of the mass and onto the open stretch of basement floor. "Your brother is looking for you," he shouted in my ear, and led me through a side door, up a short flight of stairs to a back alley. Ilya was standing in the cool dark of the morning, looking up at a few vague stars. In the east, the sun was just starting to rise. I stared up, trying to count the stars as they disappeared before the advancing, shimmering waves of pink. My ears felt numb. After the sheer decibels of the music, the morning was pure silent movie.

"Did you hear Kumé singing?" Nolo, also half deaf, shouted to Ilya. I realized he was talking about the woman I had heard singing so slowly while Mei-mei read my cards and at least one other time while I danced. Though I hadn't seen her, she must have actually been there, in the basement, a live singer and not a recording.

Ilya nodded. "She's good."

"Better and better," Nolo said. Nolo lit a cigarette, then lit another and offered it to Ilya. My brother took it, inhaled, blew the smoke out through his nose. Nolo offered me the pack. I started to take it. Why not? I'd never smoked, but what was the point in saying no? But Ilya put his hand on the cigarettes, pushing the pack back to Nolo.

Nolo laughed. "Yeah, got to look out for your little sister, right?"

Ilya coughed, then kept coughing, until he was bent over. When he stood up, he tossed his cigarette over the railing into the darkness. "Actually," he said to Nolo, "Vera is older by a whole minute, or so our mother always said, so she's only my little sister if you are talking about size."

I was still staring up at the stars as they winked out, one by one. I didn't want them to. I didn't want it to be the start of an ordinary day. I put out my tongue, full of the idea I could taste a star like a snowflake. I wondered what the world had looked like to me during that long minute when I'd been alone in the world. If Ilya, still in the womb, had missed me, wondered where I had gone.

"Time to go home, comrade," Ilya said to Nolo. "You and I work today."

Nolo groaned. "You got the wrong attitude, friend. It's too late to sleep. You can do that later. You can do that when you're dead."

We left Nolo smoking in the alley and walked home, passing other late night partiers, hearing music from clubs we passed. It was cool, the morning air damp. Ilya pulled off his blue sweater again and gave it to me. "Here," he said. "What happened to yours?"

I shrugged. It was either back in the basement or already on its way home on some other dancer's chilled arms. This time, instead of wearing it like a shawl, I pulled Ilya's sweater over my head. On him it was long, but on me it reached to my knees.

We passed a bar where more men and women were spilling into the street. In Paris, on a Saturday night, my brother said, either you went home early, before the Metro stopped running, or you stayed out until morning when it started again. Ilya stopped at a bakery off the Boulevard de la Villette and bought a flute of fresh bread. He offered me a bite. I shook my head, but he insisted, and we took turns eating chunks as we walked home. On the way, the shimmering pastels returned to ordinary colors. The air became once again only air. Whatever Mei-mei had given me, my liver, that busybody, was washing it and the wondrous visions that went with it from the bloodstream of my dance-worn body.

When we reached the entrance to the Place Ste-Odile, I heard the voices of a man arguing and a woman answering back. I recognized the voice of the neighbor. What was she doing out so early? Then a man came stomping through the arch, dressed in a white hospital uniform, not like a doctor would wear, but a practical nurse or an orderly. He glared at Ilya as he strode past. Ilya shook his head, disapproving.

Inside the courtyard, the neighbor was sitting quietly on her chair, giving no sign there had been any disagreement. She was darning a heavy pair of men's socks, digging into the coarse wool with her needle.

She nodded at us. Ilya ignored her.

"Good morning, Madame," I said, not wanting to be as rude as my brother.

She nodded again, willing to meet me halfway. She pointed her long curved needle at my feet. "Nice boots," she said.

Ilya unlocked the front door, locked it, unlocked the apartment door, locked that one behind us as well.

"What's her story?" I asked.

He tossed the keys on the kitchen table, lit the burner on the stove. "What do you mean?"

"I mean she lives in that courtyard. What is she, just professionally nosey?"

"It's her place of business," he said, as he put the coffee pot on. "She sells," he paused for a moment, "pharmaceuticals."

"Drugs."

He tilted his head to one side in that French way that meant, *Not exactly.* "You saw the orderly?"

I nodded. "Yes, and yesterday there was a doctor there. I'd seen him in the courtyard at the hospital."

"Yes, the doctors come during business hours. They're the customers. The orderlies, janitors, they're the suppliers. Usually they come before dawn. That one was late and, no doubt, that was part of the argument."

"I still don't get it."

"Doctors and pharmacists at the hospital, at any hospital, get tempted. They are around so many drugs. If they are tired, they can take a little of the therapeutic grade cocaine from the surgery or write themselves a prescription for a nice amphetamine. If they have trouble sleeping, first they can try sleeping pills, then codeine. Then, if it gets really bad, morphine injections." Ilya poured the coffee, our current drug. "After a while, if they keep it up, they get caught. *Boom*, no more job, no more wife and children, no more life.

"On the other hand, what the workers like the orderlies at the hospital need, more than extra energy or sleep, is money. They have big families, here and back in the countries they left. They're willing to risk getting caught stealing if the reward is big enough. The doctors, who have money, would rather pay for their drugs and stay doctors. So enter our neighbor, the spider. She used to be a nurse, they say, a long time ago. Now she is the middleman, the store that buys wholesale and sells retail. She buys the drugs the orderlies have stolen, and she sells them to the doctors, making a very nice profit. All she risks is jail and, honestly, what would she do there so different than what she does all day in front of her house? Sit, scrub, mop. With the muscles she has on her, she could certainly take care of herself. Think of it as the perfect expression of capitalism. Think of it as the way money always finds its way in the world. Our mother," he finished his cup of coffee, "would hate it."

"But you do, too. Why?" I asked. "What's it to you?" His friend, Mei-mei, had just given me a smiley faced tablet.

"It isn't money she takes from people. It's their life. They start easy enough, once a week maybe, I see them. Then every day. Twice a day." He set his cup in the sink so hard I thought I heard it crack.

"Okay," I said, surprised at his outburst, surprised he cared about something enough to get angry. I hadn't seen any sign of that until now.

Ilya stood at the sink a moment, took a deep, raspy breath, let it go. He looked at the clock on the stove. It was nearly 7:30. "Poof," he said, blowing air out through his lips. "Where did the night go?"

Ilya gave me an old shirt to sleep in, a towel, and pointed the way to the bathroom, which was two doors off the kitchen. Inside was a toilet, a claw-footed tub—no shower—and an old-fashioned pedestal sink. I sat on the edge of the tub and pulled off my boots, tossed them into the far corner. My socks stank. I peeled off my stolen clothes. They were soaked in sweat and smelled strongly of smoke. I dropped everything in the corner. I knew I was just as sweaty, but I was too tired to face the bath and settled for washing my face, doing an index-finger-as-toothbrush routine. Then I put on the shirt Ilya had given me. It was very fine, very worn cotton with a subtle blue pin stripe and what had once been elegant French cuffs, now frayed to soft Kleenex. The shirt must have been one of Mosjoukine's.

When I came out, Ilya called me from the living room. I could sleep in the front bedroom. "Mine is back there, off the kitchen," he said, leading the way. "But this is the better room." He opened the door, and I saw I was wrong in thinking that the living room was full of odd furniture because the bedrooms had been emptied. This one had another carved armoire, two marble-topped dressers, a couple of upholstered chairs, a fainting couch, a bedside table, and a double poster bed of the same dark mahogany as the other furniture. There was hardly room to move between the heavy, footed pieces. The high bed was made up with a half-dozen feather pillows and a vast hump of feather comforter.

Ilya took the comforter off the bed, opened the window, and gave it a vigorous shake. Dust and feathers flew. Down below, I could hear the neighbor first sneeze, then cough twice. "Stupid Jew," I heard her say.

"Bless you, too, Cow," he called back. He slung the comforter back on the bed.

"Good night, Vera," Ilya said, yawning. "Good dreams. Or none at all." I had climbed onto the bed and tucked my feet under the comforter. He turned to leave.

"You know,'" I said, "everyone else in the world calls me Emma."

"Do you want me to call you Emma?" he asked.

I shook my head.

"I'll tell you a secret," my brother said.

"What?"

"The name on my birth certificate is Ivan Ilyich."

"The same as Mosjoukine's?"

"Yes."

"Our mother named us *Vera* and *Ivan?*"

99

"Yes."

"Is that romantic or sad?" I asked, thinking of Sophie, giving birth alone in Paris while Mosjoukine was God only knew where.

"Sad," Ilya said. "Very sad."

Then he closed the door behind him and, as soon as he did, I fell asleep.

I didn't dream about the car accident or my dead parents. I had the influenza dream again, the one in which I was Vera Holodnaya and I couldn't breathe, no matter how many pillows were propped up behind me. "Vera!" I heard coughing and someone calling, "Vera!"

I opened one eye. I was in the bed from my dream, pillows, comforter. Light was shining through the open window. Awake, thank God, I could breathe. Ilya, standing by the bed, was the one who was coughing. "I have to go to work," he said. "I'm late already. Here are keys to the front door and the apartment." He set them on the bedside table, and I heard the click of brass on marble in the base of my skull. How long had I slept? An hour? Two? How long had he? "I have a double run today. Three hours to La Villette, lunch, then three hours back, so I won't be home until after dark. In the meantime, if you want to spend time with our father . . ." Ilya said as he opened the doors of the armoire.

I raised myself on one elbow, expecting to see rank on rank of vintage, custom-tailored suits to match my rag of a shirt. Instead, I saw a small TV and a video player stuck in one corner, their cords in a tangle, and beside them an untidy pile of tapes labeled with black marker. I saw the titles *Michel Strogoff, L'Enfant du Carnaval,* and half a dozen more I couldn't quite decipher. "Don't go crazy," Ilya said.

I sat up in bed, rubbing my eyes. "My God," I said. "You have everything. Don't you want me to wait so you can watch them with me?"

He shook his head. "I never want to see another silent film if I live to be a hundred." He picked up his violin case. "Especially not one with Mosjoukine."

By the door, Ilya turned. "Don't forget to eat something," he said. "I made coffee." Then he was gone. I closed my eyes. In a minute, I would get up. In a minute, I would figure out how to set up the TV and the video player. Ben had always laughed at my inability to use even the simplest electronics. I always threw my hands up in despair, and he had taken over. Julia had been a whiz compared to me, had known her way around a remote before she could reach the TV and would offer to help me. Now I would just have to do it myself or it would not get done. Then I rolled over and went down like a drowning sailor into the deep sea of sleep.

When I woke, I lay in bed for a moment, taking inventory. First a physical inventory: my head hurt, the soles of my feet felt like someone had beaten them with bamboo rods, and I had a stabbing pain in my back over my left wing bone. I sat up in bed, tried stretching. Even the muscles under my arms hurt. Who knew you had muscles in your armpits? What had I been doing? Dancing or rowing a slave galley like Ramón Novarro in the silent *Ben-Hur*?

Then an emotional inventory: what did I feel besides stiff? I felt around gingerly, my thoughts a tongue probing my soul for sore spots. Sophie, *my mother*, was dead. Back in New York, I had imagined it would be Sophie I found, Sophie who let me into her apartment, her kitchen, her life. Now what Ilya told me about our mother was all I would ever know.

Yet I felt less sad than excited. I felt a buzz, a static of anticipation. I wanted to watch the tapes in the armoire. I wanted to see Mosjoukine's movies, all of them that still existed. I wanted to see more of this once-famous father of mine or, rather, of ours. That was the real shocker—not that my parents were dead, that was bitterly familiar territory—but that I had a brother, a twin brother. I didn't know what I thought of that. It did mean I had family, something I'd hurled myself halfway around the planet to find. But not much family, not a house overrunning with nephews and nieces, aunts, uncles, cousins. Instead, I had gone from being the last member of a nearly extinct tribe to sharing my desert island with one other human. A human with as few ties to the rest of humanity as I had. Or so it seemed.

The truth was, I didn't know. Had Ilya ever been married? There was a question. I thought of Ilya dancing last night at the party. Did he have children? For all I knew, he could be like Mosjoukine. He could have children with eyes that matched his, matched Mosjoukine's, in every arrondissement in Paris. Meimei seemed to know him well. The truth was my brother could be a thief or a pedophile or a junkie. Had he gone back to school after he escaped the boys' home? How had he survived on his own since fourteen? Had he any education at all? Held any job besides tour guide? I didn't know this new brother of mine any better than a talkative stranger who sat next to me on a train.

Outside the window, I heard the bang of a bucket, the splash of a mop. I got out of bed and peeked through the curtain. The neighbor was on duty, scrubbing the stones so hard with her thick, muscled arms it was a wonder she didn't wear them away. The doctor in the gray suit was there. This time I saw him slip the bills into the pocket of her housedress while she was busy slopping soapy water on the pavement, then take out a small packet wrapped in white butcher paper.

I went to the kitchen and got myself a cup of coffee. The coffee was cold, but I didn't care. I added milk, the last in the refrigerator, and three heaping tea-spoons of sugar. I thought about bread—there was a half-loaf on the table—but it seemed too tough to chew, too hard to swallow without Ilya there to force-feed me like a stubborn bird.

I went into the bathroom, stripped, and crouched in the tub. There was no plug, just a length of tubing attached to the faucet. I hosed my body, soaped toe to head, scrubbing even my hair with the bar soap, then rinsed. I had to search the tall cupboards on one wall for a towel. For lack of anything else, I put Mosjoukine's shirt back on. I needed my last pair of clean underwear, but where had I left my purse? I found it beside the chair I'd sunk into after getting my first look at Mosjoukine's apartment. I thought about getting the makeup bag out, too, but in all honesty, the life I was living made the circles around my eyes deep and dark without cosmetics.

I gathered up my clothes from the floor and carried them into the kitchen. I was going to miss the sweater I'd tossed into the dancers. It was early in spring to go sleeveless. I washed the pants and the shell, my underwear and socks in dish detergent, laid them out on towels on the tub to dry. Then I stood for a long minute in front of the second door off the kitchen. It was Ilya's room. I had no excuse to go in. I should stay the hell out. But I had to see where my brother slept, the room where he lived. I opened the door. The first thing I saw were old soccer posters on the walls. A map of France like a schoolboy might have.

I guessed this had been his room since Mosjoukine brought him from Prague, maybe from when he was little, living here with Sophie. Had I ever slept in this room? Had we both slept here that summer after Livvy had given me back? Or had we been little enough to sleep in the big bed with our mother? For furniture, there was only a futon, a metal desk, and some impromptu board and block bookcases. Clearly, this was the source of the extra furniture in the living room. I imagined a teenage Ilya pushing all the dark, waxed mahogany out of his space, across the kitchen linoleum, and into the living room where the armoire and dressers stood now.

I hesitated, then stepped into his room. I imagined he had built the cases for books like the Houdini biography I'd seen him reading, or maybe model cars or trophies, the things the teenage boys I'd known always had on display, but now the shelves were dusty and bare. He'd swept that part of his past away. A corkboard hung over the desk, but it was empty except for two snapshots, one on top of the other, stabbed through with a single pushpin. I unpinned them. The first was a picture of a younger Ilya in a fencing outfit with a pretty, red-haired woman at his side. He looked like he was in his late twenties. He was smiling, his weapon raised in mock salute. He had his arm around the woman's shoulders. His hair was long and wet with sweat, as if he had just finished a fight or a round or whatever a match in fencing was called, and his eyes said, as clearly as they would have in any silent movie, that he had won. Both victory and this woman belonged to him.

The second snapshot showed Ilya standing by the canal boat. His hair was even shorter than mine, his head nearly bald. He looked pale, seasick maybe. The sun must have been directly overhead. His eyes were cast down, and I could see the lines etched in deep shadow on either side of his mouth. He looked years older than in the first picture. Was he? Probably. I looked at the backs of the photos, but there was no way to tell. I carefully pinned them back as I'd found them. The Ilya who thought he would always win blotting out Ilya alone.

A stack of folded, well-worn jeans sat on the desk. Beside them was a pile of neatly rolled socks. All fresh from the laundry. I took a pair of jeans off the top, held them to my waist. They were six inches too long but otherwise a good fit. I put them on, then a pair of socks. I rolled the jeans. If I wanted to go out, I could tuck them into my boots. A pair of jeans and clean socks seemed within the limits of what one sibling could borrow from another, even without asking, though it was hard for me to be sure. I peeked in the desk drawers and saw only pens and a roll of double-sided tape. I saw nothing that could have been Mosjoukine's. No silk ties or engraved cufflinks.

I went back to the bedroom I'd slept in and wrestled the TV out of the armoire, carried it into the living room. Then I did the same thing with the tape player and the tall stack of dusty tapes. I set the TV and VCR deck up on the floor, brought pillows and the comforter from the bed, and made myself a small nest on the carpet. Then I sorted through the tapes. I got John's faxed list from my purse, smoothed the sheets of folded paper, compared it to the labels on the tapes. The earliest film Ilya had was *Father Sergius,* filmed in Russia in 1917. "In this film based on Tolstoy, Mosjoukine ages from age 18 to 80," read the description on John's fax. If I was going to work my way forward through my father's film life, it looked like *Father Sergius* would act as a sort of preview, a fast forward through his aging. Then I would watch the others, one by one.

It would take all my attention. Ben swore there'd been no popcorn in theaters until sound. With silents, you couldn't take your eyes off the screen. You had to watch to catch every gesture, every expression, had to read what dialogue there was. You had to pay absolute attention. "We should live life like that," he'd said.

I put in the first tape.

11

THE TITLE FOR *FATHER SERGIUS* APPEARED. Sergius was deadly serious from the beginning, Mosjoukine's expression fierce, his nose and eyebrows drawn in with dark lines. His character, a prince, becomes a solitary monk, renouncing flesh and the world. Then, in the middle of a long winter night, a divorced woman seeks him out to seduce him. She slithers around his cell, trying to tempt him. To resist her, Father Sergius picks up his ax and, with a swift blow, cuts off his own finger.

I turned off the TV and went into the kitchen. I wasn't sure I could watch Mosjoukine's work if more of his films were like *Sergius* than *Kean.* I wasn't nearly Slavic enough for such grimness. I could hear Ilya's voice, "Don't forget to eat something," so I found a banana on top of the refrigerator, peeled and ate it, washing down each bite with a mouthful of water. I felt as dry as dust, as if by crying so much in the weeks since the accident I'd been emptied of everything living or moist, even my own spit. My eyes felt gritty, my eyelids scraping each time I blinked. I sat at the table, moving crumbs around with my finger—the same finger Mosjoukine chopped off with his ax in *Father Sergius*—as if the crumbs were parts of a complex jigsaw puzzle I couldn't quite solve.

I thought about going out for a walk. I thought about going to the bakery, the butcher, the market to buy food and make dinner. I had loved to cook for Ben and Julia. I closed my sand-dry eyes, remembered Ben at the table, saying, "Look at all this wonderful food your mother made us!" Food was love. Food was showing every day you cared. Now I couldn't remember a thing I'd made them. I took the water and went back into the living room, afraid that if I stopped now, after *Father Sergius*, I would never start in again.

The next film, *L'Enfant du Carnaval,* was as different from *Father Sergius* as the setting, semitropical Nice instead of Siberia. A smiling Mosjoukine appears in a harlequin's outfit. This is Mosjoukine transformed, as if leaving Russia had let centuries drop from his shoulders. He stands beside a dark velvet curtain, then he yanks it aside to reveal dancing carnival crowds below.

L'Enfant du Carnaval, John's list said, was the first film Mosjoukine directed as well as wrote. The plot was standard farce. A woman abandoned by her husband leaves a baby boy on the rich playboy Mosjoukine's doorstep. Thinking the child is his, he tries to care for the baby alone without knowing so much as how to fasten a diaper. Then enters the baby's mother, hired as the much-needed nurse. Just another comic turn, but Mosjoukine falls in love with her, and his intensity changes the film. They both love the baby, a boy Mosjoukine names Paul. Mosjoukine has no idea the woman is the baby's mother. But love, like a tight band, pulls them closer and closer. Mosjoukine's character finds meaning in his son, in family. I wanted to believe this. Believe, if given a chance, Mosjoukine would have been the best of fathers. Every time he cooed at Paul, I thought, That's my father, looking at Paul the way he would at Ilya, his own little son.

The plot builds toward happiness, and I found myself hugging my knees, I wanted a good end so badly. The woman is told her husband has gone down on an Atlantic steamer. By now, Mosjoukine knows she is the boy's mother and that he is not the real father. He asks her to marry him, begs her, finally overcomes her objections. Happiness is about to break out. But returning home from their wedding, whom do they find but the missing husband, waiting to reclaim his family. Mosjoukine says good-bye to his new wife, in a scene where he is limited to straightening her collar, to touching the flowers on her dress. He lets her go. Then in the last scene, Mosjoukine runs to the balcony, throws open the doors, and cries out not for his wife but for the boy he loves as his own, *My son, my son Paul! How can you take him from me!*

How could Ilya watch this and doubt that Mosjoukine had it in him to love a son. I ran the last scene again. I wanted to cry and cry more. I tried, I felt it, but my eyes stayed as dry as the dust in the carpet. I was watching it for the third time when I heard Ilya's key in the lock. He came through the door, violin in one hand, a net bag full of groceries in the other. When he saw what I was watching, he froze. "My son, my son," the last title on the screen read, then Mosjoukine's face filled the screen, his eyes wet and shimmering.

"The old bastard," my brother said. "Always a close-up with tears in his eyes."

I turned off the tape, a rush of static filling the TV screen. Ilya stepped over me without a word, heading for the kitchen. I trailed after him, wrapped in the comforter. "You told me to watch his movies."

He shook his head, not meaning *No* but more *That was a mistake.* "I know," he said. He took a bottle of wine out of the bag, a head of cabbage. "Did you eat?" I played with the bottle, tipping it this way and that. Picking it up to look at the label without reading it. I wasn't sure, but I thought we were about to get into a real fight.

"A banana," I said.

"And?"

"A glass of water?"

He sighed. "When you were a mother, did your daughter have to feed you?"

I banged the bottle on the table. "You have no right to say that. I was a good mother. I fixed Julia a hot breakfast every morning. I packed her lunch. I made her dinner every single night." Organic vegetables, I wanted to say. Made her drink her milk for the calcium, eat her spinach for the beta-carotene. So she could die with no cavities. So she could die with strong bones.

"Okay, okay," he said. He had his back to me, coring the cabbage in the sink.

"Go to hell," I said, and slung the wine across the room at the wall beside him. I imagined exploding glass, wine red as blood running down Mosjoukine's faded wall. Instead the bottle bounced off the wall and hit Ilya hard in the shoulder. I heard it thud to the floor, roll across the linoleum.

Ilya spun around, the cabbage in one hand, kitchen knife in the other. His face was a blank of surprise. Then, just as quickly, he held the cabbage in front of his face, and pretended to draw the knife across his throat. Then he dropped the cabbage, and we stared as it rolled across the floor as if we were citizens of the Republic taking a day off to watch executions at the guillotine. It rolled under the table and came to rest next to the unbroken bottle of wine.

"Feel better?" Ilya asked. I looked up at him. His eyes were twinkling a bright blue. The corners of his mouth turned up in a sly smile.

"Good acting," I said.

He tilted his head, acknowledging the compliment. "Like father . . ." he said.

At dinner, he let me talk on and on about Mosjoukine, though he spent a lot of time moving the cabbage around his plate, cutting the sausage he'd cooked to go with it into smaller and smaller bites without actually eating much.

I told him about my theory of Mosjoukine's movies rehearsing what was to come in his life. I explained about my novel set in Paris ending with a birth I had yet to experience. As I spoke, I realized the novel also opened with the unexpected death of a husband. What did that mean? I put down my fork, but Ilya seemed to be a beat behind.

"You wrote a book?" he asked.

"Yes, a novel."

"And published it?"

I nodded, "In hardback and paper. There were even German and Japanese editions." I remembered how strange it had seemed to see my name on a book filled with words I couldn't read.

"But not French?"

"No."

"Even though it's about Paris?"

"Everyone writes about Paris," I said. "And, besides, the French write plenty of their own books."

"I'd like to read it, though," he said. "I can't in Japanese or German or English."

I hadn't thought about that. It had been a long time since anyone had asked to read something I'd written.

"Did you write other books?"

I shook my head.

"Why not?" I could only shake my head again. "You aren't the only one, you know," Ilya said, pushing his plate away.

"Only what?"

"Illegitimate child of Mosjoukine who turned out to be a writer."

I looked at him, one eyebrow raised.

"Oh, no, not me," he laughed. "People say the novelist Romain Gary was Mosjoukine's son. Do you know who he was?" I didn't. "He was a pilot with the Free French, a bit of a hero, then a diplomat. His mother was a Polish actress who had known Mosjoukine in Moscow. Gary wrote a novel that won the Prix

Goncourt. Then he wrote another novel and won it again, making him the only writer ever to win twice." Ilya laughed.

"So?" I said. I didn't get the joke.

"The rules say an author can only win the Goncourt once, so Gary wrote the second prize-winning book under a pseudonym, Émile Ajar. It was a scandal."

"Mosjoukine was his father?"

Ilya shrugged. "Gary wrote a memoir, *Promise of Dawn*. It's mostly about his mother, who loved him more than life. The book tells about how poor they were, how she struggled to get them to France, to turn Gary into a French ambassador. She did, too. When she is really desperate, she sends off a letter and a picture of the boy to someone. Money appears by return mail. Mosjoukine is there in the book. Taking the boy to tea at a fancy hotel, sending him a red bicycle once."

A red bicycle. I looked at Ilya. He nodded.

"I don't think you would have trouble reading between the lines. Besides . . ." Ilya got up from the table, went into the living room. I heard a drawer open and shut. "What do you think?" He handed me a book with Romain Gary posed, chin on hand, on the back cover. He had Mosjoukine's eyes, the high forehead, and strong nose. In his long hair and a beard, he was a dead ringer for Father Sergius. Amazing, another brother.

"Do you know him? Does he live in Paris?"

"Lived," Ilya said. Of course, I thought, of course, he was dead. "I never met him." I looked at the book again. Above the author photo were some comments by a critic, talking about Gary in the past tense. "The unifying element of Gary's life," the jacket read, "was the problem of identity. In his life, in his work, in his physical appearance even, Gary never ceased changing, superimposing faces, names, identities, ending up writing his own life like one of his books." A chameleon like Mosjoukine, I thought, as if I needed more proof. What was it with us?

"Gary committed suicide," Ilya said, "in 1980."

Suicide, even worse. "Why?" I said, though I don't know what I expected Ilya to say, how he could answer for this long dead possible brother.

"Do you know who Jean Seberg was?"

"The actress in Goddard's *Breathless*?" I told him I had a friend from Iowa, Jean Seberg's home state, who was obsessed with her, obsessed with how the FBI had hounded her over her connection to the Black Panthers, had spread the lie she was carrying a black child, had tormented her until she miscarried. This friend even had a tape of the press conference Seberg had called to prove the child had, after all, been white. He tried to get people to watch it when he had parties at his house, which was odd, and sometimes they did, which seemed even odder.

"That was Romain Gary's child," Ilya said. "Gary and Seberg's."

"Seberg committed suicide, too." I knew that from my friend.

"Then he did a year later, though by the time she died, they'd been divorced for a decade."

"Jesus," I said. More Slavic endings. A whole family history with nothing but these special sad denouements where, instead of being rescued, every last soul on the ship drowns.

Ilya stood to make coffee, but started coughing, bending over the table. He sat down again. I went to put my hand on his forehead. "Do you have a fever?" I said. He knocked my hand away.

"You're not my mother," he said, struggling to catch his breath.

I stepped back. "No, no, I'm not that."

He pushed himself up from the chair, went into the bathroom, and locked the door. I could hear him coughing, harder than before, then it stopped. I cleared the dishes, washed up. Then I went into the living room and sorted through the rest of the tapes, trying to decide what to watch next. I picked *The Late Mathias Pascal,* the one that had given Mosjoukine his French alias, Adrien Meis.

I heard Ilya come out of the bathroom. The door to his bedroom opened, closed, then I heard him behind me. Before I could think of what to say and turn, he had unlocked the front door and was gone.

So I settled down with our father in *The Late Mathias Pascal.* Mosjoukine, as Mathias Pascal, works in a ramshackle library where he spends his days fishing for rats with kittens on strings, letting them wander through haphazard piles of decaying books hunting. When they catch a rat, he gently reels them in. But then tragedy strikes. Mosjoukine carries his dead baby daughter through a storm in a futile attempt to satisfy his dying mother's wish to see her only grandchild. Pure melodrama, but Mosjoukine's face and body are racked by such sorrow, such anger and frustration, that I leaned toward the screen trying to catch each current of emotion. The plot might be contrived, but he knew loss, and I did, too. I had felt what he was feeling, the need to grieve, the need to laugh at the absurdity of such a loss, the urge to turn toward God and curse or bow—but he did none of these, only stood as the rain came down like blunt, absolving blows. So what if he was just acting. He would have understood what I had lost and what those deaths had cost me.

Then Mathias Pascal is mistakenly thought to have committed suicide. He declares, "Death is freedom!" He escapes debt and a bad marriage to be reborn as the joyful Adrien Meis. Just as Mosjoukine must have felt born again when he slipped out of the hospital in Neuilly-sur-Seine, when he escaped from the postwar Soviet Union, maybe every time he left a life, a country, a lover. Maybe the deaths of my loved ones had set me free, too. Here I was, the newly rechristened Vera, living in a new country, speaking a language my daughter would not have understood. I shook my head. This wasn't a vision of myself—or my father—that made me happy.

Mathias Pascal ended, and I thought about going to bed. I had no idea what time it was, but it was late. Instead I put in another tape, an earlier film, *L'Angoissante Aventure,* the first movie Mosjoukine and his Russian friends made on coming to France. As it played, I fell asleep, woke up, fell asleep again. As I drifted off, I kept seeing Mosjoukine's face, in turns grieving and mischievous. I saw his face layered on my brother's face. Both more familiar than my own to me somehow. The last thought I remember having was *Where is my brother?* I wanted to tell him how very much he looked like our father, but Ilya still wasn't home.

I woke up, wrapped in the comforter on the floor. The TV was full of static. I stood, then almost fell over. My right leg was asleep. I opened the velvet curtains. It was late morning. Had Ilya ever come in? I limped into the kitchen, rubbing my numb leg. A fresh loaf of bread was on the table along with a small bunch of bananas. The bathroom door and Ilya's bedroom door were closed. I knocked on the bathroom. No answer. I opened the door. It was empty, but my wool pants, the sleeveless shell, socks, and underwear were folded neatly by the tub. I changed into them, folding Ilya's jeans and Mosjoukine's shirt and putting them in the cupboard.

I knocked on his bedroom door, once, twice. "Are you awake?" I called. "I'm coming in." I opened the door slowly, giving my brother a chance to grab the sheets if he slept naked. The bed was empty. I went back to the kitchen. He'd been in and then he'd gone out. Was he working? I looked on the table for a note. Nothing. I went back to my nest in the living room, ejected the tape from the deck. Had I seen enough of *L'Angoissante Aventure?* Should I watch it again from the last thing I remembered? I looked at the tape, but it wasn't *L'Angoissante Aventure*. It was *Michel Strogoff*, the movie Ilya said I should watch. He must have put it in for me. Okay, then, brother, I thought, I can take a hint. I got myself a banana and settled in for another movie.

I could see why Ilya had recommended it. It was an epic swashbuckler with a plot that would have appealed, as they used to say, to audiences from nine to ninety-nine.

Strogoff is a secret courier for the czar, smuggling a message to Omsk besieged by the Tartars. Disguised as a trader, he helps a young woman, Nadia, get a visa by pretending they are brother and sister, and they journey as a family. I couldn't help comparing the scenes where the brother and sister spar, tease, flirt, get to know each other, come to each other's defense, to Ilya and me. Mosjoukine, hands down, was more charming than Ilya. But I was no sweet blushing Nadia, either.

When the Tartars whip his mother, Strogoff reveals himself and is captured. Their Grand Khan orders him blinded. Strogoff asks his mother not to hide her face, to keep looking at him, to be the last thing he sees as the red hot sword is pressed to his eyes.

Strogoff, led by Nadia, still tries to reach Omsk. At the end of their strength, they take refuge in a village the Tartars have pillaged. Strogoff asks Nadia to leave him and save herself, but she refuses. As they sit against a cold stove in the deserted hut, Strogoff realizes he can just barely see the light of a votive candle flickering in front of the icon on the wall. His tears for his mother protected his eyes and saved his eyesight. A miracle! He can see!

Is that what Ilya liked so much about the movie, that Strogoff was blind and then, because his love for his mother was so strong, was made whole again? Had Ilya's love for our mother done either of them any good? Or was the message more universal, that love alone can save us? As much as I wanted, I couldn't quite believe it. I had loved, and still loved. It hurt like hell. Love was not saving me.

I rewound the tape to an earlier part of the movie. In it, a coach with Strogoff and Nadia runs wild in a storm, the coachman thrown aside by the panicked flight of the horses. Mosjoukine stands up, taking the reins in one strong hand. This is Mosjoukine at his most intense, alive, nearly manic. One hand around Nadia's shoulders, he shouts above the wind, "Never be afraid."

I stopped the tape, rewound it, played it again. *There,* I felt my father was talking to me. Never be afraid. I had always been afraid, and what had it got me? Caution had only slowed me enough for disaster to find my family and strike. From now on, I wanted to swear to the frozen image of my father, "I will fear nothing."

But what exactly did that mean on a late afternoon in Paris for a new widow, an orphan two times over? I wanted to see my brother. I turned off the TV, went into the kitchen. It was nearly two. If Ilya was working, the canal boat might be passing by the hospital on its way down from La Villette any time now. I grabbed a helter-skelter picnic from the kitchen, a bottle of wine, bananas and bread, a bar of chocolate. I stuffed them in a string shopping bag. Then I got my boots from the bathroom, pulled them on, and ran down the stairs.

12 ॐ

LA SIRÈNE HAD MADE IT FURTHER THAN I EXPECTED. I spotted the canal boat from the Swing Bridge of the Barn of the Beautiful and ran to the lock, just as the boat floated to the top. Nolo was casting off the lines, but the gates of the lock were still closed. He saw me and broke into a broad smile. He gave me his hand and helped me jump onto the bow. Ilya had his back to us, reeling out his story of the canal. Nolo held his finger to his lips. He wanted me to be a surprise. I knelt beside the coiled rope, keeping low. "I need a hand!" Nolo called, as if he were having trouble with the lines, and Ilya finished his spiel and jumped onto the roof of the cabin, the soles of his boat shoes squeaking on the polished wood, and headed forward. He did this with the light grace of our father. He did this the way he always did.

He jumped down into the bow, saw me, and smiled, too, though not quite as instantly, as enthusiastically as Nolo. I held up the string bag. "Lunch," I said, though it was now nearly three.

"If it's lunch, you're late," he said. I raised one shoulder by way of acknowledging the truth of what he said. I was late, but here I was.

We finished the tour, motoring out of the lock into the long dark stretch of the tunnel and finally out into the Seine. I watched as the tourists, schoolteachers from the south of France this time, disembarked on the quay. They were even bigger tippers and kissers than the Polish grandmothers. The last one off, a petite brunette with bright pink lipstick, clung to Ilya's hands for a moment, standing on tip-toe first to kiss him on the cheek, then to whisper something in his ear. My brother laughed. "If I get to Nice," he said. He watched as the teacher rejoined her colleagues, as she turned one last time to wave. I felt a rush of jealousy that made my cheeks burn.

Nolo appeared with some coffee cups for the wine. He jabbed Ilya in the back with his elbow. "Stop working," he said. "Let's eat."

Jacques, the captain, joined us on the back deck for our picnic. He opened the wine and chipped in a small can of pâté and a jar of gherkins. "Emergency supplies," he said. We ate paté sandwiches and slices of banana with chocolate. We drank the wine.

Ilya poked me in the ribs and said to Nolo, "I told you she couldn't cook." I poked back. We really were brother and sister. The late afternoon sun shone down on all of us.

"Play us something," Jacques said to Ilya after a while. "You always play a good tune. Not like that other stuff." Jacques looked at Nolo and rolled his eyes.

Ilya opened his violin case, rosined the bow. He played a jig with more enthusiasm than the Bach I had heard him play. Then *Scotland the Brave,* a song Julia had learned when she first started lessons. He played with feeling and a relaxed, idiosyncratic sense of rhythm that might have shown a natural gift for jazz, though it was hard to say. Finally he played his usual, the clunky *Gavotte.*

"You should practice more, man," Nolo said. "You could get good if you tried."

Ilya laughed. "It's just for the tourists. I'd do just as well with a harmonica, but since my wife left me the violin, I might as well . . ."

"Wife?" someone said. It was me.

It was Nolo's turn to laugh. "Oh, look what you forgot to tell little sister."

Ilya made a face. "Nothing to tell," he said, then he turned to me. "You know the old joke, yes?"

I shook my head. No, I didn't.

So he told it to me. A lord, showing a visitor around his castle, points out a large framed painting and says it is a portrait of his dear departed wife. "I am so sorry," the visitor says. "When did your wife die?"

"Oh, I didn't say she died," the lord says. "I just said she departed." Ilya laughed. Nolo didn't.

"She left?" I asked Ilya. "Just left?" He didn't answer.

Jacques brushed off his hands on his coveralls and stood up. "Speaking of wives, it's home for me. Don't forget to tie down the tarps." He wagged a finger at Nolo as if this were a sore point. "Good and tight." Then he got his gear and jumped off onto the quay. "No tours tomorrow, boys," he said. "See you Wednesday."

"No tours," Nolo said, shaking his head. "Man, I could use that money. He should buy more ads, put some investment in this tub. I mean, I'm depending on a good season. I got things I need." He stomped off to get the tarps.

"Jacques owns the boat?"

Ilya nodded. "Jacques used to work on the canal when it was real work. For him, this is more like retirement. Nolo, he wants more." Ilya watched his friend muttering, dragging the heavy blue canvas over the benches where the rows of tourists sat for their trip up the canal. "If he were careful with his money, he could buy Jacques out. But most days he thinks if Kumé, his girl, makes it big as a singer, he'll leave all this behind."

"She was the one who sang the other night?" He nodded. "You wouldn't want to own part of the boat?" I asked him.

Ilya laughed, "Me? The boy our mother raised to be such a good communist? I don't think so."

"What do you want to do?"

He made a sour face. "I want to help Nolo get those tarps right for once, then get out of here."

I gathered up the banana skins, the empty wine bottle, the chocolate wrapper. I heard Nolo and Ilya behind me cursing and wresting with the tarps. "Vera!" I heard Ilya call. I turned. He had the long pole he used to steady the boat in the lock. "Jump," he said, and he swung the pole in a low arc across the deck of the boat, aiming for my ankles. I jumped, clearing the pole by a good foot. "See," he said to Nolo, "she can move her feet."

Nolo shook his head. "You are going to get me in trouble with your sister, friend. Leave me out of this." He finished the last knot on the tarp.

Ilya turned to me. "Nolo says you walk like this." Ilya dragged his feet across the deck of the boat as if imitating someone wearing concrete overshoes.

"I went dancing," I said. "Nolo saw me dancing." Nolo voted himself out of the argument by leaving the boat. He waved as he started down the quay.

"Wednesday!" he said.

"You never picked up your feet, even when you were dancing," Ilya said. He swung the pole, faster this time. "Jump!" I didn't, and he caught me smartly across the ankle.

"Damn you," I said, hopping on one foot, holding the other where I could feel a good bruise rising. "Stop it. I can't help it if I'm less graceful than you are. I'm a klutz. I have always been a klutz. Leave me alone."

Ilya came up beside me, taking my elbow to help me balance. "No, you aren't. You just think you are. Those people," he said, and by that I knew he meant my American parents, "those people, they put lead in your blood. Remember," he was whispering in my ear now, his voice suddenly fierce. "Never be afraid."

I looked at him, so shocked I didn't know what to say, except, "*Michel Strogoff.*" He knew what part of the film I was meant to see.

"Come on." He grabbed the violin case. "I've got an idea."

We took the Metro to a neighborhood where I had never been before. We were walking by a big lycée with an endless line of chained bicycles, when my curiosity—okay, my impatience—finally got the better of me. I asked my brother, "Where in the world are we headed?"

I expected him to say, "Wait and see," but instead he said, "My fencing club."

"Your club?" I remembered the photograph of him with the mask and sword. The redhead. Had she been his wife?

"Well, once upon a time," he said. We climbed a wide flight of stairs up to some kind of gym. Ilya banged the double doors open like he owned the place, like we were Mosjoukine making a star entrance.

An old man in heavy black glasses sitting at a desk in the foyer sprang up, as if standing at attention. "Monsieur Desnos!" he said, holding both hands out.

"Petrov," Ilya said. Petrov looked as if he has seen the ghost of the czar, but Ilya just waved as we went by. We climbed another flight of stairs. Ilya threw open a second set of doors, a little less vigorously this time. Inside was a long, high-ceilinged room. On the opposite wall, there were windows high up on the wall, and the last light of day flooded across the polished hardwood floor. At the far end, a match or a lesson was in progress. Two fencers in white padded jackets and wire masks lunged, retreated, lunged again, their shoes sliding forward and backward across the floor.

He nodded toward the pair. "That's épée," he said. He pointed at a rack of thinner bladed weapons against the wall. "These are foils, but for what we're doing, either would do." Ilya took a foil from the rack. He whipped it, experimentally, through the air, then put it back, took another. "For the beginning students," he said, as if explaining some obvious lack of quality I couldn't see. We were standing on a narrow strip of rubber matting. Ilya stepped onto the wood floor, then looked at my feet. "Take off your boots," he said to me, "or you'll leave marks on the floor. You can do this in your socks." I leaned against the wall, pulled off the boots, then set them by the rack.

I looked over at the fencers in their protective gear. Ilya followed my glance. "You don't need all that," he said. "You won't be fighting anyone but yourself." He handed me the foil. I took it the way I had been trained by the colonel to shake hands, firmly, fingers together, thumb curled. It wasn't heavy. It probably only weighed a pound, but I found holding it level to the ground, away from my body, surprisingly tiring. Ilya stood behind me, his arms wrapped around me. He adjusted my grip, "Like this," he said, rearranging my fingers. "Looser. It won't run away."

He kept his arms around me, his hands on my hands, his knees behind my knees, "Forward, like this," he said, and we slid forward, lunging the way I had seen the other fencers do. "Then back." We retreated. Lunged, retreated. "Keep the tip up," Ilya said. We lunged. "Don't drag your feet." I felt I was getting a sense of the rhythm, but it was like dancing the tango with a master. I was being moved by Ilya. My movements had nothing to do with me. I was holding the foil, but I wasn't the one fencing. Ilya must have felt the same way. He let go and stepped back. I let my arm drop. Already my fingers were starting to feel numb.

Ilya sighed and pushed the hair that had escaped from his ponytail out of his eyes. "Okay," he said. "Let's try something else. I just want you to move. For once, you should move without worrying where all the pieces of your body are. *You know.* It's your body. You know." He took the back of my neck between his thumb and forefinger. "Here," he said. "Everything is centered here. Don't think about your arms. Don't think about your feet. See what you want to reach, what you want to hit, and you will be there without having to move an inch. It's like flying," he said in my ear. "Like flying in a dream."

I closed my eyes and raised the sword. I moved forward. I moved back. I lunged. I retreated. I can't say I moved with startling grace, but I felt what my brother was talking about. I felt my body moving as a whole inside its flexible skin, and it seemed I could feel, not just see, the fluid ease that Ilya shared with our father. The body answering the brain before the message was sent. The foil as an extension of the body, the body a part of the soul. I felt sweat under my arms, running down my back. I felt the knit suit of my muscles. I kept going, again and again. Lunge. Retreat. *Lunge.*

A man's voice called, "Ilya!" I opened my eyes. My brother let go of my neck, and I went limp, like a marionette whose strings are cut. Then the unaccustomed exertion hit me, and I bent over, panting. One of the fencers was bounding across the floor, pulling off his mask and glove as he came. "Ilya!" he said again. Then he grabbed my brother in both arms, in a bear hug, and lifted him off the ground. He thumped him hard on the back.

"Georges," Ilya said. "You're going to break me in half."

Georges put Ilya down. "What are you doing here?"

Ilya nodded at me. "Giving a lesson. We just started."

"No more," I said, still trying to catch my breath. "Not tonight."

"Here then," Georges pulled off his jacket and held it out with the glove and mask for Ilya to take. "You can finish mine." He waved to the other fencer, who was watching us, one leg bent like a dancer at rest. I could see she was just a girl, maybe thirteen or fourteen.

Ilya looked at the gear in Georges' arms. "Okay," he said. "Why not? Since you are too lazy." He pulled off his sweater and handed it to me. He put on the jacket, tucked the mask under one arm, then took the épée Georges offered hilt first. Ilya bowed slightly, then turned his back on us, tried a lunge. He walked across the gym to the waiting student, bowed to her, put on his mask. They stood en garde, then the lesson began. From the moment Ilya took Georges' weapon, he was a different person. No, that's not right. He was completely himself, at ease, for the first time since I'd met him. He moved like water. He moved like a man happy on his feet.

I was sweating like a pig. Georges offered me a towel, then a cup of water from the cooler by the door. "You're a friend of Ilya's?"

"He's my brother."

"You're kidding," Georges said. He looked at me. "No, I take that back. I can see you're his sister. I just didn't know he had one."

"Have you known him a long time?"

"Since we were ten and our fathers brought us here for lessons."

Our fathers. So Mosjoukine had started Ilya fencing.

"Listen," I said, sensing a chance to learn something about Ilya beyond what he'd been willing to tell me. "If he fenced for so long, why doesn't he do it anymore?"

"You know about Barbara?" Barbara, I guessed from Georges' tone, was the dear departed wife. I shrugged, as in *I know a little*. "Yeah, well," Georges said, "he doesn't like to talk about her. That's when he quit. Right before the Championships."

"Was he good?"

"Ilya? He was ranked tenth. Not in épée, in saber. And everybody knew that ranking was low. He was about to move up."

"Tenth in France?" I was impressed.

"In the world."

I looked at Ilya. He had his mask off now, was smiling at the girl he'd given the lesson. I had never seen him smile like that. But then, I had known him no time at all. "Mademoiselle," he said, bowing. She bowed back, then headed for a door at the far end of the room that I guessed led to the locker rooms. Ilya came over to join us. "Thanks, Georges," he said, tossing Georges his épée. Georges caught it. Ilya stood, wiping his face with a towel. He was breathing hard, more out of shape than I would have guessed.

"Any time, old friend," Georges answered. "Any time." Then Georges took my hand in his and bowed over it. I had never seen so much bowing. Formality seemed to come with the sport. "Look after your brother," he whispered to me, loud enough for Ilya to overhear him. "He needs it."

I caught Ilya looking at me sideways, wondering what else Georges might have said while he was fencing.

"Come on," Ilya said. "I'm sweaty as hell, but we might as well walk home to shower. I don't keep clothes here anymore." He took his sweater from me, and I followed him out of the gym.

The old man at the desk was on the phone when we got down the stairs. He called after Ilya, "Come back, Monsieur Desnos, please! Don't be such a stranger! People still call to ask if you are taking students!" Ilya waved a hand over his head as we went through the door, making no promises that I could see.

The air outside struck me as chill. I felt the sweat on my chest and back dry, then goose bumps start up on my bare arms. I shivered. Ilya peeled off his sweater and pulled it down over my head. "I'm going to buy you one," he said, shaking his head.

"Why did you stop fencing?" I asked. "Georges says you were very good. Was it Barbara?"

"Oh-ho, so Georges was wagging his tongue, old dog," Ilya said. "Barbara. Now you have a name."

"Stop joking for once," I said. "You don't take anything seriously. I want to know."

Ilya stopped and looked at me. He opened his mouth, seemed to think better of it, and shut it again. It was the perfect silent movie pantomime of indecision, but he wasn't acting. We were passing a church. Ilya sat down on the steps with a motion of complete collapse, the way Mosjoukine might have done if this were a comic scene. Then Ilya patted the cement beside him. I sat down. "Okay," he said, "okay, you're right. Barbara was my wife." I thought of the snapshot on his corkboard in his room. His beautiful, red-headed wife.

"And . . ." I prompted.

"She was a doctor. That's how I met her. She fenced a little—she wasn't good. So we signed her on as team doctor. For her real job, she worked at the hospital."

"At St-Louis?"

"Yes," he said, "in surgery, not the usual specialty for a woman. They were tough on her. She worked the worst hours. She worked harder than any of them. She made a point of it." Late hours, St-Louis, this was beginning to sound familiar, and I felt a sick vibration in my stomach. Ilya nodded, guessing what I guessed. "Yes, I told you this story already, only without the names. She started to take cocaine, then mixed it with pills. She'd come home, and there was nothing I could do." He stopped, perhaps remembering all that he had tried. "Nothing could help her sleep. So more pills. I was stupid. I was blind. I thought, she's a

121

doctor. She knows what she's doing. And, I mean, I was an athlete. I knew what guys did, even in my sport. You did what you had to. That's what we all said.

"Then everything seemed to get better. She got a promotion. The old bastard who had given her the worst time got an even bigger promotion, and suddenly he wasn't there, holding her sex over her head. She started sleeping again, eight, ten hours. No problem. And I was on fire. In matches, I just couldn't lose. I had my pick of students, no matter how much I charged for a lesson. I was headed everywhere I wanted to be. Then," he put his head down for a minute, "it got even better. Barbara was pregnant. We were so damn happy. Georges was going to be the godfather. Barbara was the happiest. She was ready to forgive everyone. Even the bastards at the hospital. She wanted me to feel the same way. If the baby was a boy, she wanted to name him after . . ."

"Mosjoukine," I said, though it didn't really need saying.

"'Forgive and forget,' she said. She really wanted a little Ivan. The tapes you watched? I got them for her. She said she wanted to see what the first Ivan Ilyich was made of. Then . . ."

"Yes?"

He took a deep breath, let it out slowly. "Then I went to a tournament in Zurich. Georges, too, though he wasn't ranked. I got back late, had to take a taxi from the club. I saw the lights on and thought Barbara had waited up." He rubbed his palms over his face. His hands were shaking. "I went into the kitchen and the first thing I saw was blood, everywhere, across the floor, into the bathroom. She was sitting on the floor next to the tub." He stopped. He stood up, as if this were the end of the story.

"I don't understand."

He sat down again, less a change of mind than a failure of will or muscle, as if he found he hadn't the strength to get up after all. "She'd been on morphine the whole time." Oh, I thought, the neighbor, the bloodsucking spider. "That was why Barbara was sleeping so well. That night she went into premature labor but was too high to do anything about it. Too out of it to care. She'd given birth to the baby, but she was just sitting there. Just sitting there with the baby beside her on the cold bathroom floor."

"But she was okay."

"Oh, okay. Sure. She's okay even now."

"She didn't die?"

He gave me a look of complete irritation. "What is it with you and dying? Not everyone dies. The truth is you can do terrible things in this world, to yourself, to other people, and in the end, you just go on living. Look at me. I'm alive."

"What did you do? You didn't do anything wrong."

"She was my wife. She was pregnant with my child, and I was off playing games in Zurich. I should have known, but I refused to see. Does that make me innocent or even more guilty?"

"What happened to Barbara?" I said.

"She moved to Australia," he said. "They let her practice medicine there. I hear she is married again. I hear she has a son."

"Was it a boy you lost?" I asked.

"Lost?" he said.

"The baby, the miscarriage."

"I didn't say the baby was dead."

"I don't understand . . ."

Ilya took me by the arm. His fingers pressed hard into my skin, each one a small circle of bruising. "Listen, I am going to take you somewhere. But when it's done, you are never, ever to mention it again. Do you understand? You are not even to imply to me you know. Not even look at me like you know. Get it?"

I used my hand to pull his fingers off my arm. "Yes, I get it," I said, though I didn't.

We turned around, heading east. Ilya walked so fast I could barely keep up. I was already tired from the fencing lesson. My arm was sore where he had grabbed me, and the ankle where he had whacked me with the barge pole hurt. I was beginning to think my brother was crazy and maybe even dangerous.

Now we marched further from anywhere I had ever been, until I thought we would cross the Périphérique, fall out of the city into the sad outer ring of suburbs. We stopped just short, though I could hear the roar of the traffic beyond.

Ilya led the way up a wide flight of stairs to a white cube of a building next to a church. Ilya opened the glass double doors gingerly, though with the same determination as the doors to the fencing club. As soon as he did, I smelled disinfectant and cut flowers and urine, the smells of a hospital. Inside, I saw it wasn't a hospital exactly, more a nursing home. There was a large lobby with one knot of elderly men and women arranged around a television set with the sound down and another half-dozen facing each other in a conversational grouping that didn't seem to include any actual conversation. One pair of old men played dominoes. The clicking of the tiles was the loudest sound in the room.

As soon as we stepped through the doors, a nun materialized from behind a counter. She was young, I could tell that from her face, but she was wearing what a lapsed Catholic friend always called the Full Penguin, the kind of black-and-white floor-length outfit American nuns didn't seem to wear anymore. She recognized Ilya, but she didn't look especially glad to see him.

"Monsieur," she said, but Ilya did not stop. He went straight for a flight of marble stairs. On the landing, another nun sat behind a small desk doing paperwork. She, too, recognized Ilya. "Ah, Monsieur Desnos. I'll have to ring for permission. I thought we agreed last night . . ." She picked up the phone, but Ilya did not stop. I followed him left, down a hall. I heard the nun hit a buzzer. Off to the right were hospital rooms with children in the beds. All sleeping, though it seemed early, and certainly the old people downstairs were still awake. Some of the rooms were painted bright colors, with posters covering nearly every inch of the walls. Some were bare. Ilya was moving so fast I fell behind.

I passed a room with a nun bending over an enamel basin. I stopped. She was bathing one of the children, and then I saw why the children were so still. It was a boy, probably a teenager, but he was hardly bigger than Julia had been. His eyes were opened but unfocused, his mouth gaped. He was profoundly retarded. In high school I had volunteered for a while at a state hospital, one that had been emptied of all but the most severely mentally handicapped, that tiny portion who needed help with everything. Even there, some had been able to move, understand a bit of speech. Not this boy, if I was any judge.

The nun saw me and smiled. She stroked the boy's hair, and I heard her say, "Look at the pretty lady, Jules. Doesn't she have the prettiest blue eyes?"

Behind me, I heard the starchy rustle of nuns. I turned to see the young nun from downstairs and a much older sister who I guessed by the way she walked, heel toe, heel toe, was in charge, the Mother Superior, if that was the right title for this brand of nun. Ilya had disappeared, but they were rushing to find him. I followed.

We found him through another set of double doors in a ward with two facing rows of hospital beds. All of the beds were empty except for one at the end of the room, and it was closed off with movable glass screens, designed, perhaps, so a nursing sister could see in, while offering a little quiet, a little privacy. The whole setup looked like a fish tank. Inside a tiny girl lay in a fetal position with tubes in her nose and stomach, intravenous lines running into one outstretched arm, which was tied with gauze to a padded board to keep it straight enough for the fluids to drip into the small veins.

The Mother Superior had reached Ilya before he reached the girl in the aquarium. Or maybe Ilya had stopped on his own, because she wasn't touching him or restraining him in any way. They just stood there, watching the nothing that was happening. As far as I could see, the girl wasn't even breathing. No, she was, but barely. Her chest rose a little, sank.

I turned to find the young nun standing beside me. Where had she been? I thought she'd been in front of me.

"Is that Monsieur Desnos's child?" I asked her.

"Yes," she said. "Anne-Sophie." *Anne-Sophie.* A child named after not our father but our mother. Ilya took a step forward, but the Mother Superior put her hand on his arm. He stopped.

"How old is she?" I asked.

"Fourteen." Six years older than Julia. I remembered Ilya saying that at least Julia had had eight years. I'd been sorry for all the things she wouldn't get to do, but Ilya must have thought of all the things Julia had done—crawling, walking, running, talking, reading—that Anne-Sophie never would. Ilya was still standing in front of the glass wall, his hands limp at his sides. "Why can't he go in?" I asked. "He's her father."

"He used to go in," she said, "but now she has seizures whenever anyone goes near her. Still, he comes. He was here for hours last night." She shrugged. "The doctors have tried every medication. They can't control the seizures. Each attack does more damage to her brain."

I looked at her, and she saw my doubts.

"I know, I know, she never had more than the mind of a two-month-old at best. But she could see."

I sat down on the empty beds behind me. She was blind. God, even that.

The sister looked down at me. "Now, the littlest sound or change sets her off. The nursing sisters have to go in at the same time, try to do any procedures quickly. Impossible, but . . . what can we do? The doctors say she won't be with us much longer."

Now Ilya was standing with his hands raised as if they were pressed to the glass, but he was a good two feet away and not actually touching the partition, not daring to risk even that noise. He was Mosjoukine standing in the storm in *The Late Mathias Pascal* with his dead daughter in his arms or Mosjoukine on the balcony in *L'Enfant du Carnaval* crying out for his lost child. Unlike Mosjoukine, Ilya wasn't acting. Looking at my brother, I felt what he felt. It was a red hot saber. It was much worse than that.

"You know," the young nun said, looking from Anne-Sophie's glowing cube toward the other rooms, "once they are baptized, these little ones are without sin. They are saints, really. I try to remember that. They suffer for our sins." She bowed her head.

I had an impulse to punch her in her small nose, to see blood streak her wimple. But then why did I want to insist that Anne-Sophie and the other children suffered for no reason? Or for no reason but that their parents had been stupid? Maybe not even that. Insist they suffered because the universe was unrelentingly, remorselessly cruel? These nuns took care of these children every day. I thought of the nun down the hall stroking the boy's hair, saying, "Look at the pretty lady!" with no hope of reply. They thought they were blessed to do it. I had spent enough time at the state hospital to know how rare that kind of care was. Who did it hurt if they needed to believe it was all part of God's great plan?

Maybe it was just my fatigue, my arriving at the far end of my nerves, but the light from Anne-Sophie's cube flowed across the floor like liquid gold. What if love was not an abstraction but a fluid, clearer, more viscous than blood? Then maybe my care and love for my own daughter—the oatmeal, the hot baths— had flowed out into the universe and continued to circulate even now that Julia was gone, keeping a child in some cold place like Siberia safe and warm. Maybe, I thought, wanting to believe it. *Maybe.*

The Mother Superior put her hand on Ilya's shoulder, whispered something in his ear. He shook his head. She whispered again. This time he nodded, and she led him away, holding his arm as carefully as if he, too, had been struck blind.

The young nun gestured toward the door. "You can wait for him on the first floor. She has some papers for him to sign."

I descended the marble stairs alone, sat on a divan near the old men playing dominoes. Each click of a tile made me jump, as if it was the tip of an épée touching my bare skin.

After maybe a half hour, Ilya came down. He didn't look at me. He didn't even seem to see me. I followed him onto the street, walking a few feet behind him. When we reached the boulevard, he noticed I was missing. He stopped and waited for me to catch up. "What were you doing back there?" he said. "Your shoe come untied?" He looked down at my boots. I thought he might laugh—or that he expected me to—but he let it go.

"Why . . ." I started. He raised his hand, like he might actually strike me, but I didn't stop. "Why didn't you go back to fencing?" He looked at me, decided that was a question he could allow. He let his hand drop.

"I got sick," he said, "after Barbara left." He said *sick,* and I thought *sick with grief.* I thought *breakdown,* remembering the photo of him with hair as butchered as mine. "By the time I was well, I was out of contention."

"You could have trained again, right? Started over. Georges still fences."

Ilya blew air out through his pursed lips in that French gesture of complete dismissal. I could tell what he thought of both Georges still competing and competition itself. "It's a game," my brother said. "It's only a game. Being sick taught me that. You saw the blunt tips on the épées. How can it be real if nobody dies?"

13 ✑

WE WENT BACK TO THE APARTMENT. The neighbor, wise woman, was not outside as we passed. By the time Ilya unlocked the top door, I was asleep in my boots. After the fencing lesson and the visit to the nursing home, I was numb and tired clear through, muscles, heart, and brain.

I wished my brother goodnight, keeping my promise not to ask anything out of bounds like, Will you be okay? He'd been okay for forty-two years. Who was I to presume otherwise now? I'd run from the Place Ste-Odile and into the colonel's arms that morning so long ago, abandoning Ilya, without a second's hesitation. I hadn't been with him when he was uprooted and moved to Czechoslovakia by our mother. I hadn't been at the hospital with Ilya when Mosjoukine left never to return. I had been growing up in Florida, in a bedroom full of Barbies, in a house surrounded by tangerine trees. I hadn't driven with him to Prague to find our mother already dead and gone for a year. I hadn't been there when Anne-Sophie was born or at any difficult moment of the fourteen years of her life. I had gotten married and had my own daughter by caesarian section and not even under the truth serum of anesthesia had I remembered, or even dreamed about, my lost brother. I pulled off my boots sitting on the bed, then fell backward onto the feather mountain of pillows. I was asleep before I could take off my socks.

I dreamed I was riding in the carriage in *Michel Strogoff*, sitting next to Mosjoukine in Nadia's place. Just as in the movie, we were riding through a terrible storm, with the horses running mad through dark, whipping trees.

I was waiting for Mosjoukine to reassure me, to stand holding the reins in one hand and tell me, *Never be afraid.* Instead, he turned toward me slowly, as if the film were running at half speed. "Watch out, little Vera," he said. "It isn't the end yet." Then a tree came crashing down in front of the carriage, and I was watching the movie again. Nadia was back on the seat next to the dashing Strogoff, secret courier for his czar. Someone was shouting. Gradually I realized it was not in my dream but outside my window, in the courtyard. One of the voices was my brother's.

I jumped out of bed and opened the curtain. It was still dark, but I could see Ilya in the light from the lamp over the passageway. He was standing talking to the neighbor, waving his arms. She stood with her hands on her hips. I thought about his joke with the knife in the kitchen, about Ilya swinging the barge pole at my feet. After what he had told me about Barbara's addiction, I was afraid. I opened the window. "Ilya?" I called. He turned, looked up to see where my voice was coming from.

"It's okay," he said, waving me away. "There's nothing going on. Go back to bed." The neighbor sat down on her chair and crossed her thick arms across her broad chest. She didn't seem worried she was about to be murdered. Still I wanted him upstairs, away from the spider.

"The telephone is ringing," I said, lying. He looked up again. Then suddenly it was.

"Really?"

"Yes."

"Don't answer it," he said. "I'll be right up."

I ran for the kitchen anyway, slipping across the linoleum in my socks. My heart was pounding, partly because of my adrenaline dash out of my dream, but also because I had never heard Ilya's antique telephone ring. I hadn't known it was connected.

Ilya bounded up the stairs, through the living room, into the kitchen. He grabbed the black handset off its hook and held it hard against his right ear as if the message might be coming from a very long way off. He leaned his back against the kitchen wall, panting hard, trying to catch his breath. "Yes," he said. "Yes, Sister. Of course. No, no, I understand." Just that, then he hung up and slid down the wall onto the linoleum. He sat there, his hands in his lap. I knew without hearing the nun on the other end of the line that Anne-Sophie had not made it through the night.

"Ilya?"

"Go to bed," he said. He looked up at me as if he were afraid I might hit him, that I might say those most unforgivable, most painful words—*Anne-Sophie.* "Please."

"Okay," I said. "Okay."

In bed, I lay listening to Ilya coughing in the kitchen. Then I heard banging, the rustling of paper. Once I thought I heard a faint sound of breaking glass. But I stayed in bed, made my eyes close. I wanted to know if he was all right, but if I couldn't mention Anne-Sophie, if we couldn't talk about the news that she was dead, how was I supposed to ask? The nun who called wouldn't have said *dead*, I thought. Surely, she said on the phone that Anne-Sophie was with her Savior at last.

I woke early and headed for the bathroom, still half asleep. In the light of morning, nothing about the night before seemed real. In the living room, I noticed that all, not just some, of the picture frames were empty. I was puzzled. Where were the photographs? The TV and video deck were still on the floor, but the tapes of Mosjoukine's movies were gone. I padded into the kitchen in my socks. The bathroom door was shut, and I could hear running water. It seemed like a good sign that Ilya was up and getting ready for another day. I knocked, then waited. I really had to pee. I knocked again. No answer. "Ilya! It's Vera. I'm waiting my turn." This must be what it was like having a real brother, one you grew up with, waiting for the bathroom, wondering if you should knock politely again or kick on the door.

I turned to see if Ilya had started the coffee, thinking if not, I might as well. On the table were two shopping bags, the kind with the waxed string handles they gave you when you bought something heavy or awkward like my boots. I peeked inside. In one were all the tapes of our father's movies and in the other were all the photographs, stacked together, neatly removed from their frames. On top I could see the snapshot of Sophie with Ilya and me. Under that was Mosjoukine as Father Sergius. So that was what I had heard last night, the rustle, the broken glass. What was Ilya up to? What, exactly, did these bags full of Mosjoukine mean?

The lock clicked, and Ilya came out, his hair wet around his face where he'd splashed it with water, his eyes sleepy. I pointed to the bags on the table. "What's all this?"

He didn't seem to hear. He brushed by and got the coffee pot out of the sink.

I still had to pee. So I went in for my turn in the bathroom. The coffee would be ready in just a few minutes, but I didn't feel like hurrying if Ilya wasn't speaking to me. This, too, was what real brothers and sisters were like, to judge by Aunt Z and Livvy. It wasn't like Aunt Z was a peach or Livvy was easy to live with. Still, Livvy had called her sister that last morning of her life, wanting to make that connection—blood to blood, sibling to sibling—one last time. Now Ilya and I had a death to talk about. I just hadn't had enough time with Ilya to know what to say. So I took the time for a hose bath, washed my hair, then put my stolen clothes back on. My bare arms were cold in the early morning damp of the old house. Ilya's blue sweater was hanging on the back of the bathroom door, so I pulled it on.

As I did, I saw a flash of white in the trash can by the toilet. I reached down and picked it up, the way a magpie will if something catches its eye. It was a small square of butcher paper, the same kind the neighbor used to wrap pharmaceuticals for her customers. I moved the tissues below it aside with one cautious finger, my heart careening in my chest. At the bottom of the can, I found what I was most afraid that I would find: a used, disposable hypodermic and an empty glass vial. Morphine sulfate, the label read.

I sat down on the closed lid of the toilet. This was why he'd been with the neighbor last night. He'd been buying this from her. Why? *Why?* How long had he been using the same poison that had almost killed his wife and had killed his daughter, though it had taken all these years? My brother, who was so thin and ate so little, was an addict just like Barbara had been. The topic of Anne-Sophie might be forbidden, but we would have to talk about this.

I couldn't bring myself to touch the vial or the syringe. I made myself pick up the paper. That would be enough. When I opened the door, Ilya looked up, steaming coffee pot in one hand. He saw what I was holding out in front of me. Then, in one fluid motion, with that grace he alone really shared with our father, he threw the pot and sent hot coffee hurtling across the kitchen, crashing into the wall next to my head.

"Jesus, Ilya."

He stood with his arms wrapped around his chest, breathing so hard he was wheezing. "I want you out," he said. "I packed everything." He nodded at the shopping bags on the table. I stared at them, letting what he'd said take a minute to sink in. Even last night, he'd been planning this. Even last night, he had wanted me gone. "Go now," he said. His jaw barely moved when he said this. His face was rigid, his breathing labored.

"I..."

"Now," my brother repeated.

Then I was angry, too. I'd done nothing to deserve this. I'd lost a daughter, too. A husband. My whole family. Had he forgotten? What a bastard. What a prick. I banged open the door to the bathroom. Inside, I pulled on my boots. I got my purse from the living room and slung it over my right shoulder with such force that it bounced off my backbone hard enough to hurt. Then I grabbed the two shopping bags. Ilya hadn't moved. I took a deep breath. "But you're my brother."

"Leave the keys," he said. I dug them from my purse and slapped them on the kitchen table. "And the sweater." I yanked it off and threw it on the table beside the heavy brass door keys. It slid, with a lonely swoosh, onto the linoleum.

"Ilya, you can't keep..."

"Don't," he said. He held up his hand, palm out, the universal symbol for *stop now.*

I couldn't. I said, "I'll go, but I want you to know. I'm coming back." *My brother.* My bastard only brother.

"Don't," he said again, but sagging a little this time, putting one hand on the stove to hold himself up.

"Shall I let myself out?" I heard myself saying next, as if this were a drawing room drama played out on a musty provincial stage.

"Please," he said, so softly I hardly heard him.

As soon as I was on the stairs, I heard Ilya lock the door behind me. By locking me out of our father's apartment, he was cutting me off, the way our mother had cut herself off from Mosjoukine. Damn family history, so much pathetic and tedious repetition. I stood facing the front door and thought about banging on it, the way I had on the bathroom door. But that wouldn't do me any good. Later I would find Nolo. He would care. He would help me figure out what to do.

Someone was watching me. I turned. The neighbor was peering out from her front window, safe behind glass. She shook her head as if she disapproved of me, as if she disapproved of everything about the people who lived in 44 Place Ste-Odile. At that moment, so did I.

14 ✒

I TOOK THE METRO TO THE HÔTEL BATIGNOLLES. Since I was paying for a room to store an empty suitcase and a couple of extra credit cards, I felt I might was well stash all my Mosjoukine loot there, too. I waited while the clerk checked for messages, though I had no reason to expect any, since no one knew I was staying there. There were none, the clerk said, handing me my room key. The clerk didn't seem surprised to see me. I'd only been gone three—or was it four?—days. So little time. It had been Friday when I arrived in Paris. What day was it now?

I asked the clerk. He blinked twice, registering more surprise at my question than he intended, then he answered smoothly, "Tuesday, Madame."

"Tuesday," I repeated. I had promised John I would call on Tuesday.

"Is there anything else we can do for you, Madame?" the clerk asked.

"No," I said, "but thank you for asking," and left it at that.

By the time I reached my room, I'd decided I would call John. That was something I could do. I called from the phone by my bed, asking the clerk to put the international call through, knowing that it was both the easiest and most expensive way. Another charge on my card at this point wouldn't make any difference.

I tried John's office, but as it rang and rang I realized it was two in the morning back home. I stretched out on the bed, turned on the black-and-white TV. The world was still there. As usual, there was a war on. *Always, things fall apart,* I could have sworn I heard the French news announcer say. I managed to make myself wait until noon. Then I called John and woke him up.

"Good God, Emma, it's five in the morning here! What's wrong?"

I thought about lying. I thought about telling the truth. I picked a middle ground. "My niece died, John," I said.

"Oh, Jesus Christ, I'm sorry. I didn't know you had a niece." I could hear him fumbling for the light or maybe his glasses. "Was she in France?"

"Yes," I said, "in Paris." Then I felt guilty. I was breaking my promise to Ilya. "John?"

"Yes?"

"Wasn't I supposed to call you today?"

"Well, actually, I think we said tomorrow. Unless it's a day later where you are."

"No," I said, "not in Paris."

"Good," John said, yawning so hard I heard his jaws crack. "Glad we settled that. Listen, I haven't been able to get anywhere with the Cinémathèque Française. I am supposed to call them again today. I was going to wait until I got to the office, and I have my big lecture this morning. Then tonight there's a screening for the class. We're watching *Rashomon*. Can I call you back?"

"I'll call you, John."

"Listen, Emma. This is crazy. Where are you staying? Can't you at least tell me that?"

I almost said, "44 Place Ste-Odile." Then I thought, I'll give you the address, but just try and find it. Except now that isn't true, if it ever had been. My brother has thrown me out.

"I'm at the Hôtel Batignolles," I said.

"Ah, the Batignolles." John sounded relieved. He, along with half the faculty, had stayed there. "Good, then I can reach you if I have time this afternoon between the class and the screening. If I find something else that might be useful. Otherwise, it will be post *Rashomon*."

"I'll try to stay put," I said. Already I was restless. I wanted to find Nolo. I had to talk to Ilya, make him listen. He had to stop taking morphine. "But if I am out, you can leave a message."

"Do you have to go to your niece's funeral?"

"Funeral?" I hadn't thought of that. I imagined Ilya at Anne-Sophie's funeral this morning surrounded only by nuns. "I don't know. I don't know the arrangements yet. Listen, John, this is costing me a fortune." I wanted to appeal to the miser I suspected lay in the hearts of all men. I was wrong.

"Your father was cheap, Emma," John said. "Ben was cheap. Not me. That's why you should let me call you back. That's why you should have married me when you had the chance." We were both silent for a moment, racking up the overseas charges. This was a lie and the truth, in complicated proportions. John had never asked me because we both knew I would have said no. For some reason I couldn't quite remember now, I hadn't wanted to be someone's third wife. Then I'd met Ben, and John had met wife three. Now even the smallest allotment of marital bliss seemed like water in the desert. I bit my lip to keep from sobbing or cursing. I honestly wasn't sure what sound was welling up in my throat. "Tricia sends her love," John said, saving us both more time hanging foolishly on the line.

"Give her mine," I said, hanging up. There was a terrible metallic taste in my mouth, as if I'd been sucking on old pennies. Was that the taste of regret? Not over John. Over Ilya. I went into the bathroom and brushed my teeth, rinsed my mouth. I brushed again. It didn't help.

After that I called information, trying to get a listing for Ilya's number. The ancient phone had rung. There was no listing for an Adrien Meis or an Ilya or Ivan Desnos, or an Ivan or I. I. Mosjoukine at any address, let alone at 44 Place Ste-Odile. Then I remembered there were no cruises today. So how was I going to find Nolo? I would go by the building where he'd had his party and try to find him that way. The dance party had seemed like a regular thing. Nolo and I would bang on Ilya's door until either the neighbor called the cops—something she would be reluctant to do—or my brother let us in. If I couldn't find Nolo, I would beat on Ilya's door by myself. But Nolo would not be hosting a dance party at noon.

I lay down on the bed on my back, crossed my ankles, and closed my eyes.

The phone rang an hour later. John must have called as soon as he got to the office. He sounded businesslike, as if he'd purposely left his office door open or a student or colleague was sitting on the other side of his desk. "No luck yet with the Cinémathèque, but there's a private collector, a film scholar. She said if you go to her apartment—she works at home—she thinks she can show you some Mosjoukine material. I'm not sure she has much, though. She said she was glad to do it for your husband."

"For my husband?"

"You told me you were finishing Ben's last book. She knew him, of course. So if you were, well, fudging a little, be careful what you say to her. She told me she had no idea he was working on Mosjoukine. She said she was very surprised to hear it."

"Okay," I said. I wasn't sure I had any reason to go see this film scholar who sounded jealous of Ben. "I'll be careful." I wrote down her name and phone number.

I had two bags full of Mosjoukine beside me on my bed. What more could she show me? But I couldn't think of anything else to keep me busy until the evening, so I called the film scholar working at home. She sounded charmed to hear from me. Yes, yes, I should come over. She would be happy to be as much help, under difficult circumstances, as she possibly could. She gave me directions to her apartment in the Marais. I pulled on the heavy black turtleneck I'd worn over on the plane. Compared to the stolen sweater I'd lost, or even Ilya's old blue one, it felt like a hair shirt. It felt like a punishment I didn't quite deserve.

I took a cab for no reason except I couldn't bear to be underground on the day when Anne-Sophie might or might not be buried. The film scholar welcomed me. She was probably in her sixties, though her hair was dyed an inky black and she was tiny, barely five feet. A pair of heavy, fiercely intellectual black-rimmed glasses balanced on her upturned nose. She looked like a librarian elf. Or maybe a French Marxist librarian elf. She kissed me on both cheeks. She was sorry, so sorry about my husband. Such a shock. She didn't mention Julia, and I didn't either, unsure whether John had not told her or whether she felt any mention of my daughter's death would be an unprofessional intrusion into my husband's personal life.

She led me into her living room, which was buried in books and equipment. It looked just like Ben's study. "I really don't have much on Mosjoukine," she apologized, pushing the glasses up on top of her head. "I thought I had more when I talked to John, honestly I did. Today, all I could find is a print of *Casanova*. It has the stencil tinted sequences, though. Have you seen those? Very lovely."

She set up the film for me on a Steenbeck, the film viewer that archives and scholars use because it doesn't stress the delicate emulsions on the old films. Watching a film on one was always like watching a movie in the world's smallest theater on the world's tiniest screen. The film scholar's Steenbeck was in one corner of what had been a kitchen, where the stove should have been. Maybe she spent her life eating out or dining with friends.

Then she left me alone in the kitchen to watch *Casanova,* in which my father made love to all the women in the world, or nearly. It was a beautiful print, a beautiful film, set in Venice during the carnival. Mosjoukine, from his powdered wig to his white shapely calves, pirouetted throughout the film, as if he had never been so happy, in love with woman after woman after woman. That was the plot, basically. He watches a sword dance performed by women artistically removing their clothes, then he carries the most beautiful from the room. All in all, the women he loved and left took it well, thinking it a wonderful part of life's game. Except the one who retired to a convent. I couldn't help but think of her as Sophie, gone off to seek paradise in Prague. In the final scene, Mosjoukine bids a tearful farewell to a girl he has rescued from her wicked guardian, and he does it with the tears for which he was famous, only to turn and see another woman on the ship he is about to board. His face lights up instantly with love as if the sun has come out from behind a dark bank of clouds.

In this, I found myself thinking, my father was like God—who, as a Father, is said to love all His children impartially. But in that case, it wasn't exactly like Mosjoukine loved me, was it? Or would have loved me, if he'd had the chance? Most of all, watching Mosjoukine reminded me of my brother, so mercurial and graceful, my brother who I was worried about, who I wanted to see. I looked at the clock on the kitchen wall. It was five, still too early for catching Nolo, but probably time to leave the film scholar to her private life.

I rewound the film, put it back in the can, and wandered into the living room to find the film scholar peering over her glasses at the contents of a folder. "Ah," she said. "There you are. I was just looking through my files. I thought I had some more Mosjoukine material here. Maybe some interviews with surviving actors from Albatross. But all I found are these," she laughed, holding up two pieces of paper. "Such strange things to have together in one file." She handed me the first, a yellowing section of newsprint. It was a page in Russian. There were ads, a couple of smeary black-and-white pictures. "It's from a paper put out by the Russian exiles," she said. She took off her glasses and tapped the page with the frames. "An obituary for Mosjoukine."

I looked more closely. I couldn't read a word of the text, but there was a photograph of Mosjoukine in a bed looking very thin, very ill.

"I would guess that's from the hospital where he died," the film scholar said. I nodded. I had no intention of telling her that Mosjoukine had, as if commanded by Jesus, taken up his bed and walked right out of the hospital and into a much longer life.

"The other is this," she tapped her glasses on the second paper. "I get the craziest mail."

"What is it?" I asked.

"Oh," she rolled her eyes. "It's a letter from a film student in Moscow claiming to have seen Ivan Mosjoukine alive and well as of," she glanced at the page in her hand, "April of last year."

"In Moscow? The letter's from Moscow?"

She nodded. "It says Mosjoukine is in a Russian orthodox monastery outside the city somewhere." She made the poofing gesture with her lips, dismissing the idea. She slipped her glasses back on. "Ridiculous, Mosjoukine died in . . ."

I finished her sentence. "1939."

"When he was, what?"

"Forty-nine," I said.

"So if he were alive now, he would be," she paused doing the math. I let her. I was thinking *Moscow*. She laughed again. "He would be 112."

That stopped me. I heard Ilya's voice: *Then one day I counted up the years and realized the son of a bitch must be dead.*

"Could I have a copy of the letter? I'm interested in how strongly people identify with dead film stars, with someone they've only seen in movies, never in real life." I was babbling. I was talking about me. She pursed her lips as if considering this, then nodded, *Why not?* And went off to the kitchen to the copier I'd seen next to the sink where a refrigerator should have been.

She gave me the copy of the letter, as warm as if she had just popped it out of the toaster. She gave me her card. She slipped off her glasses again, and we kissed cheeks.

I waited until I was outside to read the letter. It was in French:

DEAR MADAME:

I saw your short article on the films of Ivan Mosjoukine, the great Russian silent film actor, and I thought you might want to send a researcher to Moscow to interview him. He is living under the name of Father Ivan at the Monastery of St. Stefan and receives visitors on Thursdays and Fridays from noon until two. I happened to go to the monastery with my grandmother and recognized him at once. I hope you will take advantage of this opportunity. If you need any assistance, please feel free to contact me.

I also thought you might be interested in this poem by the constructivist artist and filmmaker Vladimir Mayakovsky, which records the reaction of the new Soviet filmmakers to the old style, prerevolutionary Russian cinema. Personally, I cannot agree with his assessment of Mosjoukine.

Cinema and cinema

For you, cinema is a spectacle.
For me, it is a design of the world.
Cinema is the vehicle of movement.
Cinema is the innovator of literature.
Cinema is the destroyer of aesthetics.

Cinema is intrepid.
Cinema is a sportsman.
Cinema is the diffuser of ideas.

But the cinema is sick. Capitalism threw gold dust in its eyes. Cunning contractors parade it through the streets. Pile up money by stirring the heart with tiny weepy plots.

That must end.

Communism must tear the cinema from the hands of the speculators.

Futurism must evaporate the stagnant water of slowness and false morality.

If not, we will have more imported slapstick from America or the eternally tearful eyes of Mosjoukine.

Of these two, the first annoys us.
The second is even worse.

A poem by Mayakovsky insulting Mosjoukine. I wondered if Sophie had ever seen it. I had never imagined the Red cinema of the future firing a salvo at a different sort of reigning czar. But I was more interested in the present. I turned over the letter. There was no return address, and the film scholar hadn't offered an envelope. Even the signature, which must have been on a second page, was missing. Could Mosjoukine possibly be alive? Or was what I had said to the film scholar true—this was a person too interested in Mosjoukine for his own good. *Someone like you,* I imagined Ilya saying.

The Mayakovsky poem reminded me of something I'd forgotten until then, a much better known bit of film history, one still taught in every beginning film class as the Kuleshov Effect.

The Soviet filmmaker Lev Kuleshov had taken stock footage of a bowl of soup, a dead child, and a beautiful, nearly naked woman and spliced them in after close-ups of an actor's face. The actor, I remembered now, had been Ivan Mosjoukine. Then Kuleshov showed the clips to audiences who were convinced Mosjoukine's unchanging face conveyed completely different emotions depending on the image that followed, saying he was starving, grief-stricken, or full of lust and longing. According to Kuleshov, it proved that editing was king, that the film editor controlled the audience. Acting was dead. That actor, the dead one, had been the great Mosjoukine.

Was he dead now? He hadn't been in 1939, I knew that much. He'd gotten my mother pregnant in 1959 and had abandoned Ilya in 1972. Kuleshov was right in one way. Context *was* everything. I looked at Mosjoukine in his films and saw what I needed to see: a loving father. As an observer, I couldn't be trusted. I looked at the letter again. Was it that I needed to find him alive or at least believe he might be? The Monastery of St. Stefan. *Moscow.* Impossible, but I had to go and see. Not only that, but I wanted Ilya to go with me.

15

I WENT STRAIGHT TO 44 PLACE STE-ODILE, ready to bang with knuckle, fist, and boot on the door. But I didn't have to. Ilya had just come home and was unlocking the front door as I crossed the courtyard. He heard me but didn't turn around. We'd played in this courtyard as children. We were here still. I wanted to play again, to be Ilya's adored little sister. I put my hands over his eyes. "Guess who?" I said.

"Emma," Ilya said. I flinched. Siblings knew where to stick the knife, where the soft underbelly was hidden, but you had to be tough and take that.

"Ouch," I said, making a joke of it, trying to keep this light enough to charm my way through the door and up the stairs. "But wrong." I didn't move my hands. Ilya was feeling around for the doorknob, trying to fit the key into the lock. I pressed my thumbs, hard, against his eyes.

"Vera?" he said this time.

"Bingo," I said. He lifted my hands from his eyes. He turned around, letting my left hand drop, holding my right hand in his. He looked awful. A blood vessel had burst in one eye, and the red had spread across the white next to the deep blue of his iris, spread too far for me to have just done it with my thumbs. He saw me looking at it and shrugged.

"The tricolor," he said, meaning the French flag: blue, white, and red.

"Are you angry that I came back?" I asked him.

He shook his head. "But it would have been better for both of us if you hadn't. You should have flown home to America on the next plane. After yesterday, anyone with sense would have."

"I'm your twin sister. You can't expect me to have more sense than you do."

He frowned. "You should never have come to Paris." He sounded like Apolline.

I shook my head. "Once you start that, the regrets never stop. Maybe it would have been better if we'd never been born."

"Don't say that," Ilya said. He squeezed my fingers, let them drop. "Be glad you're alive. I am."

"In spite of everything?"

"Yes," he said. "But I still wish you'd gone home."

Then he let me come upstairs, a greater concession than our mother had granted our father. We went into the kitchen. The coffee pot was back on the stove, although the wall by the bathroom still boasted a long rusty brown stain. Ilya opened a bottle of wine and poured us each a glass.

I thought about it, then broke his rule about not mentioning Anne-Sophie. I risked a glass of wine in the face, another trip down the stairs and back to the Hôtel Batignolles. "Was there a funeral?" I asked. "Or will there be?"

Ilya didn't throw anything, just shook his head. "I signed the papers for the Mother Superior," he said. He took a deep breath. "They baptized her; they cared for her. They want to bury her in the cemetery with their order of nuns. She belonged to them, really. Not me."

"Did someone tell her mother?"

"Barbara?" he said. "Yes, I called this morning. The nuns had her number."

"What did she say?"

Ilya raised one shoulder, let it drop, then did it again as if one shrug in a case like this could never be enough. "She said she appreciated my letting her know." He took a long drink of his wine. "She said she hadn't realized Anne-Sophie was still alive. Such a long time, she said. Unusual." He filled his glass again.

"What a bitch," I said. "How could she not have known her daughter was alive?"

Ilya waved a hand, like Ben had after my parents' deaths. *Let it go, let it go.*

"*Bitch,*" I said again, because he wouldn't. Then I fixed us dinner, though Ilya was suspicious of what I put on his plate. "It isn't an omelet," I said, trying not to sound defensive. "It's scrambled eggs. In America, we make them this way on purpose." Then, when we were done, I showed him my copy of the letter the film scholar had found.

143

He read it, handed it back to me. "That's interesting," he said.

"Interesting, as in that's unbelievable because no one lives to be 112? Or interesting, as in you think it's true and that's our dear old dad?"

"At the home where Anne-Sophie lives," he corrected himself, "*lived,* there's a woman who's 114. I don't think she's even the oldest woman in France. But Mosjoukine isn't 112. He told me he lied about his age when he ran away from home to act on the stage. He added ten years to his age. He didn't want juvenile roles; he wanted to play serious parts. So he's only 102."

"Then you think it might be true?"

"No, I don't. Mosjoukine has been dead for years. I'm certain of it. Otherwise, he would have turned up here. He was a man of habit, our father." Ilya sighed. "Want to risk coffee?" he asked me. "I promise not to throw it at your head."

"Okay," I said, though this reminded me of the syringe in the trash can. It reminded him, too. "We still need to talk about that, you know."

Ilya looked at me with his lips pursed, his eyes narrowed, that expression you see on Parisian faces at the market as they size up the worth of a chicken, the freshness of an artichoke. Then he said, "All right, little sister, but later. First, what do you want to do about this letter?"

"Go to Moscow," I said. "And I want you to go with me."

"No," Ilya said, without a second's hesitation. He was adding the ground coffee to the bent pot. "Absolutely not."

"Why not?"

"Mosjoukine's dead. I told you that. Even if he isn't—and *he is*—he's dead to me. If he sent me a postcard, a birthday card, an engraved invitation to Moscow, it wouldn't make any difference."

Postcard. The word tickled something in the very back of my head. I went to the living room to get my purse and dug out Apolline's postcard of Mosjoukine. The photo, I recognized now, was from about the same year as *L'Enfant du Carnaval,* 1925, maybe 1926. I'd assumed it was a souvenir Mosjoukine had sent to Apolline or maybe to Sophie, who had, in turn, passed it on to her when they were roommates. I turned the card over.

Now I could recognize my father's handwriting, the same huge looping letters of the autographs on the photos, *Ivan Mosjoukine.* But it was still a puzzle trying to make out the words of the message, the letters so large and stylized. *Bonne Année,* I decided. Happy New Year. The card had no other greeting or salutation, no *Dear Apolline* or *My Sophie.* Also no address. The message and signature filled the entire back, so if it had ever been mailed, it must have been sent in an envelope, maybe along with a letter. But it did have a date. I looked closer, thought I could make out a looping *2 0 0 0.* I blinked, but the numbers stayed the same, which meant the card had been written by Mosjoukine—not in 1926 or even 1957, the year of our conception—but just last year. Sent, I was guessing, from Moscow to New York, as a New Year's greeting from an old friend.

If so, Apolline had known all along Mosjoukine was alive and well in Russia. She had kept her mouth shut, just as she had about the existence of my twin brother. Instead, she sent me after Sophie. I took the card into the kitchen, showed it to Ilya. "Why would she do that?" I said. "Not tell me this came from Moscow last year?"

"If it did," Ilya said. He flipped the card onto the table. "She wouldn't want you going there any more than I do. What do you think you'll find? A senile old man who shouts, *Girl, come closer!* Do you think he is going to remember who you are? Who you are out of all the children he fathered? You're going to get your heart broken. Either that, or you will find out this Father Ivan is some total stranger and find out that Mosjoukine has been dead thirty years. Is that what you want? More weeping? More ghosts standing next to you when the next gypsy reads your fortune?"

"No," I said, leaving the card of Mosjoukine where it lay on the table, but doubling my bet. "I just want an ending. Come with me. We might find him alive. We might find him dead. You, Ivan Ilyich Desnos, can spit on his grave or in his old wrinkled face if that's what you want. Then it will be over. I promise it will be over. I promise to turn my face to the future and never look back."

"You promise?" He sounded doubtful.

I crossed my heart. "And you can, too, Ilya. Start over. Please, brother, I can't do this without you."

He sighed. The coffee pot wheezed steam, boiling away on the stove. "All right," he said. "I'll go with you to Moscow. Besides, I'm not sure I trust you to make the trip by yourself, as crazy as you've been. But I won't see him. You can do that part alone."

"I could make the trip alone, Brother," I said. "I just don't want to. I found you. I can find him, if it is him. But you," I reached across the table and took my only brother's hand, "you can't keep on with the morphine. You know where that will get you. You know." I looked at him, but he was looking at the floor. "I don't know how long you've been using it, but you have to stop."

"Not long," Ilya said, but faintly. "The morphine, not long at all. It will stop. I promise." He took both my hands in his. "After Moscow."

"After Moscow," I said, and we shook on it.

16

"YOU HAVE A CREDIT CARD, YES?" my brother asked after we had finished our coffee.

"All Americans have credit cards." I emphasized the plural. "Even the poor ones. Like Europeans have passports or identity cards. In America, you are your credit rating."

Ilya raised an eyebrow. "So we can use one to buy plane tickets for Moscow? We should fly."

"Yes," I said. "We can do that."

"Good. I have a friend, Pavel, in Moscow from my fencing days," Ilya said. "We can stay at his place."

I thought about Aunt Z. "I'd rather stay at a hotel."

Ilya shrugged. It was my money. "Okay, he can arrange that, too. He has connections. He did in the old days, and he still does. He's one of the coaches of their fencing team. He can advise us about the tickets and visas."

"You still need a visa to go to Moscow?" I had imagined the wall of bureaucratic paperwork fallen along with the one in Berlin. "I can go anywhere in the EU without so much as showing my passport."

"Russia is still Russia," Ilya said. "Czar or commissar or capitalist—Russians don't trust foreigners."

Ilya put our coffee cups in the sink and went to the telephone to call his friend. Things had changed that much. In the Soviet days, Ilya hadn't been able to get a letter through to our mother in Prague, let along ring her up from her old kitchen. "Pasha, my friend!" Ilya said, then added something in Russian, a language I could guess now he had learned in school in Czechoslovakia.

Then Ilya switched to French, and I listened as he asked how quickly we could get visas. Ilya nodded, listening to the answer. "I'll check," he said, covering the mouthpiece with one hand and turning to me. "Pavel says he knows a travel agent in Paris who can get us visas by tomorrow, but the overnight charge is five hundred euros."

The price of a pair of Jean Gabot boots. "For both?"

"For each." He looked at me, trying to read my face. After all, the trip was my idea. "Okay?"

In for a penny, in for a thousand euros. "Okay, then," I said, nodding.

Ilya wrote down the address of the travel agent. "Okay, Pasha," he said to his friend over the phone. "I'll be in touch." He hung up, coughing. He bent for a moment with his hands on his knees, then straightened up. "We'll have to hurry. Our visa applications have to be done by eight."

"I'm ready."

Ilya ran his hands over his face. He looked pale, the circles under his eyes so dark they looked painful. "Give me a minute."

He disappeared into the bathroom. I washed the cups and the coffee pot, splashing water in the sink to make him think I was too busy to know what he was doing. No more morphine after Moscow, he had promised, but first we had to get there.

When he came out of the bathroom, Ilya looked as if he'd had a blood transfusion instead of a syringe full of morphine, his color was so much better. He looked like my brother again, also like our father, that cat with nine lives. Ilya smiled, reborn for now. "Okay," he said, rubbing his hands together. "Visas."

The travel agency was in Belleville, not far from where we'd gone to dance in Nolo's basement. The windows were papered over with posters offering special rates on flights to the countries in Africa that had been French colonies and to Poland, Russia, and Vietnam, all the homelands of Paris's working poor. Ilya opened the door, waved me in ahead of him.

The travel agent was on the phone and motioned for us to sit in the chairs across from her. I'd been expecting her to be Russian, but she was African, nearly as dark as Nolo, and she was beautiful, her head shaved and polished, her brown eyes the shape of a cat's. When she hung up, she leaned across the desk and touched my brother's hand lightly. I'd been slow to realize it, but this time it struck me how women were drawn to Ilya—Polish grandmothers, French tarot readers, and schoolteachers from Nice alike.

"I'm Ceci," the travel agent announced. She nodded to me, then turned, smiling, to Ilya. "How do you know Pavel?" she asked him.

"We fenced together. Drank vodka together."

Ceci laughed.

"And you?" my brother asked.

"Oh, I met him when I was in Moscow on scholarship. I'm from Angola. In the old days, I was a good Marxist. Or at least as good as I had to be." She smiled at Ilya again, resting her white teeth on her dark red lower lip. She said something to him in Russian, and my brother, fellow child communist, said something back. They both laughed. I felt a sudden flush of irritation at being shut out.

I cleared my throat. "I assume I can charge the visas to my credit card as well as the plane tickets?" I said, realizing as I did that I was throwing my plastic money on the table to show who was in charge.

Ceci turned her lovely cat eyes in my direction. "Of course, dear," she said. "But first, there is paperwork." She looked at Ilya again, gave a little shrug of apology. "Always for Russia, there is paperwork."

She left us at her desk with a stack of forms and two pens while she tapped away on a computer in the back, booking our flight.

"There's no need to be jealous," Ilya said.

"I'm not jealous," I said. "You're my brother." Though as soon as Ilya said the word, I knew he'd put his finger on the absurd inappropriateness of what I'd been feeling. If he was channeling Mosjoukine, I was playing the possessive Sophie. And neither of us were our parents. I tapped my pen on the visa application. "Okay," I said. "Point taken, but I just want us to get this done in time."

The application was a long one, with questions still full of Soviet Cold War paranoia, such as "Do you have any specialized skills, training, or experience related to firearms, explosives, or nuclear, biological, or chemical activities?" Another asked for "Other names ever used (maiden, family, pen-name, stage name, holy orders, etc.)?" What would Mosjoukine have put down for that one?

Ilya held out his application so I could copy Pavel's name as the person who was inviting us to Russia. I had circled "widowed" under marital status.

149

I noticed Ilya circled "divorced." After "Have you ever abused drugs or been a drug addict?" I saw he had firmly circled "No." An even more heavily inked "No" followed "Do you have family in Russia? If so, who?"

I'd circled "No" for that one, too. A "Yes" seemed too complicated to explain (as in "my father—maybe"), but I felt guilty about it. Ilya, I suspected, did not.

"Good," Ceci said, looking over the applications after she came back from the computer. Then she stood us against the wall and took Polaroid head shots of us. "Here are your tickets. I have you booked for an evening flight tomorrow, so let's hope the embassy staff is wide awake tonight. With luck, we should have your visas by tomorrow afternoon."

"Thank you," I said.

Ilya said nothing. He looked tired.

"You are most welcome," Ceci said. She shook my hand; then she kissed Ilya on both cheeks.

By the next afternoon, the visas were ready. Ceci phoned to say she was sending a messenger from the agency over with them. I took the call, then I let myself out and waited by the entrance to the Place Ste-Odile for fear he couldn't find it. Ilya had gotten up early, then gone back to bed. All morning, I'd watched the neighbor through the living room window. She'd had customers, but Ilya, who I'd heard coughing off and on in his room, was not one of them.

When I got back to the apartment with the visas, Ilya was up and packing his rucksack with its usual load of bread, chocolate, and bananas. We had finished all the wine. He added a pair of jeans and a shirt. He watched as I put my clean underwear, socks, and toothbrush in my purse. It was getting to be a habit for me, this leaving one country for another with next to nothing. Ilya frowned at my purse-as-suitcase, then stuffed another pair of jeans in his pack. "That way we won't fight over who gets the clean clothes," he said, poking me in the ribs with one finger.

At five, Ilya and I left for the airport. I made us take a taxi. I said it was because our flight left in just a few hours, and it was a long way on the RER to Charles de Gaulle. Ilya was as pale as he had been that morning.

By eight, we were on the plane to Moscow. It was entirely too easy. No long, snaking lines. I said so to Ilya.

He laughed. "You would have loved the trip in the old days. When Sophie brought me by train from Paris, and we crossed the border into Czechoslovakia, they made us all get off the train. Made us get our bags off as well. There were guards with shiny black boots and Alsatian shepherds. I was so frightened. To me they looked like the Gestapo in the American war movies. Sophie wasn't frightened; she'd seen the real thing. The guards lined us up by the track and went up and down, searching and sniffing, while other guards checked under the carriages with mirrors and up inside the ceiling, everywhere anything could be hidden.

"Later, I understood if we had been going the other way, they would have been looking for people. It happened. There were always people desperate enough to try. But going east, it was books, pictures, magazines, cameras. You were not allowed to have cameras. I had an American comic book Mosjoukine had given me, the Justice League of America. Do you know them? Aquaman, the Green Lantern." He pointed at me, "Wonder Woman," then at himself, "Superman." I laughed. "Well, of course, they took that away. Also a book of Sophie's about the French Resistance. They were very suspicious. We stood there for what seemed like forever. I remember it started to rain.

"Then a special guard came down the line to stamp our passports. He had this briefcase strapped around his chest that flipped open and made a little desk. It had a light built into it. He looked just like a robot. I was sure he was a robot. It's a Czech word, but I didn't know that then. *Robota*—it means drudgery, compulsory work. The guard took our passports and he stamped and stamped, all over every page, as if he were killing ants, as if he were blotting out the people we had been.

"Finally we piled back into the cars, but I slowed Sophie down, and by the time we got on, there was barely room to stand, let alone sit. We were jammed on top of our suitcases inside the door to the WC. I kept telling her it smelled bad, like pee-pee, I was saying, and she kept telling me she agreed, but that there was nothing she could do about it. Then one of conductors came and got us. He took us to the conductors' compartment. Word had gotten around that Sophie was immigrating, that she was such a good party member she was coming to live the kind of life they led. I think they were flattered. I think they thought she was crazy.

"So they gave her vodka and me chocolate and put a conductor's hat on me. She was beautiful then, you know, our mother. They couldn't take their eyes off her. When it got dark, they let me sleep in one of the bunks that were reserved for them. Sophie sat up telling them they were lucky, so lucky to be building a new world, the Czech socialist workers' paradise. Listening to her, I think they almost believed it."

We were sitting side by side, and Ilya held my hand while he told me this story, as if we were Hansel and Gretel left in the forest by a father who couldn't feed us and a stepmother who wouldn't allow us back. A fairy tale too close to the truth, in our case. Somewhere over Poland, my brother fell asleep. But I didn't let go of his hand until we had our wheels on the ground.

We landed in Moscow just before midnight, but Sheremetyevo Airport was locked up tight. Not a kiosk or food stall was open. We followed our fellow passengers into a dingy basement and stood in the passport control line. A bored and sleepy official fingered our newly acquired visas and then stamped our passports. At customs, none of the three agents on duty seemed interested in searching my purse or Ilya's rucksack, though they descended on a poor African from our flight. Free to enter Russia, we wandered across the terminal, walking in a daze side by side. Then I heard someone whistle, high, shrill. "Ilya!" a man shouted. Ilya was slower. I poked him. A man with a silvery Elvis pompadour came toward us. He was as wide and tall as a door, but a whole lot thicker. Now Ilya saw him, too. For this friend he opened his arms. They hugged, Ilya clapping his friend on the back. Pavel, his Russian friend, rubbed the knuckles of his right hand on Ilya's head. Ilya let go first. He waved a hand at me.

"Pasha," he said, "meet Vera. Vera, meet Pavel."

"Enchanted," Pavel said with a much better French accent than mine. He looked around. "No luggage?"

Ilya shook his head. "We're living out of our pockets." Pavel laughed, as if this were either a joke or maybe an expression in Russian for traveling on nothing but raw nerves.

"Well, come on then," he said. "The car is parked right outside. I don't want to have to bribe the security guy twice."

Pavel's Mercedes was parked half up on the curb. Three security guards stood nearby, but when they saw it was Pavel, they all studiously looked away. Ilya got in the front seat, me in the back, and before I could figure out if there were seat belts or how to work them, Pavel put the car in gear, floored it, and we shot off the curb and into traffic as if someone had waved the checkered flag. The acceleration flattened me against the seat. "I didn't know you knew how to drive, Pasha," I heard Ilya say with what I thought was a light touch of irony.

"I didn't when I saw you last, Vanya," Pavel said. Someone cut in front of us, and Pavel stomped on the brakes, then just as rapidly put his entire weight back on the gas. "But I took lessons." Ilya laughed, took a pack of cigarettes from the ashtray in the dashboard, lit one with Pavel's lighter, then calmly smoked the rest of the hair-raising trip into town.

As we got closer to Moscow, I wiped the window with my sleeve and tried to see the buildings as we passed. This was our father's country. I expected to feel a tug at my heart strings, maybe to hear my Slavic blood start to sing. It looked vaguely familiar, but half because of old pictures I'd seen in *National Geographic*—an onion-domed church was illuminated in the distance—and half because the concrete apartment blocks looked like the same depressing structures that ringed Paris, marred Belleville, filled so many of the world's other cities. "The monastery where you are headed is south of town," Pavel was saying. "So I got you a suite in a nice old hotel just out of the center." We turned off the larger road into what seemed to be an older part of the city. "It's run by my cousin's nephew."

"Your cousin's nephew?" Ilya said.

"Well, my cousin's nephew's cousin," Pavel said. Then they both laughed, as if this were code for some deal that was vaguely shady. It felt late. It was suddenly all too hard for me to follow. In the front seat, Ilya started to cough, then seemed to stop himself through a sheer application of will. He threw his lit cigarette out the window.

"Russian cigarettes," Pavel said, shaking his head. "Everyone else buys American now, but I still like a smoke with a kick." He slammed on the brakes, and Ilya pitched forward, nearly slamming his nose into the dash. I looked out the window. We had stopped in front of a stone building with red velvet curtains in the windows like the ones in Mosjoukine's apartment, though these looked new. The sign on the awning read, *Hotel Sputnik.* "Your hotel," Pavel said. Ilya got out, opened my door.

I stepped out, and for a moment, maybe because of Pavel's driving, maybe because of the secondhand smoke from Ilya's Russian cigarette, I couldn't remember what I was doing in Moscow, the second capital city I had flown to in ten days.

"What time do you want me to pick you up for the monastery?" Pavel said, feeding me my lines like a stage prompter.

"Noon," Ilya said. "His Holiness holds court after lunch. And it's only Vera. So try and think of something else for you and me to do instead."

"Something amusing, Vanya, or something good for you?" Pavel asked.

"Vera's the one in charge of redemption," Ilya said. "So I guess amusement is the right answer to that."

17

PAVEL CAME AT 11:30 THE NEXT MORNING. Ilya had just gotten up and was sitting in the living room eating the breakfast that room service sent up, a boiled egg in a brightly painted egg cup, sliced cucumbers, and a pot of strong black tea. Our room, thanks to Pavel, was a large, two-bedroom suite done almost entirely in stiff new red velvet furniture that was a modern imitation of the mahogany that clogged Mosjoukine's apartment. The Hotel Sputnik, in spite of its name, was trying its best to appear more czarist than Soviet. Ilya was ignoring me, reading or pretending to read the morning paper in Russian. Pavel came pounding in with greetings in French and kisses for me, a crushing hug for my brother. He swept me out of the room with one huge arm around my shoulders. Ilya, he said, he would come back for.

When we were again in his car and vaulting out into traffic, he said, "I've checked out this Father Ivan you're going to see. He's the talk of Moscow, or so my girlfriend Kisa says. She has a taste for all this monarchist Orthodox bullshit."

"What did she tell you?"

"First, that he's a schema monk."

"A what?"

"Schema monk. Yeah, I had no idea what that was either. It's a sort of monk superstar, a special high rank granted by the bishop to a monk willing to surrender his life to save people's souls. He becomes a walking icon, wears some kind of special robe with crosses and other mystical craziness on it. Kisa called them 'Angels in the flesh.' Apparently a schema is usually very old, someone who has struggled long and hard in the monastic life. Does that sound like your guy?"

I remembered Mosjoukine carrying the naked sword dancer offscreen in *Casanova*. "No," I said, "except he is old."

Pavel shrugged. "Maybe it's not the same guy."

"Maybe not," I said, knowing Pavel—and Ilya—were right to doubt the connection between Mosjoukine and Father Ivan. The more I heard, the less possible it seemed. But Ilya hadn't seen our father in nearly thirty years. Maybe that was long enough for even Mosjoukine to become a living saint.

"Here," Pavel took one hand off the wheel and tossed me a cell phone. I caught it. "Just press one. It's preset for my number," he said. "I'm going to drop you off and when you are done, call me and wait inside the monastery until I come. This is a bit out in the country, and call me a city boy, but I never think you can trust the damn peasants."

It didn't look like we were out in the country. It looked only a little less built up than Belleville or Batignolles, though the street was narrow and filled with the deepest potholes I'd ever seen in a paved road. The monastery took up a whole block, with a high wall around it topped with a wicked combination of curved spikes, barbed wire, and broken glass. Pavel slammed to a stop in front of a large wooden gate. A small door, set in the larger one, stood open, and a monk in a long black robe stood there helping a steady stream of people, mostly old women, step over the threshold. I'd been wondering how I would explain who I was looking for, but now it seemed all I had to do was follow the crowd.

"Okay?" Pavel said. He had one foot on the brake, the other on the gas, and the engine was racing. "Somebody will speak either French or English. They get all kinds of pilgrims."

"Okay," I said, opening the passenger door, stepping out.

"Don't forget the phone!" Pavel said, then he took his foot off the brake and, like a gas-powered meteor, he was gone.

The monk spotted me and held out his hand. He had a long black beard and equally long hair that was parted firmly in the middle. His hair was shiny with grease, like either it was against his faith to wash it or he had slicked it down with holy Vaseline. He wore a large silver cross on a chain around his neck. He said something in Russian and, holding my elbow, led me inside, through an inner courtyard. The pavement inside held the melting snow and the spring rain like a wading pool. We splashed through one long muddy puddle. We passed a line of old women in babushkas and men with canes, sprinkled here and there with a teenager in jeans or a better-dressed woman in a fur hat and coat. The monk took me to the head of the line, using one elbow to push a man on crutches back far enough to install me in front of the door to a large stone building that was the monastery itself. Then he bowed. He stood there, bowing again. I finally realized what he was waiting for, opened my purse, and gave him a tip. Or was it a donation? All I had were euros, but that seemed fine with the monk. He tucked the money somewhere inside his sleeve, then picked his way across the courtyard to the gate, trying to hold his robes up out of the flood.

From the rear of the compound, church bells began to ring. They sounded different than western bells, more like giant gongs, and they tolled first a simple deep rhythm, then an increasingly complicated one, the way an African drummer might, without ever breaking into anything I would have called a tune. Then they stopped. Noon. The doors in front of me opened, and I stepped from the bright courtyard into a space that was both large and dim. As I hesitated, a rush of people pushed past me, forming into ranks near the front of the room. I hurried, too, then, grabbing a place in about the tenth row. There was scuffling as the room behind me filled in. I looked around. It wasn't a church. It had no altar, no icons. It looked more like a dining hall, long and narrow, with the only windows high up in the walls. It looked remarkably like the gym at the fencing club, except the wooden floor under my feet, instead of gleaming, was so worn, rutted, and dirty that it looked as if cattle or horses had been stabled there.

I wasn't sure what would happen now. Would Father Ivan come in to give a sermon? Could a 102-year-old man talk to a crowd this size without loud speakers? I looked around, but there was no sign of a pulpit, with or without a microphone. I heard, but didn't see, a door open at the front of the hall, beyond the rows of standing pilgrims, then the rubbery squeaking sound of a wheelchair. Half the crowd shifted to the left, as if they knew where the action was going to take place. For one brief moment, before the other half did the same, I could see through the faithful. A tall young monk was pushing someone across the room in the wheelchair. I caught a glimpse of a gray, nearly bald head bent forward on a chest covered by a long white beard. Mostly what I saw was a black robe stiff with elaborate embroidery—a giant, almost cartoonlike cross and, surrounding it, other designs that were harder to make out. I thought I saw Longinus's spear and oversized nails—spikes really—from the crucifixion. Dense rows of Russian text snaked between the images, making the robe look like a page from a grim comic book. The heavy robe covered the man, trailed down from the wheelchair, giving a pyramidal shape to what otherwise seemed a shapeless thing.

From the front of the room came a sharp order in Russian, and about half the people in the room prostrated themselves, kneeling and pressing their faces to the floor as if we were in a mosque. Over their bent backs, I got an even clearer look at Father Ivan. But was it Mosjoukine? His head was as overlarge as a baby bird's and was bobbing slightly, never really rising from his chest. I couldn't see his eyes. The young monk stood behind him with a couple of older monks, though neither was nearly as ancient as Father Ivan. The woman next to me reached up and grabbed the hem of my black sweater and tried to pull me down to the floor. I stayed standing. One of the monks recited a prayer, and everyone around me mumbled along. I guessed that some, after the decades of atheist communism, had as little experience at being Russian Orthodox as I did. But the older women seemed to have the hang of it. When the prayer was over, the people who had prostrated themselves stood.

Then nothing happened, or so it seemed. We stood. I couldn't see anything but the gray, permed hair of the woman in front of me. No one was speaking. The room smelled strongly of wet leather and drying wool socks. I thought about easing my puddle-soaked feet out of my boots. Then we all moved two steps to the left. After about five more minutes, we did it again. It was nearly automatic. I was moved by the people on either side of me without any effort on my part.

When I reached the end of the row, I saw a woman and a boy with a hugely misshapen head pass by in the company of one of the brothers, headed for the door to the courtyard. Father Ivan must be seeing pilgrims one by one, somewhere in front of the ranks. Now, hands pushed me forward, into the next row of pilgrims and then we all slid right two steps, then again and again until I reached the end of that row. Then I was pushed by hands behind me up into the next, one closer to whatever dispensation we were all seeking.

I was kicking myself for my hesitation at the door. I had been first in line, thanks to the monk with the sharp eye for an American tourist. If I hadn't been so stupid, I would have seen Father Ivan up close by now. One way or the other, I would know. I sneaked a peek at the watch on the wrist of the woman next to me. Already it was nearly one. I had moved up one row, with eight to go. If the monks held to this schedule, it seemed unlikely I would get anywhere near Father Ivan before the audience was over for the day at two.

I couldn't do anything about it. If I had to, I would come back to try it all again tomorrow. I closed my eyes, letting the eager bodies of my fellow pilgrims move me sideways, then forward. Seven rows to go. The pace of the audiences picked up now, the impatience in the room palpable. Six rows. In front of me, one woman shifted, but the man next to her, asleep on his feet, snoring loudly, did not, and I saw, as through a window, the front of the room and Father Ivan, who was much closer now.

I saw him put a gnarled claw of a hand on the bent head of the woman kneeling in front of him, then he looked up. His glance was the beam from a lighthouse cutting through a foggy night. I almost flinched as it moved down the row of believers. Then it touched me. *Mosjoukine.* There was no doubt about it. His eyes had not lost one bit of the power they had in his movies. They were large in his face and blue as deep water. His gaze stopped, sharpened as if his eyes were focusing for the first time. I thought, he knows who I am or at least he knows who I look like. *Him.*

Then the other pilgrims in row five shifted the sleeping man to fill the gap and just like that, my father was gone. I started to push my way forward, breaking ranks. The woman who had tried to make me prostrate myself shouted something in Russian, grabbed my sweater, and stretched it, but before she could do anything more, the tall young monk was there. Come to toss me out, I assumed. My row mate let go of my sweater. Instead, the monk said, in perfect California-flat English, "Can you come with me? Father Ivan wants to see you."

He led me out of the hall, across the wet courtyard, toward a low, modern building. "I'm Brother Paul," he said. Paul, not Pavel.

"You're American," I said.

"San Diego," he said.

"How in the world did you end up here?"

"How did you?" he said. That stopped me. I opened my mouth, shut it.

We went into the new building, which was some kind of central office. On the desks were a hodgepodge of computers—Macs, old PCs. Brother Paul unlocked a door beyond the office. Inside was a small waiting room with a couch, coffee table, chairs, and piles of old magazines like in a doctor's office. He gestured at the couch. "Make yourself comfortable. It may be a while."

It was more than a while. Just like in the reception room, the only windows were high up in the wall, and these were shaped like slits for pouring hot oil down on invaders. The whole monastery seemed to have been built for defense like a castle. I flipped through a two-year-old *Time* magazine and a *Paris Match*. Nothing in the room was in Russian except a pamphlet that, to judge by the pictures, looked like it might be the history of the monastery. There were old black-and-white photographs of other schema monks, or so I judged from their advanced age and their robes, each embroidered with a giant cross, but no picture of Father Ivan. Each copy had an envelope attached—a plea for donations?

After I'd been through all the magazines, one of the brothers, this one short and Russian, brought me tea and a plate of stiff, chewy-looking cheese sandwiches. I had just been thinking about setting out to find Father Ivan on my own. After putting my tea on the coffee table, the short monk showed me there was a bathroom at the other end of the waiting room by opening the door, turning on the light long enough for me to see the toilet, then turning it off again. Then he left. When he did, I heard the click of a lock. So much for wandering around the monastery unescorted.

I drank the tea. I picked the cheese out of the sandwiches and ate it. I stretched out on the couch and tried to take a nap, not really thinking I would fall asleep, but I did. When I woke up, I could tell it was late. The slit windows were dark. I went into the bathroom and washed my face. The seam on the vinyl couch had left a nasty red crease on one side of my face, like a Prussian dueling scar. I decided I had better dig Pavel's cell phone out of my purse and call. Ilya would be worried. Or I hoped he would be. I was worried. Just then, the lock clicked. Brother Paul was back.

"Sorry," he said. "Father Ivan had to rest. The audiences are very draining. He'll see you now." Brother Paul fixed his calm brown Californian eyes on me, as if weighing my intentions or maybe my soul. "He's an example for us all, living so long in the faith. He suffered terribly under the communists, you know."

I nodded. Stalin killed his father, he'd told Ilya, but I didn't think Brother Paul was talking about that.

I followed the tall monk out into the night, across the courtyard, and back into the deserted hall. He led me through the door at the far end, down one corridor, then another, through door after door. I was beginning to wish I'd saved the sandwich crusts for bread crumbs, when he opened a small paneled door and, ducking low, went into a room. I was right behind him. The room was nearly bare. Was this a monk's cell? Probably. Except instead of the narrow cot or slab of wood I expected, there was an old-fashioned hospital bed with a hand crank at one end. The head of the bed was raised, and a hospital tray of food was swung over the middle. Sitting up, eating his soup, was my father.

He put his spoon down, and his eyes hit me again, hot as the sun. God, he was good. When he was looking at me, the image I had of the old man with a head lolling like a bald baby bird dropped away. Instead I saw him as he used to be, as he was in *Kean* and *Michel Strogoff*, intelligent, handsome, discerning, with eyes that seemed both wise and ironic, decisive and soulful. No wonder Apolline insisted he was not old when he was with my mother, insisted that he was handsome and desirable. Ilya was charismatic, but Mosjoukine was hypnotic. No wonder he had been a star among stars.

Brother Paul put a stool by the bed and waved for me to sit down. Then he let himself out of the room. Father Ivan aka Ivan Ilyich Mosjoukine held out a slightly shaky hand, "Hello, my dear," he said in Russian-accented French. "Which one are you?"

I took his hand. The bones were so light inside the wrinkled skin, I felt I could crush them like so many potato chips, hurt him if I so much as sneezed, but his grip on my fingers was strong, pure will overcoming the limitations of flesh. No wonder he had lived to be 102. He was stronger than I would ever be. "I'm Anne-Sophie Desnos's daughter."

"Ah," he said, keeping his eyes on mine, not letting me look away. "Little Vera. Did you find your brother?"

"Yes," I said. "He's in Moscow with me, but he wouldn't come. He hasn't forgiven you for leaving."

Mosjoukine laughed softly, his voice a bit hoarse. When he did, he closed his eyes and the effect was startling, like one of those pictures of Jesus done in lenticular 3-D. If you looked at it one way, you saw Jesus risen from the tomb, then with the tiniest shift in perspective, Jesus was dead on the cross. With his eyes closed, Mosjoukine was older than old. Not like in *Father Sergius* where, though the makeup used to age his face was remarkably good, his body had stayed strong. Now he was shrunken in on himself like an old potato the cook had forgotten to throw away. Then he opened his eyes, and he was Ivan Mosjoukine again, essentially unchanged. "I'm sorry," he said. "I shouldn't laugh. It isn't a joke, but it was all a long time ago. I did go to Prague. I don't suppose your brother believes that?"

"No," I shook my head.

"I went to get your mother, and she reported me to the secret police. Can you believe that? Sophie had me arrested. That woman was tough."

"Arrested? You were in a Czech jail?"

Mosjoukine laughed again, as if at 102 the past were nothing but one long string of good punch lines. "Deported," he said, "sent back to Russia. She knew I was a Soviet citizen, no matter that I had a French passport."

"And then?"

He shrugged one shoulder, a gesture that matched Ilya's perfectly. "Russia," he said, "is a prison inside a prison inside a prison." He made a gesture with his hands, as if he were opening nesting dolls. "It always has been. Soviet or czarist, or now, under our new democracy of plutocrats. Nothing really changes. I ended up in the east, in Siberia."

I gestured at the cell, the monastery beyond. "And in Siberia, you found God?"

This time he didn't laugh. "That's the wrong question, Vera." He tapped his knuckle on the metal hospital tray. "God is never lost." I remembered a philosophy class I had in college on Spinoza. *God is in the table; God is in all of us.* Then Mosjoukine smiled again, bent his head close to mine. "Though the church did get me out of Siberia and back to the capital." Now he closed his eyes, and his hand loosened its grip on mine. I thought he had fallen asleep, and started to slip my hand out of his, but his eyes opened. "I thought about trying to get to Paris. There are Orthodox even there. I did want to see it again. See your brother if he was where I thought he would be." If Mosjoukine knew Ilya would be living in the apartment at 44 Place Ste-Odile, why hadn't he written to Ilya the way he had written to Apolline? "But I knew he would never forgive me. And I don't travel easily anymore." He nodded toward the wheelchair, folded in the far corner of the cell.

"Why wouldn't he believe you?" I said. "If he knew you went to Prague . . ."

Mosjoukine waved my protests away. "Because it isn't about me. He loved his mother. I took him away. He loved his mother more than anything." He looked at me, as if weighing what to say. "Except maybe you. He never forgot you. But his mother didn't love him back, not like that. She loved him less than she loved Marx. Maybe even less than me. Me, at least she cared about enough to have arrested, cared about enough to hate. Her children, she gave away, or let other people take."

"Why?" I said. "Were we so unlovable?"

He shook his head. "That was Sophie. I think something terrible happened to her in the war. She wouldn't talk about it, but she never grew up, and a child can't be a mother. She was always a ten-year-old girl inside, the world all in black and white, her soul full of this terrible hunger for perfection. That was the attraction communism held for her. It promised perfection, inhuman, unforgiving perfection. If it hadn't been communism, she might have ended up a nun or a Zionist. Sophie had no patience for people. They were too prone to weakness, to failures of will." He tapped my hand.

"But she loved you."

My father nodded. "For a while. I think I reminded her of someone, her father perhaps." He laughed. "Maybe her grandfather. She thought I was the one person on her side. Then I failed her, too. I wasn't there when you and your brother were born. She never forgave me." He shrugged.

"Did you love her?"

"Yes, of course," he said. "She was so fiercely alive. She reminded me of . . ."

"Of Vera Holodnaya?"

He waved his hand. "Only her eyes. In temperament, she reminded me of myself. She reminded me of the way I used to be when I was that young. And," he smiled wryly, self-deprecatingly, "I always did love myself. It was my tragic flaw. My great sin, really." He waved his hand at his cell. "Though I pray I have finally gotten over it."

"Did you love us?" I asked him. I held my breath.

"Of course," he said. "I loved all my children." He squeezed my fingers. "But I wasn't a good father. I don't lie to myself about that anymore. I was only a good father in my movies. It's the great occupational hazard of acting, confusing the role with reality. That and poverty. Oh, and drink."

The door opened. Brother Paul peeked in. Mosjoukine made a shooing motion, and the door closed again. "How is the colonel?" he asked me. "He was one of the most intelligent men I ever knew, not that it did him any good. An army is a hard place for a smart man. I could have told him he would never become a general."

"He's dead," I said. "His wife, too."

"So young?"

"They were both in their eighties," I said. He nodded, though I guessed from his vantage point that still seemed tragically young.

"You'll live much longer," he said. I shook my head. I doubted that.

"My daughter died," I said. "My husband, too. I don't want a long life alone."

"Your daughter?"

"Yes."

He put his hand on my head the way I had seen him touch the pilgrims. I rested my forehead on his other hand, the one I was still holding. He was quiet so long I wondered if he was praying. Or if he had fallen asleep. I looked up. Tears were running from his blue eyes, into the deep folds on either side of his nose. They were dripping with little splashes into his half-finished bowl of borscht.

"I'm sorry," I said. Meaning, I think, *I shouldn't have told you.* He had been Julia's grandfather.

"I'm the one who is sorry," he said. "If I had led a different life, I might have at least seen her play." He might have stopped by with a red bicycle, I heard Ilya, my cynical brother, say. We were twins, but we were not the same. I believed Mosjoukine. I had to. He said he had loved all his children, loved Ilya, loved me. He had confessed his neglect of us and repented. He would have loved his granddaughter, if only fate had given him the chance. I kissed my weeping father's shaking old hand.

"Vera," he said, "what I'm going to tell you now is true. Doubt anything else I say but this. Tell me, how old are you?"

"Forty-two," I said.

"I almost died when I was forty. Your forties are the hardest time. You want so many things when you are young or maybe even have them and lose them, then there comes a day when you're alone, when everything you had is gone. You think your life is over. Do you hear me?"

I did. I said, "Yes, Father."

"But if you can get past your forties, it's easy. Look at me! Have you ever seen anyone older and uglier?"

"No," I said. But he wasn't ugly, I thought, and he knew it. Old, yes, but never ugly. Not Ivan Mosjoukine. At least, not with his eyes open.

"I've never been happier. You'll live to be one hundred, Vera. I know these things."

He looked at me with those amazing eyes, and I believed him. He looked at me, and I could see a good future, faint and pink, on the horizon. I would be okay, Ilya, too. We would both live long enough to be happy again. We would both live to be one hundred. Older, even. I clung to my father's hand.

Brother Paul reappeared and stood by the bed, giving no sign of leaving. Mosjoukine's eyes closed, opened. "I had better go, Father," I said, kissing his palm.

"I am glad I was here to meet you, my daughter," he said, his eyes shining, "Tomorrow . . ." he paused, "God knows. I may not be here. Go with my blessing." He made the sign of the cross in the air in front of me. "Go and promise me you won't look back, won't come back." I opened my mouth. I wanted to see him again, and he knew it. "Remember," he pointed one bent finger, fixed his eyes on me. "Never be afraid!" My father, Ivan Mosjoukine in the flesh, not in a movie, said this to me. I felt the words move through my body like electricity. Then his eyes were closing again. "And give your brother my love."

Brother Paul stayed with Mosjoukine. The short Russian monk led me back through the maze of the monastery, across the courtyard toward the outer door. As soon as I felt the night air, I thought, I have to come back. I needed to bring Ilya to see Mosjoukine. Then we could both turn our faces to the future.

It wasn't until I was on the street and I heard the monk bolt the heavy monastery gate behind me that I remembered Pavel's warning. It was the middle of the night, and I was in a neighborhood I didn't know, God-knows-where in a city I didn't know, in a country where I spoke exactly one word of the language, *nyet*. I fumbled for Pavel's cell phone, but before I could push a button, a car parked down the narrow street roared to life, the lights clicked on, and it squealed forward. Pavel leaned over and opened the passenger side door. "Get in," he said. "Your brother is worried about you." I got in, and he took off before I had the door closed.

"Where is Ilya?" I asked.

"He's not well," Pavel said, stopping at the corner by smashing on the brakes, then heading into a roundabout with the gas pedal flat on the floor. I clutched the dash.

"How not well?" I asked.

Pavel cleared his throat. "I sent him to see a friend of mine, who runs a pharmacy."

"Oh," I said, thinking, *that kind of not well.* What was I going to do?

Pavel looked sideways at me, but didn't say anything more. After we had jerked, raced, jerked, and raced across half of Moscow again, he pulled up with a final squeal in front of the hotel. "Did you find what you were looking for? At the monastery?" he asked.

Mosjoukine. I had almost forgotten. "Yes," I said. "Ilya has to see Father Ivan." Pavel looked skeptical, and I wondered how much Ilya had told him.

When Pavel spoke, his dismissal was more universal. "This interest in the old religion," he said, "I don't get it. What do people see in it? The communists lied to the people. Before that, the church lied. Now the church is all holy again. What's next? The return of the czar's cousin's nephew?"

"I don't know," I said. "I hope not."

He waved a hand, dismissing me, himself, Russian history. "Nothing changes. Go see how your brother is." He leaned across me to open my door. I got out. "If there's any trouble," he pointed a finger at my purse, at his cell phone, which was inside. "Call me. Okay?"

I nodded, then shut the door and he squealed off.

Inside our suite, Ilya was sitting on the couch, moving pieces around on the heavy onyx chess board on the coffee table in a way that made me guess he knew more about the game than I did. Did he think he was fooling me? Because he looked fine. He looked rested, and his color was good. But I knew that somewhere in the apartment was an empty vial, a used syringe. He'd stop when we got back from Moscow, he'd said. We were still here.

He was also halfway through a bottle of vodka. "So," Ilya said, moving the black queen, "was it Dad?"

"Yes. No question about it." Ilya looked up at me, the white bishop dangling between the fingers of his right hand. "Listen, Ilya," I said. Ilya looked down at the chess board again. "He tried to bring Sophie back. He did go to Prague. She had him arrested."

Ilya laughed. "That's good."

"You don't believe me?"

"No, no, I believe you," he said. "It's just what Sophie would do. I don't know why I didn't guess that was what happened. Blind, I suppose."

"So you'll come with me to see him tomorrow?"

Ilya stared at the board, took a pawn with his knight. "Was that move legal?" he asked. "I haven't played in so long. I should ask Pasha."

"Ilya?"

"Go to bed," he said. "Go to bed. If it means so much to you, I'll go on the pilgrimage with you. I'll get down on my knees and kiss the old bastard's ring, if that will make you happy." He was still fooling with his pawns. "Will that make you happy, little sister?"

"I want *you* to be happy," I said. "I want you to be well." I put my hand under his chin, lifted his head so he was looking at me.

"Oh," he poured himself another shot of vodka, "I am happy."

I left him on the couch, took a shower, and went to bed. I dreamed I was a real pilgrim, walking on my knees over rocky soil. Russian grandmothers all around me were on their knees, too, puffing and coughing. We were trying to reach a church so distant it looked like a toy, like a Christmas ornament. We coughed and coughed, the air full of something like cotton, like dandelion fluff.

I woke up. The coughing, of course, must have been Ilya. Had he sat up, drinking, all night? The fluff was stray feathers from the hotel pillow. Somehow I'd torn the ticking open.

I put on my clothes and went out into the living room. Ilya wasn't there, though someone had won the chess match. The white king lay, surrendered, on its side. The bottle of vodka was empty. I checked the other bedroom. The bed was untouched. I ordered breakfast. It took a long time coming, but there was still no sign of Ilya. When it was nearly 11:30, time for us to go if we were to have a chance of seeing Father Ivan, just as I was thinking the words *lying bastard* about my only brother, I heard a car horn outside the window. Ilya was calling my name. I stuck my head out. He was standing, half in and half out of a cab. "Pavel couldn't come," he said. "Hurry or we'll be late."

I hurried, cursing Ilya under my breath.

The taxi, even though it drove with what I was coming to think of as Moscovian abandon, took nearly twice as long to reach the monastery. As the driver picked his way slowly down the long blocks from the highway, trying to steer his way around the larger potholes, I could already see the crowd in front of the monastery gate. It was even larger than the day before. I frowned at Ilya. We should have come earlier. If this worked as it had yesterday, we were in for a long wait. Unless I could get one of the brothers to take a note to Mosjoukine. I wondered how many euros I had on me. The driver stopped. The crowd was blocking the street. He raised his hands off the steering wheel, let them fall. This was as far as he was going. I gave Ilya my wallet so he could pay off the cab.

As soon as I got out, I could tell the crowd was different from yesterday. People were shouting and angry. Yesterday there had been a bit of shoving, but nothing like this. Ilya came up beside me and took my arm. "What's going on?" he asked me.

"I don't know." The gate to the monastery was closed, and an old woman was pounding on it with her cane. I looked at the digital clock on the cab's dash. 12:30. It should have been open. Could Father Ivan be ill?

Ilya turned to the people closest to us in the crush and tried his Russian on them. One old man spoke back, his voice a stream of complaint, spit flying from under his heavy, white moustache. Ilya nodded. "What is he saying?" I asked.

Ilya shrugged. "I have no earthly idea. I couldn't understand a word. Let me try someone else." He pushed ahead, and I saw him talking to a well-dressed woman in fur. She pointed at the monastery, at heaven, then at the closed gate. Ilya nodded vigorously, *yes, yes.* He had to use his elbows to get back to me. "She says they won't let anyone in." He raised his hands, palms up, to his shoulders, let them drop. "She says the monks told them Father Ivan isn't here."

"Isn't here? Where else would he be?" Ilya started the pantomime with the hands again, and I turned away disgusted. I looked down the street. There, near the market on the corner, I caught a glimpse of black hem. One of the brothers must have come out a side gate, taking a risk, to do some shopping. "Come on," I said, grabbing Ilya's hand, pulling him out of the crowd. We jogged down the block. "In there." I pointed at the shop.

The monk was stepping out of the shop with a liter of Coca-Cola. It was Brother Paul. I grabbed his sleeve. "Where is he?" I said. "What's going on?"

Brother Paul tried to pull away, but now Ilya was there, standing with one foot on the hem of the monk's robe. The shop clerk just inside the door was pointedly looking the other way, as if she didn't care one way or the other what happened to these servants of God. "He left," Brother Paul said. His eyes were red, and as he spoke, he looked as if he might start crying again. "Sometime in the night, after I went back to my cell. When I went to get him this morning, his bed was empty."

"How could he?" I said. "He was there when I left."

Brother Paul frowned. "You weren't the last. There was another girl. She looked a lot like you, but she was younger."

Suddenly Ilya was laughing. He was laughing so hard, he nearly bent double. Had he gone crazy? He waved a hand by his head, as if brushing the whole thing away. Then he started to walk into the street. I caught at his sleeve.

"What! *What?*" I said to him.

"You don't get it, do you?" he said. He was wiping tears from his face with the side of his hand. He had been laughing that hard. "It's *Father Sergius.* Suddenly the saint is gone. He just can't stop. He's still living out his damn movies."

Ilya was talking about the scene near the end of *Father Sergius* where the monk flees into the night. I had a hard time imagining the man I had seen last night fleeing anywhere. At least, not without help. I looked around for Brother Paul, but he was gone, no doubt making a run for the safety of the monastery walls. He had said the girl who came to visit had looked a lot like me. "Which one are you?" Mosjoukine had asked me. I had a vision of another sibling, someone younger, the product of Mosjoukine's long years in Siberia. Some young Russian girl who owned a fast car. He'd told me not to come back because he knew he was leaving.

I couldn't believe it. Surely Mosjoukine was inside the monastery. It was just these crowds he didn't want to see. He would want to see me and Ilya. "We're going in," I said and tried to push through the solid mass of people drawn by the general air of outrage, the chance to shout and be angry for no particular reason except that life was hard and getting harder every day. I had to see for myself. I was willing to climb over or under or beat my way through. The crowd was not going to get in my way.

Then I felt Ilya's arm around me, across my chest in a fireman's hold. I kicked my legs up, tried to break away, but his arm was an iron bar. He might be shooting his body full of morphine, but the muscles from his years of fencing were still there. He dragged me backwards, out of the crowd. "Stop it," he hissed in my ear. "You are going to get yourself hurt." I let my body go slack. He loosened his grip, thinking I had come to my senses. I swung around, my hand already a fist, and hit him hard on the side of his head, catching him across his left ear.

"You, you . . ." I spit at him. I wasn't sure what the end of the sentence was going to be, except that this was his fault. If he had come with me the first time, if he had cared a little, just a little, we could have been a family.

Just as fast, he hit back, slapping me hard across the face. "You are fucking crazy," he said.

He was right. At that moment, I was more than insane, but before I could hit him again, he was down, first bent over from his waist, then on his knees, coughing. I went down on my knees beside him. "I'm sorry. Oh God, Ilya, I'm so sorry," I said, over and over. He nodded, too out of breath to talk. I felt something wet on my face and looked up. It was snowing big white flakes. It was a March snow storm. White swirled over the crowd, settled on the fur hats and knotted scarves of the angry believers.

It fell on Ilya's bare head. He put his hand on my shoulder, and together we got up. I looked around, wishing I knew the Russian word for *doctor*, when I saw that the taxi we'd come in was still there. It had been trapped by the crowd and was inching its way past us, trying not to run over too many feet. I opened the back door as it passed, shoved Ilya in, and hopped in myself.

The driver looked back, said something in Russian, probably *Get the hell out of my cab.*

"The hotel," I said. "We need to go back to our hotel." He knew where we'd come from. He could damn well take us back.

He glared at me and at Ilya, slumped in the corner. Someone in the crowd beat on his trunk, then someone else joined in banging on the hood. He shrugged, stepped on the gas, and we were out of there.

By the time we were on the highway, Ilya was sitting upright. "Don't look so worried," he said, pulling out another old joke. "It only hurts when I breathe." Neither of us laughed, because what he said was too obviously true. It was snowing harder, a real blizzard, though the snow melted as it hit the dark pavement of the highway. It stuck on the trees and on the tulips open in the window boxes we passed as we entered the city.

We arrived at the hotel nearly as quickly as if Pavel had been at the wheel, the taxi driver eager to be rid of us. I held out a wrinkled wad of bills, and he carefully picked through it. Ilya was outside, leaning against the cab, still breathing hard. Then he shifted to the skinny tree caged in the sidewalk by an iron paling. Snow was building up in a small drift at its roots. Just as the taxi driver finished his careful examination of my euros and took a couple of bills, including what I assumed was a once-in-a-lifetime-sized tip, I saw out of the corner of my eye that Ilya was bent double again, hanging on to the sapling with one hand, coughing harder than ever. He was sick, really sick.

I went to help him into the hotel. Looking down at the fresh snow I saw bright red blood. Ilya raised his head, and his lips were just as red. I wiped his mouth with the sleeve of my black sweater. "Come on," I said, "just a little further and we're home." The *home* part wasn't true, but we did make it to the hotel room, and he went straight to the bathroom. I heard him retching in the toilet, then coughing again, as if his lungs might come up. I took Pavel's cell phone out of my purse and pushed the number one. The phone rang and rang. I threw it on the couch. Ilya was out of the bathroom now. He sat on the edge of the bed in his room, his head in his hands. I glanced into the bath. There was blood spattered on the lid of the toilet, drops splashed across the bright white of the tile.

"We have to call an ambulance," I said to Ilya. I headed for the house phone by his bed. "I'll call the desk, they'll know . . ."

"No," Ilya said. He raised his head. His lips were crusted with blood.

"We have to. This isn't a joke. You're really sick."

"Yes," Ilya said. Just that. *Yes.* Then I saw it. I had been blind, but now I could see. Blind was better.

"Oh, God," I said, my hands flying to cover my mouth, to hold back the words. "You're dying."

He nodded. He had told me he'd been sick after Anne-Sophie was born. I had seen his picture with almost no hair.

"Cancer?" I said.

"In one lung the first time," he said. "They operated. Did chemotherapy. They thought they'd caught it in time."

"And now?"

"I know it's come back." He pointed at his chest, made a motion as if he were crossing himself.

Suddenly, stupidly, I was angry again. I said, "I can't believe it. I find you. I just find you, and now my brother is dying."

Ilya held out his hands. "I'm not your brother," he said. I blinked, shook my head. Was all this some kind of scam, some hallucination? Was I really that crazy? I closed my eyes, opened them, half expecting to see a stranger who looked nothing like me sitting on the bed. It was still Ilya, a man with my eyes, my nose, my face. He said it again, "I'm not your brother," holding out his hands, empty, palms up, beckoning me.

I took his hands, sat down beside him on the bed. "You are."

He shook his head. "I don't want to be if this is all it brings you. Three months ago, when I started coughing again, I thought my only worry was not dying before Anne-Sophie. Now . . ."

"Shhh," I said, holding up one finger. "Shhh."

"I couldn't tell you, not after hearing about your family. I tried to get you to go home. I threw a coffee pot at your head, for God's sake." I could feel his pulse racing in his wrist, but he wouldn't be quiet. "In Romain Gary's memoir, Gary survives the war so he can tell his mother he's become a pilot and a hero of France just for her. Did I tell you that part?" he asked. I shook my head. Ilya drew a shaky breath, went on. "Gary gets letters from his mother all during the war, but he's never sure his are getting through to her. Then, after D-Day, he makes his way back to Nice—only to find his mother's been dead for three years." My brother shook his head. "Knowing she was dying, she wrote him hundreds of letters and left them with a friend to mail, so he wouldn't know she was gone until the war was over." Ilya paused. "I thought, if I could get you to leave, I could write you for as long as I could, then just disappear. You'd never need to know..."

I put my finger to his lips. "It's better to know," I said. "It's always better." I told him how, when I was in kindergarten, I'd come home one day to find my parakeet Ginger, the one the colonel had bought me at Woolworth's, missing. Livinia told me while she was cleaning her cage Ginger had flown out the open kitchen window. "For weeks I looked in every tree, calling *Ginger, Ginger, Ginger*. I was sure she would starve without her birdseed bell. 'No,' Livinia said, 'someone else will find her and give her a good home.' Then, years later, Livinia confessed to me that she'd lied about Ginger. 'I found her on the bottom of her cage. Feet up, eyes closed,' she said. 'I wanted you to think she'd gone on to better things.' I just sat there, unbelieving," I told Ilya. "How could she believe it was better for me to worry about Ginger every day than to know the truth? I'd rather know. Even this, I'd rather know."

Ilya shook his head again. "Two weeks ago, you didn't know you had a brother. You didn't know I existed. You could have gone on not knowing."

"I knew," I said. "I must have. Why else did I fly to Paris with nothing but a toothbrush?" I rested my forehead against his. His skin was hot and dry. I could feel his body shaking. For the first time since I'd known him, Ilya was the one crying.

18

I PUT ILYA TO BED AND COVERED HIM. He was shivering, though the hotel room was overheated and stuffy. I laid next to him and wrapped my arms around him to warm him. He was on his side, trying to catch his breath, trying not to start coughing. How could I have not known he was so ill? How had he kept going? I'd seen him fencing, damn it. I could feel his heart beating, feel the energy there, the will, the fierce control that I'd felt during my visit with Mosjoukine in the monastery. It was what kept them both alive. Another trait of our father's I didn't share.

His eyes closed, drifting into sleep. I stayed awake.

I thought about Mosjoukine. Where was he now? If he had known I was coming, would he have asked me, not some younger sibling, to take him away? Would he have asked me to take him back to Paris?

"Too old," Ilya said, without opening his eyes, and I realized I must have said what I was thinking aloud. I poked him.

"He was a young 102," I said, joking. Even at 102, Mosjoukine was not too frail for life in Paris.

"Not him," Ilya said. "You. He always goes for the younger woman. It's the movie star in him."

I said, "Forty-two is young to a man over 100." Ilya started to laugh, then cough, and I had to get him a wet towel and hold his head. When he was done coughing, I could feel his heart beating in his chest, as if it were a bomb ticking, as if his life were a clock running down.

Ilya woke up at dusk. The morphine he'd gotten from Pavel's friend was wearing off, and his eyes were bright and wet with the pain. His breathing was fast and shallow. "You'll have to go to the pharmacy for me," he said. "You can take Pavel's note."

So I went out into a new snow, because I couldn't say I wouldn't, even though the idea of buying drugs in this illegal way in a city I did not know, in a country in which, as Mosjoukine had told me, there were prisons inside of prisons, scared me so much my hands shook. The pharmacist let me charge the drugs to my credit card. He gave me three vials. He spoke perfect English. He told me he'd studied one year at the Mayo Clinic. Did I know the Mayo Clinic in Rochester, Minnesota?

Yes, I said, I certainly did. It was near my house in America, or at least only a few states away.

He liked Minnesota, he said, except that the winter was so bitterly cold. Colder, he insisted, than in Moscow. Then he counted out three disposable syringes with needles, still sealed and sterile. "These are harder to get than the morphine," he told me. "So don't lose one." Then he gave me instructions. I could give my brother no more than two injections in six hours.

"What would happen if I did?" I asked. I was pretty sure Ilya had been taking them nearly that often. What if it wasn't enough?

"An overdose will suppress his heart rate," the pharmacist said. "He'll stop breathing."

Back at the hotel, Ilya sat dressed on the couch with a fresh bottle of vodka, trying to work on the pain shot by shot. He took the bag from the pharmacy into the bathroom. I had the strong sense it wasn't good to mix the two, but we had moved beyond that, really. We were way out to sea in the fog of what-the-hell-difference-does-it-make. He looked better when he came out. It was past dinner time, but neither of us mentioned food. "I should show you how to do that," he said to me. "Are you squeamish about needles?"

"No," I said. "I don't think so. Not about getting shots anyway."

"You might have to do it for me, sooner or later."

Later seemed overly optimistic. "No problem," I lied just a little. "I can do it. I do tougher things every day." He kissed me on top of my head.

"Take me back to Paris," he said. "I want to sleep in my own bed."

"Now?"

"Now," he said, handing me the cell phone off the couch. I rang Pavel, and this time he answered. I handed the phone to Ilya. Whatever Ilya said, he managed it in Russian. I looked out the window, pretending not to be trying to listen, pretending not to wonder what he'd said. "Pasha's bringing the car around," Ilya said after he got off the phone. I went downstairs and paid our bill with my miraculous credit card. We sat side by side on the couch until Pavel knocked on the door.

Pavel took us right to the gate at Sheremetyevo Airport, though there were concrete barriers that implied parking was forbidden. He took us to the door of the Aeroflot plane. He hugged Ilya, whispered something in his ear. Ilya laughed, a flush of color rising in his cheeks. Then Pavel gave me a bone-cracking squeeze. "Take care of your brother," he said, whispering in my ear. "He's a good man. He deserves to be loved." After a round of rapid-fire Russian from Pavel directed at the gate attendant, we were on a flight on which we had never booked a seat, without anyone so much as checking our passports or tickets.

"What did Pavel say to you?" I asked when, after a steep and bumpy takeoff, we were finally up in the air.

"Pasha?" Ilya said. "Just now?" He took my hand. "He asked me how come if we were friends, I never told him I had such a good-looking sister."

I told Ilya that as soon as we got to Paris, we would take a cab to the nearest hospital.

Ilya shook his head. "No," he said. "I won't go. I know what will happen."

I started to protest.

He put his fingers over my lips, leaned close to my ear. "I won't end up like Anne-Sophie." I thought of her glass cell, the snaking clear tubes.

"I won't let them do that to you," I told him. "No matter what. I promise. But I have to know they've done everything. Did the doctors tell you there was nothing more they could do?"

Ilya looked away from me, shook his head. "No."

"Then we have to try. We have to go to the hospital."

"All right," he said, nodding. "But I want to go home first. Just for one night, okay? What difference could that make?"

I hesitated. I couldn't frog-march him to the hospital against his will. I needed his cooperation.

He took my hand. "Please?"

I gave in. "Okay. We'll go to the doctor tomorrow."

"Tomorrow afternoon," Ilya said. "I think I deserve to sleep in."

We landed in Paris at midnight.

We walked slowly through Charles de Gaulle, past the immigrant workers mopping and waxing the vast terminal floor. Then we went outside and got into a cab. Ilya closed his eyes until we were almost into the city, then he opened them and smiled like a child when he saw the lights of Paris.

"Oz," I said.

"Heaven," he said. "Or, at least, earthly paradise."

The taxi driver parked his cab at the entrance to the Place Ste-Odile. He helped me get Ilya, who was unsteady on his feet, down the passageway and to the front door of Number 44. "My God," he said, looking around the deserted courtyard. "I bring people to the hospital to visit relatives and see doctors all the time, and I had no idea this was here." I gave the driver the last of my cash.

Ilya insisted he could get himself up the stairs, and he did. As I unlocked the door, I realized that the phone was ringing, and Ilya pushed past me to answer.

I followed, carrying his rucksack. Ilya was leaning against the kitchen wall, talking into the receiver. I could see his legs shaking with either the effort or a chill.

"Yeah, Nolo, I believe you Jacques was pissed," I heard Ilya say. *The boat.* Ilya had stood up Jacques and Nolo, gone missing just as the spring tourist season heated up. Ilya listened to Nolo, nodding. "Tell him I'm sorry. Tell him I'm not feeling well." More nodding, more listening. Ilya had stopped shivering. "No, don't worry. Vera is here. If you want to come over, come next week. I'll be better by then. Tell Jacques you have my blessing. I knew you could do it. With enough tips you can buy the damn boat." Ilya said good-bye and hung up the phone. He sat down at the kitchen table, winded. I sat down next to him.

"Nolo did the tour himself?" I asked.

Ilya nodded. "He's heard me often enough. The old ladies loved him." Ilya gave a little hoarse laugh, too close to a cough for comfort, and I held my breath as I watched him try to catch his. When he had, he put his hand over mine and seemed to take a minute to count my fingers one by one. "Are you afraid, Vera?" he asked.

"Yes," I said. I was so afraid I could hardly breathe.

"Don't be," he said, squeezing my fingers hard.

"So the old bastard was right?" I said. "Never be afraid."

Ilya started to laugh again, then thought better of it. "I was wrong about the bastard part. His parents were married. You and me, we're the bastards. We can't help it. We were born to it. So you know what? No more worrying about anybody else, Vera." He let go of my hand and tapped me lightly with one finger on the chest. "You should think only of you."

I looked him right in the eyes, holding him with my eyes the way Mosjoukine would have. "Don't you dare tell me to leave," I said. "Don't even think it."

Ilya looked down. "No," he said. "I won't ask you to go. You have to take me to the hospital tomorrow, remember?"

Ilya stood up, putting his hands on the table to steady himself. "Wait here a minute," he said. "Close your eyes." Then he went into his room. I heard the drawer in the desk scrape open. Then he was back. "Put out your hand. Sophie gave me this. I want you to have it." He dropped something small onto my open palm. I opened my eyes. It was a red, star-shaped pin with a photograph in the middle of a boy with curly blond hair.

"Who's the boy?" I asked.

"Lenin," Ilya said. "All us good communist kids got them, like medals." He took the baby Lenin, the one child our mother could truly love, and pinned it to my black sweater. He kissed me lightly first on my left cheek, then on my right, as if he were awarding me the Croix de Guerre. "For valor, comrade," he said.

After that, I helped him out of his sweater and jeans and into bed in his shirt and underwear, not on the futon in his room but in the big bed. I propped him up on the snow bank of pillows so he would be able to breathe. I gave him the second of the three shots. He tried not to flinch when I stuck the needle into the bruised flesh of his thigh. I pulled the comforter over him.

I brought him a glass of wine and a banana. He ate a little, drank a little. Then I propped myself up next to him. We sat, side by side, together on the bed where it seemed likely we had been conceived.

"Talk to me," he said, his voice drifting on the morphine. "Tell me a story." In the dark, I told him the plot of my novel. "It's about an American woman who makes a sudden, irrational decision to come to Paris," I said. My brother laughed, and I held my breath for fear he would start coughing, but he didn't.

Then I told him what I hadn't before, how the heroine left America after the unexpected death of her husband. Ilya raised his eyebrows at this bit of art beating life into the world. "But no children die in it," I said. "I swear." I hadn't been capable of imagining that tragedy to come.

In Paris, my American meets a half-Alsatian, half-German man. "I'm not any part German," Ilya pointed out.

"So? In my novel, he's not her brother either," I said. "I mean, what kind of novel do you think this is?"

The American and the Alsatian fall in love, I told him, and then are separated. But in the end, they're reunited, and their child is born—*what joy!* A novel with a gloriously happy ending! the jacket copy read. Like fireworks. What did that say about my ability to see my own future?

"It will happen," Ilya said. "Mei-mei saw it in your cards."

"She did not."

Ilya closed his eyes. "She should have. That's what people pay her for."

Near dawn, I told him what Mosjoukine had said about how your forties were the toughest decade and how if you could just get beyond them it was easy. "'Live to be 100, Vera,' he said to me."

"More than 100, Vera," Ilya said, "Live to be 110 at least. Promise me. One of us should have a long life besides that old bastard. Live beyond all this, until there isn't any more getting sick." He was lying on his back, trying hard to keep breathing, his hands behind his head, looking at the ceiling as if he could see something there I couldn't.

I told him about my feeling that the dead were always with me. I told him it felt as if I could put out my hand and touch them, the wall in front of me an illusion, the thinnest veil.

He said, "God, it sounds like you're in the shower and your family is on the other side of the scummy plastic curtain, looking in. When I'm dead, I'm gone. Take my word."

I didn't answer him, because I wasn't planning on staying behind this time. If two shots would stop Ilya's heart, then they would do the same for mine. I would just need to get my hands on more morphine, and I knew perfectly well where I could do that.

19

THE NEXT MORNING, I GAVE ILYA THE LAST of the Russian morphine, trying not to look at the black and purple bruise on his thigh from the shot I'd given him the night before. It wasn't hard to do, if I made sure not to think about how tender the flesh was where the needle went in, didn't think of the tiny hole it made as symbolic of any larger loss. Ilya closed his eyes, felt the rush of the morphine, waited for the pain to recede. I would have a talk with the neighbor before we went to the hospital to see a doctor. I needed to have enough morphine for Ilya to make good on my promise that I wouldn't let him end up like Anne-Sophie. Enough for me as well, if I decided not to stick around either. I knew the neighbor would sell me as much as I needed, as long as I had the money. I felt Ilya's eyes on me.

"Don't even think about it, Vera," he said. "You promised me. You swore to live to be 100."

"No," I said, "110." Which was a bigger sin, suicide or lying to a dying man?

I went to get my purse, but when I looked in my wallet I remembered giving the taxi driver the last of my cash. I would have to find an ATM. There would be one near the hospital, or failing that, at a bank on the Boulevard de la Villette. I doubted the neighbor would charge the morphine to my credit card the way the Russian pharmacist had. "I have to go out and get money before we go to the hospital," I told Ilya. "Will you be okay for a while?"

"I'm lovely," he said, smiling. He was. His eyes glowed like the sea in a tropical postcard.

"Yes, you are," I said.

He poked me with a long finger. "You, too, little sister. You, too."

I didn't feel beautiful. I felt raw. I felt like I had been living on a diet of broken glass. More than anything, I wanted to keep Ilya alive and with me as long as possible, even if that meant his being in the hospital. I put some water by the bed for him and, though I didn't really think he would be reading, the paperback life of Houdini there as well. Then I put on Ilya's jeans, T-shirt, and the blue sweater. I took the baby Lenin pin off my black turtleneck and pinned it over my heart. I even put on his boat shoes instead of my boots, knowing as I did it that I was trying to keep my only brother close. I took his keys and let myself out.

I nodded to the neighbor as I went past. She was cracking walnuts into a bowl, her muscular forearms bare in the morning sun. I found an ATM inside the courtyard of the hospital. The leaves on the trees were open now, the tulips, too, a blaze of red. An old man was sitting on the bench where I had sat the morning I set out to find the Place Ste-Odile a lifetime ago. I counted the days. Jesus, just ten days had passed. Ten days. It felt like my whole life, or like one really long Russian silent movie.

I put my card in the machine, punched in my number, asked for two hundred euros. But the ATM, instead of thinking about that for a moment while it chatted with the ubercomputer in touch with my bank in America, instead of spitting out fresh bills *phit, phit, phit,* it made an odd clucking sound and a message flashed on the screen. *We are desolated, but your card has been confiscated. Please contact your home institution.* I hit the cancel button, once, twice, but the card would not come out.

What could have happened? Sure, I had been spending like a sailor, but the card had a ten thousand dollar limit, and I hadn't gone that crazy. Then I remembered John saying this had happened to him once while he was traveling through Europe with Tricia, because she'd bought too many designer clothes in one day. My spending pattern, buying tickets to foreign countries at the last minute, buying expensive luxury items (those boots!), paying for two hotel rooms in two different capital cities at the same time, must have tripped some kind of security program. Somebody, one computer told another computer, has stolen this card. The owner would never spend money this way. Take my word for it. I know.

What was I supposed to do now? The card probably had an emergency number on the back to call in case of trouble, but the machine had the card and it wasn't giving it back. I needed cash. Now.

Then I remembered the two other cards I had squirreled away in my suitcase back at the Hôtel Batignolles. I would go there, get them, and come back. It wouldn't take long. We could still get to the hospital that afternoon. I thought about running back to the apartment, telling Ilya where I was headed, but that would just take extra time. He would be sleeping. I could call, but—stupid—I still had no idea what the number was that made the antique phone in the kitchen ring. I would be fast.

I ran as far as I could, Ilya's boat shoes flapping a bit. Every burning breath I took along the way reminded me that nothing I had been doing lately was in the least bit good for me. I had the foolish thought that all this dying would be the death of me.

I took the Metro, then, panting, I half-ran and half-walked the long way from the nearest Metro stop to the Hôtel Batignolles. The clerk could barely conceal his alarm at my sudden sweat-drenched appearance. I expected him to mention the dead credit card, since it was the one I was using to pay for my room, but apparently the hotel hadn't caught on yet. So I grabbed the key from him and took the stairs, not wanting to wait for the elevator. I pulled the stolen suitcase out of the closet. The cards were still there, thank God.

I took them both, also the bottle of Percoset and my three-year-old Valium. Neither was morphine, but who knew? Maybe the neighbor would be willing to talk trade. My only question was whether I should try to find an ATM near the hotel—surely the clerk would know the nearest one—or head straight back, find something closer to Ilya. That way I would know where to go when I needed more cash. I didn't want to risk the one at the hospital again. I put the pills in my purse and kept the cards, ready, in my hand.

Just as I reached for the knob, there was a knock on the door. I opened it holding up the new credit cards, expecting to see the desk clerk with my unpaid bill in his hand. Instead, standing in the hall was a plump, middle-aged woman wearing the kind of pink flowered pantsuit that marked her as an American. "Can I help you?" I said.

"Emma, I found you," she said in English with strong midwestern vowels. Her eyes were wide in her round face. Her blonde hair needed washing, and her clothes were even more wrinkled than mine. She reached out and grabbed both my wrists as if she were drowning and I was the only hope she had of reaching dry land. I noticed that her nails, painted pale pink to match her pantsuit, were chewed to the quick. I was pretty sure I had never seen her before.

"Do I know you?" I asked.

"We met once. Don't you remember? At the College Open House. I'm Nance Olmstead," the woman said. "I work for Dr. Parcher." Ah, I thought, now it was beginning to make sense. Harry Parcher was our dean of students, the one who was so crazy about the Hôtel Batignolles that he booked our faculty and students there year after year.

"Did Dean Parcher send you?" I asked. I'd told John where I was staying and obviously he'd squealed.

"You don't know why I'm here?" Nance Olmstead looked puzzled, as if we had an appointment she couldn't believe I'd forgotten.

I shook my head. "No," I said, "not really."

"It was my son Josh," she stopped, watching my face. *Josh*, I thought, spinning the Rolodex in my mind. Former student? Classmate of my daughter? Then it clicked, and she saw the answer hit me. "Yes," she said, her voice low, "it was my son who ran the red light." She was clinging to my elbows now, and her hands were inching higher as I tried to back away. "It was my son . . ." The back of my knees hit the bed, and I sat down. I finished her sentence for her.

"Who killed my family." Nance Olmstead nodded. She looked exhausted. She looked worse than I did. I pulled my arms free from her. "It was your damn SUV," I said. She nodded, though I wasn't really sure why I said it except she was there, ready to take my anger, and her dead son was not. I put my hands on my cheeks as if I were afraid my head might come apart. She pressed her hands with their raw nails together as if she were praying for me not to hit her. Or maybe praying that I would. Something, anything to take her mind off the echoing space where she lived.

"Oh, Christ," I said. "What are you doing here?"

183

"I came to get you. I came to make sure you were okay. I know Tricia Silver. She told me where you were, how worried everyone was. I come all the time; it's part of my job. I was a French major. At least once a year, I fly over to get a junior who has broken her ankle or who the faculty think is suicidal. I'm good at it. Really. I thought, if I go, if I get there in time . . ."

What was in time? I thought. Two months ago was in time. Two months ago when your son and my daughter were both alive. Now I was dying of something a plane ticket wouldn't cure. I wanted to tell her to go to hell, but looking at Nance, it was hard to say that. She was already in hell.

So now she wanted to be the lifeguard, to save me as if I were the one drowning. She would do her duty or die trying. If she couldn't rescue me, I thought, she wouldn't be coming to shore either. I had it in my power to take both of us down. But my brother was waiting, and every minute his pain was creeping back. I stood up and backed Nance toward the door.

"I can't talk about this now," I said. "I'll call you tonight, I swear it. Or I'll come back tomorrow. You're staying here, right?"

"Don't go," she said, grabbing at my sleeve.

"Listen," I said. "You can trust me. Take my stuff into your room and check me out of mine. Then you'll know I'll be back." I waved at the shopping bags of video tapes and photographs on the bed. "It's like I'm leaving a deposit." Nance moved toward the bags and, in that instant, I slipped by her and out the door. I took the steps two at a time, and when I reached the street I ran like hell and caught a bus at the corner. I looked back to see her coming out of the Hôtel Batignolles. Even from that distance, she did not look well.

After riding the bus for ten minutes, I got off and found an ATM near the Metro station, got some money, then ran to the train. I got on, got off, and kept running, some secret supply of adrenaline kicking in. Still, it was nearly noon when I ran through the passageway into the courtyard, chest out as if I expected to cross a finish line, break the white tape. The neighbor was cracking the last of her nuts, the bowl still in her lap. I would talk to her in a minute. Whatever she wanted, I was willing to give. She could name her price. First, I had to check on my brother. I unlocked the bottom door, then the top. "Ilya?"

No answer. I looked in the bedroom. The bed was empty. I checked the kitchen, the bathroom, even his room, but the futon was as empty as everywhere else. Note? Had he left a note? Maybe he'd gone out to find something for the pain himself. I thought of the vodka in Moscow. He would try anything in a pinch.

The kitchen table was bare. I looked in the bedroom again, and there it was, in the middle of the middle pillow. Not a note, but a picture. I sat on the bed. It was a still of Mosjoukine in bed dying at the end of *Kean. Alexander died, Alexander was buried, Alexander returneth into dust.* It was torn neatly in half. There was no writing, but I could read the message clearly. There would be no long death bed scene for Ilya. No hospital this afternoon or any afternoon. I had lied to him. He had lied to me.

I looked around the room. My boots were missing. Hard to believe he had worn them since his feet, as his shoes had proved to me all the way across Paris, were at least two sizes larger. I went to the window. The neighbor hadn't moved while I was gone, but there was something different about her. I looked down at her on her chair. She was wearing her usual flowered housedress, but on her feet were a pair of five hundred euro Jean Gabot boots. More than enough for the two vials of morphine Ilya needed to kill himself. She sensed me at the window and looked up guiltily, like she might run, but I was down the stairs and across the courtyard before she could put her bowl on the ground.

"Where is he?" I said. I had her arm in my hand, my fingernails digging into her skin. The muscles underneath were as hard as wood.

"Don't look for him," she said. "You won't find him."

"Where is he?" I said. "He needs me, if he is going to . . ." I stopped.

"I gave him enough," she said. "You think after all this time, I don't know my own business?" She took my hand off her arm, but she didn't let it drop. Instead she held on to it, squeezing my fingers so hard they turned white. "I owed him that much. Take my word. It's over by now."

"I have to see him," I said. "I have to. You know where he is, don't you?"

She looked at me. She pursed her lips, considering. "Yes," she said. "I'll take you there, but if you make a scene, you'll get us both arrested."

We went to the hospital, headed for the very spot where the ATM had eaten my credit card. As soon as we stepped through the archway into the courtyard, I saw him. He was sitting in the shade, the tulips on fire behind him, on the bench where I had sat when I was searching for the mysterious Place Ste-Odile. His legs were outstretched, his arms limp at his sides, his head thrown back as if he were sleeping. "No," I said, and started forward, but the neighbor wrapped her broad arms around my chest, held me to her in a grip like a trap, and pulled me back into the shadow of the archway.

"I told you," she hissed. Her breath stank of fish and fried onions. "You'll get us arrested. What good is that going to do him?" As she spoke, a doctor crossing the courtyard saw Ilya, went running toward him. He pressed a hand to Ilya's neck, feeling for a pulse. He shook his head, then he called to an orderly. Why couldn't someone I loved die while I was there? Why did they always leave me to leave me? "It's over. It's over," the neighbor was saying in my ear as I struggled. A hospital security guard appeared, talking into his two-way radio. Was he calling the police?

The neighbor kept her arms so tight around me I could hardly breathe, both of us half-hidden in the archway, while the orderly came back with a gurney and gently loaded my brother's body. I struggled against her without making a sound as if this were the moment the world finally went deaf, turned once and for all into a silent movie. The orderly rolled Ilya away, but the doctor didn't follow. He sat down on the bench, picked up the needle that lay on the ground. Then he looked across the courtyard, straight at me and at the neighbor. The doctor was the one I'd seen buying drugs, her best customer. The guard was following the orderly, but at any moment he might turn and see us.

The neighbor said nothing. For a moment I stopped struggling, and we stood looking back at the doctor. Then the doctor stood, dropped the used needle in the pocket of his lab coat, and followed my brother inside. I kicked the neighbor hard in the shin, or as hard as I could in Ilya's boat shoes, and pulled away. She grabbed two handfuls of my brother's old blue sweater and hung on, holding me back. "What good would it do him?" she said again. "His sister getting arrested. If they think you helped him, that's against the law."

"Are you threatening me?" I said, turning on her. "Let me go, or I'll scream."

She released me. "Listen to me," she said. "He's dead—that's what he wanted. If you think it's such a sin, then go to church, if that is something you people do. Go pray for his soul."

I glared at her. Spider, Neighbor Death, Angel who had helped my brother out of his pain. "I'll pray for you," I said. I spat at her feet. Then I walked away.

When I reached the quay, for no reason, I ran. *If I was a Jew, if Ilya was, too, would it be right for me to go to a church?* I wondered, running. If not a church, where could a mongrel like me go to pray? I'd never set foot in a synagogue or temple and had no idea where to find one in Paris.

I went to a church, not a famous one or a big one, but the first one I found open, off the Canal St-Martin, that ribbon of water leading to a city of death. I meant to light candles. I knew that was what Catholics did. I would light every candle in the place, then go down on the floor on my face in front of the altar. It would be dramatic. It would be what Mosjoukine would do in a movie. I hoped it would hurt. I hoped it might knock me unconscious.

There weren't any candles inside this church, only electric lights arranged in what looked like giant versions of the candelabras Americans put in their windows at Christmas or oversized menorahs, each bulb the shape of a flame. They stood by each of the side altars; one for the Virgin; one for St. Joseph, her husband, the patron saint of cuckolds; one for St. Barbara, who cut off her own breasts with a knife. The largest candelabra stood in front of the main altar with its Christ in carved agony. I walked down the side aisles flipping the little switches, turning on all the electric votive lights. Here, *here*, welcome the soul of my brother.

Then I took the two hundred euros I'd gotten out of the ATM and stuffed it into the tiny box labeled *Tronc,* meant to hold nothing but small coins to pay for the electricity. I stepped back to look at the effect. It wasn't impressive. It wasn't the blaze I wanted to signal God that my brother was on his way. The small bulbs looked too much like the lights in the Mémorial de la Déportation, that too subtle marker of the Holocaust in Paris. Where had God been then? Or during that last hour in Terezine, the camp already liberated, when He looked the other way as Robert Desnos died of typhus?

So I walked back down one aisle and up the other, knocking over the racks of lights, stand after stand. They fell with a satisfying clatter, the bulbs exploding with a popping sound like Christmas ornaments knocked from high on the tree. Finally, I tipped over the largest set by the main altar. That must have thrown the circuit breaker, because the church suddenly went dim. The only illumination was the evening sun bleeding through the smog-darkened windows. I heard someone open a door to the left of the altar. Then, a second later, I heard the door shut again. The priest had taken one look at me and was calling the cops. Who could blame him?

Then I saw the two real candles on the altar, tall white ones as thick as the neighbor's forearms. The least I could do for Ilya would be to light those. So I climbed over the railing and up onto the marble slab of the altar. I looked up and saw the crucified Christ, his ribs so painfully thin, the scar of the wound on his side, his long hair sweaty, spilling down. I thought, Oh, Lord, that's my brother. That's my brother up there.

I was trying to climb high enough to reach him, touch him, when the police arrived, grabbed me by each ankle, and pulled me, with one hard jerk, back to the ground.

20

IN *L'ANGOISSANTE AVENTURE,* THE MOVIE I had largely slept through in Ilya's apartment, Mosjoukine, desperate for money to buy medicine for his daughter, breaks into his childhood home and opens the safe, only to be discovered by his estranged father, who attacks him. They fight, and Mosjoukine kills his own father. In the apartment, I'd woken up to see this nightmare playing out on the tape.

What ending could be more sadly Russian than that? Then—*unbelievably, astoundingly*—the film changes. It pulls the world's oldest trick. Mosjoukine, young again, boyish, wakes up on the couch in his father's study where he has fallen asleep. Every bitter moment of the film had been nothing but a dream. It was an impossible ending, one too silly for words, but I was overjoyed. Anything was better than the story turning out to be true.

Now I wanted to pull the same trick, *wake up.* But that wasn't going to happen. My brother, Ilya, was dead.

When I told Ilya my dead were with me always, he'd laughed. Now, as the police hauled me from the church, as my eyes closed from whatever opiate they'd stuck in my arm, I thought, where is my brother? I felt the air around me for him, for at least some sense of him.

He wasn't there. The others—the colonel, my mothers, my husband and my daughter, and Anne-Sophie—were gone, too. The world was flat and empty. The world was full of nothing but the strangers lifting me into a midnight blue police van. Only one dim light, a candle more distant than a star, was flickering, almost going out, but not quite. Somewhere out there, Mosjoukine was alive still. I wished I had my hands around his throat. Why did he live and not Ilya? I wanted to find Ilya in the kitchen. I would have taken him angry—about to throw a coffee pot, knives. I would have settled for an Ilya who was not speaking to me, just to have a living brother who would stay in this world with me.

But I was alone.

I woke up in the local police station, in a cell that looked remarkably like a budget hotel room, with a bed, a TV, and a table with two cheap upholstered chairs. "Every day some tourist goes crazy in one of the churches in Paris," the sergeant in charge would tell me later. "At least you did it in the 10th Arrondissement and not in some church filled with treasures of French patrimony."

Patrimony, that was where this had all started. I had asked, *Where did I come from?* Now the question left to be answered was, *Where will I end up?*

The next morning, after a policewoman finished taking down my side of the story of why I had felt moved to desecrate a church even though I wasn't a Catholic, there was a knock on the door and the sergeant came in with Nance Olmstead, the other survivor of this deadly drama we were in. The sergeant disappeared and left her with me. They were hoping she would take the trouble that was me off their busy French hands.

She sat opposite me at the table and took both my hands. I noticed that my right hand, the one I had used to strike down the candelabras in my scuffle with the church, was dotted with small cuts the exploding light bulbs must have made. The blood was dry, but as Nance squeezed my hands for all she was worth, one of the cuts reopened. There was blood, first on my hand, then on her hands, which seemed rather appropriate, considering. She didn't notice, only leaned across the table, holding on as if she thought I might get away again, as if she couldn't believe she had found me, apparently well, or at least still alive.

"You had the key from the hotel in your purse," she said, explaining how the police reached her. "You forgot to turn it in when you left in such a hurry." That was putting it mildly, since I'd almost knocked her down to run away from her. "Last night I was standing at the desk at the hotel, checking you out like you asked me to, when the police called to ask the clerk if you'd come to Paris with anyone, if there was anyone at the hotel who knew you."

"Good timing," I said. Then, as she clung to my hands, I explained how my life had become such a bloody tragedy, though maybe one that bordered on farce. I told her everything that had happened to me since Aunt Z appeared on my doorstep. I talked and talked. I couldn't shut up. She listened. Maybe she thought she owed me that much. I told her about the trip to New York, about Apolline leading to Ilya, about Mosjoukine and Sophie. I told her about the trip to Moscow. I told her more about Mosjoukine than she ever wanted to hear. She was my confessor or the nearest thing I had to one. "Oh, Lord," she said. She bit hard at one fingernail, "Oh, Lord," reduced to using repetition for emphasis the way good midwesterners did.

When I finished telling her about Ilya's death, she put her head on the table. I remembered seeing the bloody gurney with her son rolling across the intersection after he had killed both himself and my family. I felt sorry for her, and also—God forgive me—I took pleasure in causing her pain, in the name of my husband, in the name of my daughter. Then that bitter satisfaction passed and a little healing began.

She raised her head and looked me in the eye. She was looking better. She had found some time between when I had seen her at the Hôtel Batignolles and her appearance at the jail to shower, wash and blow-dry her hair, and change into fresh clothes, a mint green pantsuit this time. She'd put on pink lipstick and taken an emery board to what was left of her nails. I could tell she was a woman used to being both tidy and in charge. If she could rescue me, then she could still do good in this world. If she could save someone as childless, as bereft as she was, she could go on with her life.

Maybe she could save me. She, more than anyone else, knew what I had lost before I came to Paris. Our children had died at the same bloody moment, as if they'd fallen together in the same battle of the same useless war. After I finished my story, Nance sat for a moment. She took back her hands, let them fall in her lap. When she did, I realized I had been hanging on to her just as hard as she'd been holding on to me. Now I felt frightened, like the black pilot standing on his own at the top of the swaying Eiffel Tower.

She leaned forward. "Listen," she said. "I have to know the answer to one question."

"Okay," I said, though I couldn't guess what the question would be. "What is it you need to know?"

"Are you going to kill yourself?"

I started to answer, but she stopped me, raising her hand. "If you say yes, I'm going to leave you here. If you say yes, I can't stay. You wouldn't be here if it weren't for my son. I feel responsible. I know at least half of what you're feeling, if only half. But if you die while I'm with you or while I'm watching or when I'm in the next room, it's going to kill me. It will be the end of me, too." She was crying, and the mascara she'd put on ran down her face like dirty water, turning the hairs above her lip a sad gray.

There we were, the two who didn't die, like Horatio and Fortinbras at the bloody end of *Hamlet*. I thought of my mother, my father, Ilya, all slipping away, leaving me alone in the room. I made my decision. I took Nance's hands back in mine. "I won't," I said. "I promise I won't do that to you."

21

THE POLICE MADE IT CLEAR they expected me to leave Paris at the soonest possible opportunity. I would be sent a bill for the damages to the church. They would have liked me out on the very next flight, but I'd had enough of last-minute flying and I wasn't ready to leave, not until I'd buried my brother. So they released me into Nance Olmstead's custody, warning her to keep me in the strictest charge. I was to stay out of churches, and also, they said, under no circumstances was I allowed to ascend the Eiffel Tower. I could see that last bit got her worried.

I wanted her to go back to the Hôtel Batignolles, to trust me to meet her there later, but she took the police warning seriously. So she went with me to the Hôpital St-Louis. We entered through the door I'd seen the orderly use with Ilya, but once inside there was no desk guarded by nurses, no signs pointing this way to Emergency, just a long white hall punctuated at intervals by empty wooden benches and by tall doors, most closed. "French hospitals are always like this," Nance said. Clearly, it was not her first time in one. I remembered what she'd told me back at the Hôtel Batignolles about flying to France to rescue students. "To us, St-Louis looks like an octopus that's all arms and no head. The French don't need registration desks manned by clerks whose job it is to collect insurance information. They don't have to worry about getting stiffed for the bill." she went on. "But there's always someone around who knows what you need to know. Shall I ask?" I nodded, thinking better a reassuring matron in soft pastels than someone clearly a lot less stable, possibly crazy.

Nance headed down the hall with me trailing behind until she found a nurse in a room lined with filing cabinets. I stood a few feet away as Nance talked to her. Nance's voice was low, reasonable. The nurse pointed down the hall, said something that sounded like a room number. Nance looked startled. Stepping forward, she whispered a question. The nurse, with a puzzled frown in my direction, followed Nance's lead and whispered her reply.

"What?" I said. "What?" Nance turned toward me, one hand outstretched.

"Your brother isn't dead," she said. "He's in the room at the end of the hall."

Her words buzzed in my ears. I shook my head like a spaniel coming out of the water. "Say that again." She did.

My brother, I thought, and my body took me down that hall in one fluid motion, for once moving the way my brother did every day. I hit the tall door still running, pushed it open. And there he was. His face was half-hidden by an oxygen mask. His blond hair, wet with sweat, fanned across the pillow above his head as if he were under water. A tube ran from his chest into a bubbling tank. My brother as merman. But I could see his chest rising and falling. He was breathing. He was alive.

It was *L'Angoissante Aventure*—and I had just woken up. My heart turned over in my chest with a painful thud. But Ilya was not awake and smiling like the father in Mosjoukine's movie. For my brother, the day before had been more than a bad dream. With the chest tube and an IV dripping into his arm, he looked frighteningly like Anne-Sophie. Still, I took his hand and it felt wonderfully warm. His eyes fluttered, opened. I expected him to be angry. I'd let the one thing happen to him I had promised would not. He was in the hospital in a web of tubing. He just looked surprised. His eyes wrinkled into a smile. He pushed the mask up with his free hand, and I saw a goofy, lopsided grin. "What are you doing here?" he asked. He was loopy, clearly stoned. No matter that he had been injecting morphine every day. I had never seen him high. Now he was flying. I wondered if he thought we were both dead.

"Where do you think *here* is?" I asked him. He gave a small, one-shouldered shrug.

"Paradise," he said. "Where else would we be?" He closed his eyes.

"You scared me, brother," I said, but he didn't answer.

I heard the door behind me open and turned, expecting to see Nance, but it was the doctor who'd found Ilya in the courtyard. He was wearing a hospital ID badge that said Dr. Bonheur. *Dr. Happiness.* If I hadn't known him as the neighbor's customer, I might have taken that as a good sign. As it was, it seemed bitterly ironic. I wondered if he felt the same.

Dr. Bonheur came to stand beside me as if we had known each other a long time. It seemed like we had. "You're his sister?" he asked.

"Yes," I said, wondering whether he knew that from the neighbor or from talking to Nance in the hall or just from looking from Ilya to me.

"Well, don't be frightened. He's sedated. A collapsed lung is very painful. We're draining the fluid." He pointed at the tube running from Ilya's chest. "We have him on a wide spectrum antibiotic, and he seems to be responding."

"Why isn't he dead?" When I said it—*dead*—I started crying. Tears made their usual way down either side of my nose. Damn, damn, I'd thought I was done with all that.

Dr. Bonheur pulled a tissue from his lab coat pocket and offered it to me. I took it.

"He didn't get enough morphine for an overdose."

"Because he was already taking such a large dose?" Dr. Bonheur laughed, as if calling the amount of morphine Ilya used a large dose was the best joke he'd heard all day.

"Because the syringe he was using was too small. He needed two injections for a lethal dose and before he could use the second, he lost consciousness. An amateur, your brother." Dr. Bonheur gave me a small smile, acknowledging what we both knew—that he wasn't one. "I thought you saw me pick up the full syringe and knew what that meant."

I shook my head. "I thought he was dead."

Dr. Bonheur crossed his arms on his chest, and we both stood there for a minute watching my brother breathe.

"The cancer caused the collapsed lung?" I asked, finally.

"Actually, the pleurisy. *Pleurisy?* Do you know what that is? Fluid between the walls of his lung. He had some pneumonia as well. Scarring from a previous surgery can predispose a patient to infections of this type."

"But the cancer is back?"

Dr. Bonheur pursed his lips. "Very likely, I'm afraid. We'll know for certain after we take a second set of X-rays. The first ones were too obscured by the fluid to get a clear picture. We are going to do more tests now."

I looked at my brother, asleep, tethered by his tubing. "Doesn't it say in his medical record? I thought he'd seen a doctor."

Dr. Bonheur shook his head. "I think he diagnosed himself. Your brother is not someone who likes hospitals. He made that clear when he woke up here."

"Damn it." Ilya hadn't even been to see a doctor. If only I had noticed how sick he was sooner.

Dr. Bonheur touched my shoulder. "Don't blame yourself," he said, and I guessed from his downcast eyes, his slightly embarrassed expression, that he was talking about Ilya's attempted suicide. "You have to remember that he was in terrible pain. In such circumstances, who can hold onto their rational nature?"

Ilya had, I thought. He'd told me he didn't want to end up in the hospital. Told me quite simply what he intended with the torn picture from *Kean,* then he'd had the courage to do it, knowing I would be angry and I might never forgive him. No, he knew I would forgive him, sooner or later. What else could a sister do? But it hadn't turned out the way he intended, and now he—we—would just take each hour as it came. No disappearing into a new life like our father, not this time, not for either of us.

A pair of orderlies arrived to take Ilya down for the tests. I squeezed his hand hard, but he didn't open his eyes. I sat next to Nance Olmstead on one of the wooden benches in the hall. She handed me a fresh tissue to replace the doctor's. Then she began talking to me about little things, the cold spring they'd been having back home, what the stock market had been doing to our college's endowment, what that meant for the possibility of a pay raise this year for her or for me. At first I didn't want to hear it, any more than I wanted to watch another silent movie. After Mosjoukine, it might be years before I wanted to watch a movie at all.

All I wanted was to hear the bad news about Ilya and deal with it. But little by little, I found myself drawn in by what Nance was saying. Were there likely to be budget cuts? What programs might find themselves sacrificed for the greater good? I found myself thinking of Gwen, chair of my department, my old friend. I knew how worried she must be, and suddenly I wanted to talk to her, to hear what plans she had for protecting the program we'd worked so hard to build. But I knew what Nance was doing. Stitch by stitch, word by word, she was trying to sew me back into the fabric of my old life.

I twisted on the bench, trying to get comfortable as Nance talked. I was sore from the day before in places I hadn't noticed until now. My breasts were tender to the touch, swollen. I cupped my palm around my right one, which felt nearly twice its usual size, odd considering how much weight I'd lost. I must have said my thoughts out loud—which was getting to be a bad habit—because I noticed that Nance had stopped talking and was staring at me.

"When was your last period?" she asked.

"My what?" Not getting her point, until I did. My periods had always been irregular. I certainly hadn't had one since I'd been traveling so light—to New York, Paris, Moscow, back to Paris. I remembered Ben, our last night in bed. We'd had, as the phrase went, unprotected sex, but we'd been having unprotected sex for eight years, ever since Julia had been born. We'd hoped for a second child, but nothing ever happened. It was absurd to think I was pregnant now. Grief and jet lag had sent my hormones into hyperdrive. It was true I couldn't seem to stop crying. Even Nance's fresh tissue was soaked.

Nance got up, then a minute later she was back with a red-haired female doctor, one too young to have known Ilya's wife Barbara when she practiced at St-Louis. The doctor looked me over from head to toe. She was wearing orange Birkenstocks with her white lab coat. Her name tag read Dr. Moreau, a name blessedly free of any obvious ironic meanings. I thought maybe she would ask me to pee in a little cup, send that down to the lab to see if I was pregnant, but instead she led me down a flight of stairs and into an examining room. "Should I get undressed?" I asked.

Dr. Moreau shook her head. "It's not necessary. Just lie down and pull up your sweater." She clicked on the monitor next to the examining table, then squirted cold gel onto my bare stomach. She rolled an ultrasound wand around on my belly, the ball tracking across my gooseflesh. Then there, on the little black-and-white screen by my side, were two small, nearly translucent fish. One moved, as if it had been tickled, then the other one wriggled, too.

"Do twins run in your family?" Dr. Moreau asked.

"Yes," I said. "Yes, they do."

She clicked the wand, and the babies' measurements appeared on the screen. "I'd guess the date of conception at March 1." She looked at me. I nodded. "Though it's hard to say with twins. They're always smaller. It could have been earlier. March 1 makes the due date December 1, but twins are often born early." She lifted the wand. "If you are going to have them. At your age, there are risks."

I knew what she was asking. Could I manage a double pregnancy at forty-two when I had been taking no kind of care of myself? What if they were born as tiny and ill as Anne-Sophie? I knew medicine had made progress in keeping premature babies alive, helping them grow into better lives than the one Anne-Sophie had lived. But there were no guarantees. I would be having these babies alone. Ben was gone, and Ilya would be gone, too.

Never be afraid, my father and brother had said to me. This time I didn't need to be told. I was not afraid, though maybe I should have been. I wanted the babies. No matter what happened, I wanted to be a mother again. I wanted to have something of Ben, of Mosjoukine and Sophie. I wanted to be part of a family again, one that did not end with me. I told her I wanted to carry the twins. I told her I wanted them to be born healthy.

"Then we'll make sure they are," Dr. Moreau said, helping me off the table. "You Americans worry too much. Drink a glass of red wine a day, and all three of you will be fine."

22

I WENT UPSTAIRS TO JOIN NANCE ON THE BENCH. "Twins," I said and watched her lips form a perfect O. It took her a couple of tries before any sound came out.

"Oh, my." She looked at me with her eyes slightly narrowed, as if measuring me. "Are you sure you want more children? Are you ready to go through it all again?"

I surprised myself. I smiled at her. I beamed. I laughed out loud. "You bet," I said, one midwesterner to another.

She smiled, too. Everyone would help, she said. I could teach part of the fall, then go on maternity leave. Maybe I still had some of Julia's baby things—a crib? A high chair? If not, people would lend things. She and Tricia would throw a baby shower.

I let her talk. I imagined my house set up for a new family. My old life retrofitted to make room for two new lives.

"Then, in the spring . . ." Nance stopped in midsentence, looked at me. "You aren't coming back to Indiana, are you?"

She was quicker than I was. I thought of Mosjoukine's apartment, the big bed where I had spent my first hours with my mother and my twin. I thought of the Place Ste-Odile. "No," I said. "I'm not." It wasn't until I heard myself say it that I knew it was true. I had a new life. Or I would soon build one. In France. With or without Ilya, I had my old life, my first life, back. I'd been born in Paris, and my twins would be born here, too.

Nance looked like she might cry. "Damn," she said. The twins were her tight-rope to the future as well, a thin strand of hope over that bottomless well of grief we both had only begun to cross.

I put my arm around her shoulders. "You can visit. As often as you'd like."

She nodded. "Well," she said, wiping her eyes with the back of her hand, "the French have wonderful prenatal care. They're still trying to make up for all those people they lost in the war."

I laughed again. Practical Nance. But she was right to count the blessings of free medical care. I had to feed and clothe my soon-to-be children. There was Ben's life insurance. I could sell the house. We would be okay. If Ilya could make his way in Paris, so could we.

Ilya's gurney appeared at the end of the hall and rolled past us into his room captained by a single orderly this time. I followed them in and waited until Ilya was back in his bed, sheets tucked carefully around the tubes.

He was awake, his eyes bright, maybe with the pain starting to cut through the morphine, maybe just bright and blue the way only Ilya's could be. "The doctor will be in with the results from the tests," the orderly said to Ilya, giving the sheets a last pat. Ilya didn't answer, in no hurry to hear the bad news.

As soon as the orderly left, Ilya pulled down his oxygen mask. It hissed faintly around his neck. "I'm sorry if I said anything crazy before."

I took his hand. "Nothing crazier than usual, brother." I was still smiling. I couldn't help myself.

"You're the one grinning like a fool," he said.

"I'm pregnant. With twins."

Ilya laughed, a quick shout of complete surprise and joy. In spite of the tubing, he managed to grab me and give me—and the twins—a fiercely hard hug. Even now, even after all he had gone through, he was stronger than I was. "You see?" he said, letting me go. "You were looking in the wrong direction. I told you life is about looking forward." He grimaced and leaned back in the bed.

"If I hadn't looked behind me, I wouldn't have found you."

Ilya made a sour face that said clearly, *Look what that got you.*

Before I could answer, the door opened. As soon as I saw Dr. Bonheur's face, I knew what the news would be. His name had been a good omen after all.

"All clear," he said, holding up an X-ray in one hand. "Not a sign of a mass or a shadow. Nothing. *Nothing!* No cancer." He slapped Ilya on the knee with the sheet of film. "You just have to learn to take care of yourself. No smoking. Honest hours."

It wasn't *L'Angoissante Aventure*—death nothing but a dream. Ben and Julia did not spring back to life. The colonel and Livvy, Sophie and Anne-Sophie stayed dead. But my brother, my twin brother, would live.

"We'll keep you at least a week, though," Dr. Bonheur said to Ilya. "Maybe ten days to make sure the antibiotics do their job."

"Thank you," I said. Then at a loss for words, I repeated myself, shaking Dr. Bonheur's hand, wringing it really. "Thank you, thank you, thank you."

"Sometimes we get a good outcome." Dr. Bonheur nodded. "That's important to remember." He took his hand back. "I should say good-bye, then. There will be another doctor in charge of your case. I am taking," he paused, as if searching for the right words, "a voluntary medical leave." He frowned, and I could see his hands were shaking slightly. I had a flash of his finding the neighbor's house empty, of morphine suddenly difficult to find. Dr. Bonheur shrugged. "Inevitable," he said. "Best to face the future."

"Yes," I said, "the future," hoping his, too, would turn out well. Dr. Bonheur took Ilya's hand and shook it. For the first time, I noticed how still Ilya was, his eyes round as pennies. He looked shocked.

"How do you feel?" I asked him.

"Like the hangman dropped me from the gibbet at Montfaucon and the rope broke," he said. "The rope broke, and I fell two stories and landed on my feet like a cat."

"Exactly," Dr. Bonheur said. "Now stay off the gallows." He bowed slightly, then left the room and, as it turned out, our lives.

I sat on the edge of Ilya's bed. I felt dizzy with our change in fortune. I worried it might all somehow come undone. "What are you thinking?" I asked. The oxygen mask still hung around his neck. His eyes were serious, his mouth neither smiling nor frowning,

"I was thinking," he said, then paused. "I was thinking that as much as I hate to admit it, Mosjoukine was right. We might live to be 100, you and I."

"With his genes?" I said. "At least 110."

I touched Ilya's hair, damp and tangled on his pillow. He was real, his skin and hair too sticky and dank to be part of any ethereal dream. I poked him gently. "You smell terrible, you know," I said.

"If I were dead," Ilya said, "I'd smell much worse."

It was evening by the time I left Ilya and took Nance with me to 44 Place Ste-Odile. My guess had been right. The neighbor's house was deserted, her lights off, her curtains drawn tight. Maybe after Ilya's failed suicide, the police had visited her. More likely, she'd decided to take a little voluntary vacation until things calmed down in the Place Ste-Odile. As I put the key in the lock, I found proof the neighbor had been there since I'd seen her last. On the doorstep were my boots, stuffed with crumpled newspapers to hold their shape. An apology? Penance? A refund? I shook my head and took them inside with us.

Nance was impressed by the furniture. Back home, she collected antiques. Looking around, I felt no attachment to the couch or piano. A kingdom of thing-dom, the colonel would have said. Only the people who lived here, had lived here, were important. I thought of my parents' apartment. The house I had left behind. People died and left rooms full of tables and sofas and empty, empty beds. The point of this apartment, of Paris, was who was here and who would be here soon. I went into Ilya's room, looked at the two pictures on the corkboard. Ilya happy, Ilya sad. I was glad the one with him smiling was pinned on top, even if Barbara at his side was a foreshadowing of the dark things to come.

During the day, I sat at the hospital with Ilya while he got well. He wanted me to teach him English. Ben's children, he said, should grow up speaking English as well as French, and he wanted to learn along with them. I bought some children's alphabet books, and we worked our way first through an ABC of fruits, apple, banana, cantaloupe, fairly useful vocabulary. Then one of animals, anteater, boa constrictor, capybara, which was a bit more esoteric, but Ilya was a quick study.

Nance hovered like a hummingbird, nervously going back and forth between the hospital, the Hôtel Batignolles, and the apartment, unable to bring herself to leave quite yet. She solved the mystery of who owned the apartment at 44 Place Ste-Odile. Her years of experience unraveling the problems of midwestern college students studying abroad had left her with no fear of the

French bureaucracy. The answer was both simple and surprising. Ivan Desnos —Ilya—owned not just the apartment but the whole house. Mosjoukine had transferred it into Ilya's name before leaving for Prague in search of Sophie, maybe foreseeing how that journey would end. When I told Ilya, for once he was speechless.

In the paperwork was an answer to a second question: how first Mosjoukine, then Ilya kept the house without ever paying a penny of tax on it. Apparently my father, the colonel, had set up a trust to take care of those before he left Paris. Whether he had done it as a parting gift or payment for his friend and fellow spy Mosjoukine or as a legacy for Ilya, the boy he had not taken to America when he took me, I could never know. Any way you looked at it, 44 Place Ste-Odile was a gift, a double gift from two fathers to two children. Now it would house a third generation as well.

Nance even tracked down copies of Ilya's and my birth certificates, listing Sophie as our mother, but our father as unknown—Mosjoukine a fact Sophie had kept to herself. Nance used that document to persuade the police I would be no danger if I stayed in Paris under the watchful eye of my brother.

On the day before Ilya was to be released, he sent me home early to nap, invoking the health of the twins. Coming in, I found Nance sitting in the kitchen drinking vodka with the air of someone who had been drinking a lot lately, as if that was what she did alone all night at the Hôtel Batignolles. I remembered that first awful night after Ben and Julia were killed and the night I'd spent drinking with Apolline. Pain cries out for anesthetic. Ilya could have told her that.

I put my hand over Nance's squat glass with its grudging French portion of ice before she could empty more vodka in it. "Don't," I said.

Nance opened her mouth. Probably to tell me to mind my own damn beeswax. I guessed I was not the first one to ask her to stop drinking. But I wasn't just anyone, not anymore. "Okay," she said. She let go of the glass and handed me the bottle.

We ate dinner together at Ilya's kitchen table. It was my turn to listen. Nance talked about Josh, her son, how she hadn't had a moment's hesitation handing him the keys to her brand-new Avalanche that last night. He'd never given her any reason to worry. He never played his music loud if she was in the house. He always kept his room neat, his clothes folded away. After he died, she'd found herself angry with him for having been so damned perfect up until that awful night. If he'd been rebellious, if he'd been trouble, she could have steeled herself, prepared herself for bad news. She'd seen other parents do that, after the third arrest for drugs or disorderly conduct. They kept their muscles tight, always ready for the sucker punch. She'd been so unprepared.

Even more urgently, she'd had the sad sick feeling that, in trying to please her, his overworked single mom, he'd missed out on life. On sex maybe, on wild dancing at all-night parties, on the exhilaration of swimming naked—God knows what else. Missed out on so many things he would never get to do. He did one bad thing, one stupid thing, and he paid such a high price—his life, two other lives. It was goddamned unfair.

I agreed. It was all damned unfair. We stayed up nearly all night talking. She left for home the next day. I stood in the Place Ste-Odile and hugged her like we might never see each other again, though that turned out not to be true.

Later that afternoon, I brought Ilya home in a cab. He was still too weak for even the short walk from the hospital. After he was settled in his room, he asked me to go to the boat and tell Jacques and Nolo what had happened. Then, two weeks later, when Ilya was well enough, the four of us went to the cemetery where Anne-Sophie was buried. Jacques and Nolo had known Anne-Sophie and used to go with Ilya to visit her in the years before she was too fragile to be touched. We stood looking at the little temporary metal marker on her grave. Ilya stepped over the low iron fence, went down on his knees on her grave. This made Nolo very nervous. He looked around for irate nuns. Jacques had brought flowers and handed them to Ilya to arrange at the foot of the marker.

Ilya had laughed when I told him how close I felt my dead were, but he pressed his palm to the soft earth over his daughter as if he was sure she knew he was there. Then he took two small white stones out of his pocket and handed one to me. We put them on top of Anne-Sophie's grave marker, neither of us caring that as a good communist and an atheist, our Jewish mother would not have approved. Stones didn't wither and blow away like flowers. They were beyond death, and so was Anne-Sophie.

In July, Ilya and Nolo bought *La Sirène* from Jacques, who was ready to retire a second time. Ilya and Nolo took turns giving their spiels to the tourists, steering the boat. The neighbor's house stayed empty. I hired workmen to fix up the empty apartments on the ground and attic floors. When the twins got larger and needed more room, we would move downstairs, give Ilya some space. Who knew when he might need it? No son of Mosjoukine was too old at forty-two to marry again, to have another daughter or a son. Meanwhile, I rented out the top floor apartment to a pair of interns from the hospital and paid our daily expenses out of their rent.

When the ground floor apartment was remodeled in August, I discovered what everyone living in Paris with a spare bed already knew. People came to visit. Nance came and then John and Tricia with their seven-month-old son. Aunt Z and Apolline each promised a visit at Christmas after the twins came. Children have a way of making family.

In October, there was a revival of Mosjoukine's reputation as an actor, at least in the world of silent film scholars. John called to tell me the film scholar I'd visited in the Marais was working on a book about Mosjoukine's French films. And a film festival in Italy screened a major retrospective. I didn't hear about it until it was over, but I wondered if Mosjoukine wasn't there, sitting in the dark in the audience, an old man in a wheelchair pushed by a pretty young woman who looked enough like him to be his daughter. And I thought, who knows if we have seen the last of him? After all, he knew where to find us, 44 Place Ste-Odile, Paris, France.

On November 20th, the twins, a boy and a girl, were born, unbelievably tiny compared to Julia, but healthy at five pounds and three ounces apiece. My future and my past. The boy was a pale blond with the calm, distant light blue eyes of a believer. My own little monk. The girl had dark curls like Sophie, but brilliant blue eyes like Mosjoukine or Ilya. The first time she looked at me, I thought, this one is fearless.

To Ilya, with only Anne-Sophie for comparison, the twins looked like giants. He sat on the edge of my hospital bed, looking down at his new niece and nephew tucked in safely at my sides. "What are you going to name them?" Ilya asked, touching his finger to his nephew's tight fist. "Promise me not Vera or Ivan."

"That would be pushing our luck," I said. I nodded at my blond son, asleep and dreaming beside his darker sister. "This is Benjamin," I said, giving my husband one more way to be remembered in the world. Then I pointed at my dark-haired daughter, "And Élodie."

Ilya curled her pink fingers around his outstretched finger. "Why Élodie?"

"Because I've never known a living soul with that name," I said. "So who knows what we can expect?"

Ilya laughed. When he first led me into Mosjoukine's apartment, he'd whispered, *Welcome to the past.* Now he bent over the bed and whispered in the twins' ears, "Welcome to the future!" Then, like the tour guide that he was, he flung his arms wide, pointing the way there—as if we had just stepped off *La Sirène,* as if the world were a pleasure park and we were in for the ride of our lives. As usual, my brother was right.

And three days later, when we brought the twins home, we found two shiny red bicycles, newly delivered, waiting by the door.

Author's Note

IVAN MOSJOUKINE is one of the greatest film actors of the silent era. Born in Penza, Russia, on September 26, 1889, Mosjoukine was the son of a patrician landowner. Educated in Moscow, where for two years he studied law, he returned to Penza to announce that he wanted to go on the stage. When his father protested and put him back on the train to Moscow, Mosjoukine got off at the first station and began his life as an actor.

Mosjoukine starred in comedies and dramas alike, but became famous for his explorations of psychological realism. Mosjoukine's performances in *The Queen of Spades* and *Father Sergius* are among the finest in Russian silent cinema. After the revolution, Mosjoukine followed other Russian émigrés to France, where he created his most remarkable work as a director, the experimental film *Le Brasier Ardent*. He also starred in the classic films *Kean, The Late Mathias Pascal, Michel Strogoff,* and his last, most ambitious French silent picture, *Casanova.*

In 1926, Mosjoukine, with a Universal Studios contract in hand, sailed for Hollywood. Universal cast him in the leading role in *Surrender,* an adaptation of a stage standard about a Jewish girl and a Cossack who fall in love. The reviews were disastrous, and Mosjoukine returned to Europe to act in German productions. His last silent films were *Manolescu* and *Der Weisse Teufel.* Mosjoukine appeared in sound films, but roles for an actor with a heavy Russian accent were limited. He died from tuberculosis on January 18, 1939, in a hospital at Neuilly-sur-Seine, France, at the age of forty-nine. He was buried in a poor grave marked only by a wooden cross.

JESSE LEE KERCHEVAL was born in France and raised in Florida. She is the author of twelve books of poetry, fiction, and memoirs including *Brazil*, winner of the Ruthanne Wiley Memorial Novella Award; the poetry collection *Cinema Muto*, winner of the Crab Orchard Open Selection Award; *The Alice Stories*, winner of the Prairie Schooner Fiction Book Prize; and the memoir *Space* about growing up near Cape Canaveral during the moon race. She teaches in the creative writing program at the University of Wisconsin.